UNSEEN VOICES

PROJECT DEMON HUNTERS:
BOOK FOUR

CHRISTINE POPE

UNSEEN VOICES

Copyright © 2019 by Christine Pope

ISBN: 978-1-946435-26-2

Published by Dark Valentine Press

Cover art by Christian Bentulan

Prologue

WILL GORDON'S CELL PHONE RANG, AND FOR a second or two, he contemplated ignoring the call and letting it go to voicemail. The Adult Children of Alcoholics meeting that All Saints Church was hosting would begin in less than fifteen minutes, and he still needed to leave his office and head over to the all-purpose room so he could get the chairs set up and the refreshments laid out before people started gathering. However, he figured he'd better take a look at the phone's screen just so he could see who was calling him on Friday night, when most people in his circle knew he had a regular commitment here at the church.

But a quick look told him that it was Michael Covenant calling...and Michael didn't make phone calls just to chat.

Frowning slightly, Will swiped his finger

across the screen. Despite the tension he could already feel building in his body, he thought it was probably better to start out light. "Hey, Michael. How's Tucson?"

"Good," Michael replied. He sounded tense, and Will wondered why. Michael and his girl-friend Audrey had relocated to Tucson two months earlier so she could work on getting her doctorate in parapsychology at the University of Arizona, one of the few places left in the United States where such programs were even still offered. As far as Will knew, everything had been going just fine with the couple, although he hadn't heard from Michael recently.

Since his friend didn't seem eager to add anything to that single brief syllable, Will asked, "Everything okay?"

A long pause. "I'm not sure."

Will glanced down at his watch. Seven twenty-three. While he didn't want to be rude, he also didn't have much time to spare. "Well, tell me about it as I'm heading out of the office. I've got an ACA meeting in less than ten minutes."

"Oh, hell, I'm sorry."

"Nothing to be sorry about. I don't expect everyone to keep my calendar in their heads."

"Still hectic over there at All Saints?"

"You could say that." Will headed out of his office and shut the door behind him, then locked it. In the not-so-distant past, he wouldn't have had to take that kind of precaution, but a few burglaries in the last several years had shown that even All Saints Episcopal Church wasn't immune to petty crime. "One of our pastors took a position in northern California, so the rest of us have been doing double duty for a while." He left it there; no reason to point out that he'd been happy to take on the extra workload, if for no other reason than doing so helped to camouflage the wasteland his social life had become.

Something that might have been a sigh—or simply a released breath—came through the phone's tiny speaker. "Then I kind of hate to dump anything else on you, but I don't know who else to ask."

"You don't need to ask anyone else. What do you need?"

Another pause. Will hoped his friend wasn't second-guessing whatever impulse had led him to make the call in the first place. They'd known each other for more than five years, their paths first crossing at a metaphysical symposium being held in downtown Los Angeles at the convention center. While they were both ordained ministers, Michael had never sought a congregation, preferring instead to use his calling to rid the world of the darker forces that lurked at its edges. Even some of Will's fellow clergy thought Michael was a crackpot, but he knew better. His friend was one of the few holding the line against a foe most people wouldn't even acknowledge; if Michael was calling because he needed assistance with something, then Will knew he had to offer his help, no matter what might be involved.

"This *Project Demon Hunters* thing...." Michael began, then let the words trail off, as if he didn't quite know where to start.

Will had vaguely known about the reality TV show Michael was involved with, but he'd been busy with church activities and hadn't been in touch with his friend while the show was shooting back in the early spring. And when Michael told him it was canceled but didn't give any more explanation than that, Will guessed the cancellation must have had something to do with the sudden, untimely death of the show's co-creator and producer, Colin Turner. Since Will heard nothing else on the topic from Michael—and he didn't waste his time with the sort of celebrity gossip sites that might have continued to follow the story—he figured that was the end of it, at least as far as his friend was concerned.

"What about *Project Demon Hunters?*" he asked. By that point, he'd arrived at the meeting room, so he shifted his phone to his other hand so he could get the keys out of his pocket and unlock the door.

"It's done, but...I don't know. I've been getting a weird feeling the past few days."

Michael Covenant's "weird feelings" weren't usually the sort of thing you ignored. Will let himself into the meeting room and flicked on the lights, then said, "Anything more specific than that?"

"Not really. Just a sort of building pressure, like storm clouds on the horizon or something." A slight hesitation, and then Michael said, "I'm mostly worried about Rosemary."

"Who's Rosemary?"

"A friend of Audrey's and mine. Audrey met her over the summer, and Rosemary helped me out when I was really in a bind. She's a psychic who owns a bookstore over in Glendora."

If Michael called someone a psychic, that meant they were the real deal; he didn't use the term lightly. "Any particular reason why you're worried about her?" Will asked as he did his best to pull a chair off the stack against the far wall using only one hand. Good thing the Friday night ACA group was never very big—he shouldn't have to set up more than a dozen seats at the most.

"No. Like I said, it's just a feeling. Mostly, I wanted to give you a heads-up that I'd like to give her your contact information, let her know that if she runs into anything that makes her feel hinky, she has some backup in the area."

"Of course, it's fine if you give her my number. I'm glad to help."

"You're sure?"

"Absolutely." Will wrestled another chair over to the small circle he was setting up in the middle of the room and sent a worried glance at the clock on the wall. Seven twenty-eight. People were going to be here at any moment. "But I have a feeling everything is going to be fine."

"I hope you're right." Once again, Michael paused, this time for so long, Will wondered if his friend had ended the call. But then he said, "It's just...."

"Just what?" Will asked.

"Just...I can't shake the feeling that *Project Demon Hunters* isn't over. Not by a long shot."

Chapter 1

Rosemary McGuire trundled a cart laden with book boxes down the narrow aisle, pausing every foot or so to dig out the titles that needed to be shelved in each section where she stopped. Restocking was probably her least favorite part of her job here at the bookstore she owned with her two sisters, but the work had to be done. Of course, she found it just a wee bit convenient that Cecily had to take her son Tyler to a pediatrician's appointment and Isabel had a meeting with her financial planner on the very afternoon when their new shipment from Llewellyn Press—one of their biggest suppliers— was due, but whatever. It was a Tuesday, and those middle-of-the-week days tended to be dead in Glendora's sleepy historic downtown.

Still, Rosemary could think of about fifty

other things she'd rather be doing right at that particular moment, none of which involved meticulously placing each new title in its designated section, whether the category in question was Tarot or folk healing or meditation or astrology. But since the books wouldn't put themselves away, she kept doggedly at the task, thinking that after she got off work, she'd reward herself with a glass of pinot at the wine bar just across the street and half a block up from where Sisters We was located.

The string of Tibetan brass bells that hung from the front door of the shop jingled, and she straightened up from the lower shelf where she'd been shelving a book about Reiki. Not that she really needed to keep too close an eye on things; the shop's security cameras would have caught whoever had just entered the store. Besides, it was too early for the local high school to have let out yet. Not that she had anything against high school kids, per se, only that some of them tended to be a little light-fingered around the boxes of incense that were stacked neatly on a table not too far from the cash register. Probably, the kids took the incense to cover up the smell of pot; marijuana was legal for recreational use in California, but not if you were under eighteen.

Then a man's voice, nice and low, but sounding a little hesitant. "Rosemary McGuire?"

She swiveled and saw a male model standing at the end of the aisle where she'd been working. All right, maybe not exactly a male model, but definitely someone who wasn't exactly the type you'd usually see wander into a metaphysical bookstore. The stranger was probably around six feet tall and had sandy blond hair, regular features just strong enough to avoid being downright pretty, and brown eyes under slightly arched brows several shades darker than his hair.

"Um...yes?" she replied in response, not sure exactly what this apparition could want with her. At the same time, she was very glad that she always made sure her hair and makeup looked decent when she came into work—and was also secretly glad that today she wore a new sequin-accented skirt she'd just bought, which wasn't an ankle-sweeper like most of her skirts but only barely covered her knees. The weather had been pretty hot for early October, so she figured she could get away with something that short, as well as the black tank top and black platform sandals she wore with it.

If the stranger had noticed her ensemble, however, he didn't give much evidence of it. His gaze was fixed on her face, and she hoped she hadn't blushed. Hard to say, since she already felt a little overheated from all the shelving she'd been doing.

"Hi, I'm Caleb Dixon," he said, and extended a hand. Although she wasn't used to her customers offering to shake hands, Rosemary put out her own hand and exchanged an awkward pump before she wrapped her fingers around the handle of the cart next to her, hoping the sensation of the cool metal against her skin might steady her a bit. "I hope you don't mind me coming to see you here at work like this."

She shook her head, even as she replied, "Sorry, do I know you?" *Dumb question,* she thought. *I'd definitely remember you if we'd ever met before this....*

He grinned, showing off teeth that were as perfect as the rest of him. "No, sorry if I gave the wrong impression. I guess that sounded kind of weird. You're a friend of Audrey Barrett's, right?"

Immediately, Rosemary could feel herself tense. Of course, she was a friend of Audrey's— and of Michael Covenant, Audrey's significant other—but, considering some of the stuff the two of them had been involved with, it wasn't exactly the sort of connection Rosemary liked to acknowledge to a complete stranger.

"I know her," she said cautiously. "Why?"

Caleb's smile slipped a little but managed to remain in place. "It's all right," he told her. "I knew Colin."

That remark made Rosemary's eyebrows lift a

fraction. She definitely hadn't been a fan of the acerbic producer of *Project Demon Hunters,* but just because Colin could be a prize jackass when he wanted to, that didn't mean she thought he deserved to be murdered by demons. Sure, everyone thought his killer must have been an intruder in his rented Los Feliz home, but Audrey and Michael—and Rosemary by extension—knew better. Anyway, a friendship with Colin Turner wasn't exactly the most fortuitous connection to claim, considering what had happened to him.

But even though her spider sense was tingling all over the place, she made herself reply calmly, "Oh, did you work on one of his shows?"

Because Caleb definitely had the sort of face that should be in front of a camera.

However, he immediately said, "No. I'm a filmmaker, too—or at least, I want to be. I met Colin at a couple of local conventions, and we interacted online a few times."

Which basically meant Caleb must have known Colin in roughly the same way a bunch of people who went to the local psychic fairs could claim to know Rosemary. None of those people were friends, only clients who'd gotten a Tarot reading or had their palms read, but they knew her name, knew she was associated with the Sisters We bookstore in Glendora.

"Ah." That was about the only response she

felt willing to give right then.

It seemed to be enough for the man who stood before her, though, because he went on, "I just wanted you to know that I was familiar with his work, that I knew about his connection to Michael and Audrey." Voice lowering slightly, Caleb added, "And I know about *Project Demon Hunters.*"

Rosemary's fingers tightened on the handle of the book cart. "A lot of people know about *Project Demon Hunters,*" she returned, hoping she sounded casual and not like her heart had suddenly started beating a little faster than it had been a few seconds earlier. "I mean, it was announced on the cable network's website, even if they did end up pulling the show. It's not like it was a state secret or something."

"True," Caleb allowed. He didn't seem too put off by her comment, because he went on, "But that's not what I'm talking about. I'm talking about how I know that Colin and Michael and Audrey managed to get footage of phenomena no one else has ever seen."

Once again, Rosemary could feel her brows lift. As far as she knew, no one working on the show had openly discussed any of the things they'd seen or experienced. At least, that was what Audrey had made it sound like, although Rose-mary could tell that her friend pretty much wanted to leave the whole mess behind her. Who could blame her? Fending off demons in the basement of a haunted mansion or being an eyewitness to an actual exorcism had to be pretty traumatic. And that didn't even take into account having to face down and then vanquish an actual lord of Hell on the grounds of an isolated manor house in the Connecticut countryside....

"I wouldn't know anything about that," she said carefully. While she hated to give someone so gorgeous the brush-off, she also knew that Audrey and Michael had talked to her in confidence, and she wasn't about to betray their secrets to the first stranger who dropped into her shop, no matter how good-looking he might be. "And I really need to get back to work—"

She took hold of the book cart with both hands and acted as if she was going to push it a little farther along the aisle. However, Caleb stood in her way, effectively blocking her progress.

"I think you know something," he said.

"I really don't."

He smiled again. It was the smile of a guy who was used to getting what he wanted, and irritation stirred within her. All right, someone like Caleb Dixon probably did have people bending over backwards to help him out, just because the world wasn't full of insanely good-looking men, no matter what the movies and romance novels might want you to believe. However, that realization made her even less inclined to help the guy out. People who traded on their looks annoyed the crap out of her.

"Do you really think Colin would have wanted his work to just disappear into the ether and never be seen by anyone?"

Damn it. Rosemary wished she could retort that she hadn't known Colin very well and therefore couldn't possibly have any idea what he would or wouldn't have wanted. Problem was, while such an assertion might be partially true, she'd heard enough from Audrey to know the producer definitely had wanted to make sure everyone saw the unbelievable footage he'd captured for *Project Demon Hunters*. In fact, Michael and Colin had been plotting to release some it anonymously—heavily edited, of course —but had never managed to accomplish their goal…mostly because someone or something had killed Colin before he could upload the videos to YouTube or Vimeo or wherever he'd planned to distribute them. The hard drive on his computer had been erased, and, as far as Rosemary knew, Michael had never been able to determine whether Colin had made any backup copies.

Of course, the footage wasn't gone entirely. One copy had been uploaded to the servers of the cable network that had ordered the show in the first place, where it was locked up tight. Maybe a really good hacker could have found the footage, but she wasn't entirely sure about that. She assumed the network must have some pretty strong cyber security.

About all she could do was shrug. "Like I said, I hardly knew Colin. I won't presume to guess what he might have wanted."

That remark sounded so prim, so officious. Rosemary hated the words as soon as they left her mouth, but she couldn't take them back now. However, her reply didn't seem to have dissuaded Caleb. He hooked his thumbs in the belt loops of his jeans and only lifted his shoulders slightly.

"Well, I knew him. The day before he died, he was on the filmmakers' forum where he hung out sometimes. He was talking about how he had something really big, really exciting…and that we'd all get to see it very soon."

She wished she could shake her head and say no, of course Colin wouldn't be blabbing about his footage on some random forum where anyone could be hanging out and reading his posts. Problem was, she had a feeling that was exactly the sort of thing the producer might have done. From some of the comments Audrey had made, he seemed like the type of person who needed to inflate his accomplishments in order to feel better about himself.

And all right, that sort of description probably could be applied to at least half the people working in Hollywood, but in this case, Rosemary guessed it was probably pretty accurate. As far as she could tell, Colin Turner had operated on the fringes. He'd never had a hit show or even a regular gig. His producing jobs came along often enough that he could talk a good game and get funding for his projects, but Stephen Spielberg, he wasn't. She could easily imagine him hanging out in a forum where his minor accomplishments would still be enough to make him seem like a rock star. From there, it wasn't too big a leap to guess that he'd been talking about things he probably shouldn't, just to get some buzz going.

She let out a breath—not exactly a sigh, but something close to it—and said, "Maybe. I don't know. I probably exchanged fifteen words with the guy, if even that much."

"But you talked to Audrey."

"Some," Rosemary admitted. "Honestly, we didn't discuss Colin all that much. I could tell Audrey was pretty shaken up by the whole thing, so I really tried to avoid the subject."

"Understandable." The half-smile Caleb had been wearing disappeared completely then, as if he'd been forced to remember exactly how the *Project Demon Hunters* producer had died. Or at least, something of the manner of his death. None of the exact details had been released, probably because the LAPD still considered the murder an active case. They hadn't found any leads, though, and never would. It was pretty hard to connect a demon to a homicide. "Still, I have to wonder what happened to the footage."

Well, there was one thing Rosemary felt okay with telling Caleb, mostly because she hoped it would convince him that he was following a dead end…so to speak. "The network has it," she said.

He didn't even blink. "Everyone knows that."

"'Everyone'?" she repeated.

"Basically. That is, the show might have been canceled, but I assume Colin was still required to hand over any footage he shot."

"He was," she allowed, although she didn't trust herself to say much more than that.

"But Colin Turner was the kind of guy who would've kept a copy for himself."

There wasn't much point in arguing with that assertion, mostly because Caleb Dixon was exactly right. However, Rosemary didn't know for sure whether she should let him know that his assumption was correct.

Her silence seemed to be all the answer he needed, because he said, "What happened to Colin's copy of those files?"

"I don't know," she replied, which was the truth. That is, she knew the files in question weren't on the hard drive of Colin's iMac when Michael went looking for them, but she had no idea what had actually happened to the footage. Had the demon who'd murdered him wiped the hard drive? Maybe. Demons weren't exactly known for being computer-savvy, and yet she had a feeling that anyone—or anything—who could kill a human being so casually could probably summon the skills necessary to make sure no incriminating evidence was left behind… including footage that pretty much definitely proved demons were real. Since she didn't see much harm in providing Caleb with one small piece of information, she added, "The footage wasn't on his computer. Michael couldn't find any trace of it, and neither could the police. I don't know anything more than that."

Although most people might have found her words discouraging—to say the least—Caleb didn't seem at all put off. "I guessed as much. I mean, if Michael had actually found something, he probably would have gone ahead and released the footage, just the way Colin wanted. But just because those files weren't on Colin's computer doesn't mean other copies don't exist out there somewhere."

Rosemary didn't bother to hide the skepticism in her voice. "What, you think Colin uploaded it all to Dropbox or something?"

"No," Caleb said. He didn't sound offended by her dubious tone. In fact, even though she didn't know him at all, she thought he seemed almost encouraged by the absence of those files, which didn't make much sense. "I don't think he'd do anything that obvious. But I'd be really surprised if he hadn't squirreled away a backup copy of everything someplace else."

Maybe. She supposed Colin Turner had hit enough ups and downs in his career that he'd decided to provide himself with a cheap piece of insurance. But if he'd done such a thing, he'd taken the secret with him to his grave. Rosemary didn't pretend to be privy to all of Audrey and Michael's private affairs, but she guessed that if they'd been able to find the missing footage, Audrey would have said something. She hadn't, though. She and Michael had packed up their lives and moved to Tucson so she could finally get her Ph.D. in parapsychology, a dream she'd put away years earlier but would finally get to realize in the not-too-distant future.

And now Rosemary was living in the big, beautiful Craftsman house they'd vacated, ostensibly to act as its caretaker in their absence, but mostly because the house next to her much more modest home here in Glendora was being torn down to the studs and remodeled, and having to put up with the resulting construction noise for the next eighteen months was not something she'd looked forward to with any enthusiasm. Going to stay in Audrey and Michael's place had seemed like the perfect solution. True, she had only half the garage for her use because Michael was still storing a bunch of stuff in there, but—

Her thoughts skidded to a stop. At the time, she hadn't given the matter much thought, except to nod when Michael told her he was hanging on to some of the things that had been cleared out of Colin Turner's rented house, mostly because the cost of shipping all that miscellaneous leftover crap to Colin's sister in England would have been prohibitive. In fact, over the past few months, Rosemary had gotten so used to walking past those boxes when she parked her own little pistachio-green Fiat in the garage, she hardly paid them any attention at all.

The irony of the situation hit her. It would be pretty funny if the footage Caleb Dixon was looking for turned out to have been lurking in her garage all this time.

But no, she realized almost immediately that couldn't possibly be right. Michael had already gone through that stuff; he must have, because he was the one who'd packed it all in the first place. If he'd found anything important, he would have told Audrey, and she in turn would probably have said something to Rosemary.

Maybe.

Or maybe not.

It was a very long shot, though.

Obviously, her extended silence had gotten to Caleb, because he lifted an eyebrow and gave her a penetrating look. "What is it?"

Did she dare say anything? Part of her realized the smart thing to do was to continue to stonewall, to tell him she didn't know anything and that he was barking up the wrong tree. Because if she mentioned the cache of Colin's belongings in the garage, then Caleb would want to come see it...and that meant he'd be at the house with her. Alone. Was she really willing to let him know where she lived?

Where you're living temporarily, she reminded herself. *It's not* really *your house.*

True, but since she planned to be there for at least another ten months, if not more, her current living situation might as well be permanent. It wasn't as if she would be staying someplace else starting the next day or something.

"Well...."

Caleb's gaze only intensified. Something about that stare made her feel almost breathless, which was just silly. No matter how good-looking a guy was, he shouldn't be able to have this kind of an effect on her.

"Did you think of something?" he asked.

"Possibly," she replied, still hedging. "I don't know for sure." There, she hesitated, knowing she either had to lie and try to get rid of him, or tell the truth and let the chips fall where they may. She thought of the Fool card from her Tarot deck, that impetuous youth with his foot confidently extended over the edge of the abyss. In that moment, she thought she could sympathize with his precarious position.

Caleb was silent, still watching her. It was as if he knew he couldn't say anything, didn't dare interrupt the racing thoughts in her mind.

And what would be the harm, really? She carried pepper spray in her purse, and if he tried anything, he'd get a face full of it. Honestly, though, he seemed pretty harmless. Even now he was looking at her with those puppy-dog brown eyes, and she could feel her will beginning to waver. After all, although she wasn't a mind reader, her psychic abilities always allowed her to know what kind of person she was dealing with. She certainly didn't sense anything wrong about Caleb, didn't get the uneasy feeling that tended to settle in her stomach when she met someone with a dubious past or dark motivations.

Besides, although Michael and Audrey hadn't talked about it much, Rosemary knew that her friends were still troubled by the conundrum of Colin's missing footage. If she and Caleb actually managed to find the tapes—or the hard drive, or whatever—she'd be doing them in a favor as well.

That seemed to decide things.

She pulled in a breath. "There might be something," she said at last, a strange tremor running through her. For better or worse, she was going to cast the dice. "It's at my place. But it'll have to wait until after I'm done here."

"What time?" he asked.

"Six o'clock," she replied. "Give me your number, and I'll call you."

He nodded. "You have something to write this down?"

She nodded and went over to the cash register, which always had a hand-painted mug filled with pens standing by. After extracting one and pulling a pad of sticky notes out of the drawer under the register, she quickly jotted down the number he provided, then said, "My place is over in Pasadena. Do you want to meet me there or follow me from here?" Even as she asked the question, she wondered whether it was a good idea to give him the address before she actually got home. Caleb seemed friendly and harmless enough, but she supposed there was always the chance that he might try to search the garage in her absence.

Well, if he tried a maneuver like that, he wouldn't get very far. The entire property was guarded by Michael's highly sophisticated security system. The place wasn't exactly Fort Knox, but it was protected by motion sensors and hidden cameras, and had an on-call team that would show up if any alarms were tripped. Between all that and the anti-demon wards he'd left in place, she'd always felt close to invulnerable when inside the house.

"I'll meet you there," Caleb responded. "You can give me the address when you get home, if that makes you feel better." A certain glint entered his chocolate-brown eyes, as if he'd guessed at her misgivings about providing him with the address too far in advance of their meeting.

"Sounds good," she said, hoping she sounded neutral. "Then it'll probably be closer to six-thirty —I have to close up the store, and I never know when I might get some last-minute shoppers."

"It's fine," he said. The smile was back, probably because, despite her best intentions, it seemed as if he was going to get his way after all. "I'll see you then."

And he tilted his head at her by way of farewell, then went back out the door to the shop. The bells hanging from it jingled again, although this time they sounded vaguely accusing, as if trying to let her know that she'd just screwed up in a major fashion.

Maybe so. Or…maybe not.

After all, he was awfully cute.…

Chapter 2

To Rosemary's relief, there weren't any last-minute looky-loos, no one who came breathlessly in at five minutes until six, only to leisurely flip through book after book without making any decisions. In fact, the last customer left the store at about a quarter 'til, which meant she conceivably could have closed up early...if it weren't that she knew either CeeCee or Izzie would inevitably get wind of her unprofessional behavior and take her to task for it.

Sometimes, it was a real pain in the ass being the youngest sister in a family of psychics.

She dutifully locked up and turned on the alarm, then climbed into her Fiat, which had been parked out back behind the store and baking in the hot October sun all day, making the interior feel like a blast furnace. Rolling down the windows and maxing the air conditioning helped a little, but she couldn't help grumbling to herself about the weather. All right, it was often pretty hot in SoCal at this time of year, but she still wished it would cool down. Her brain couldn't quite wrap itself around the fact that Halloween was only three weeks away.

As she drove, she kept wondering if she'd really blown it here. Not only had she agreed to help someone she didn't even know try to track down Colin's missing footage, but she'd also been stupid enough to invite him over to the house. The far smarter thing to do would have been to offer to look through the stuff in the garage and then let Caleb know if she'd found anything. But since he was already expecting to meet her at the house, there wasn't much she could do except follow through with her plan and hope he wasn't a serial killer…or worse. She tried to comfort herself with the reminder that Michael's demon-repelling wards were still in place on the house. Those same wards had protected him and Audrey from demon attack while they were living there, so Rosemary knew they would continue to do the same for her.

Not that she'd ever heard of a demon who looked anything like Caleb Dixon.

Once she pulled off the 210 Freeway at Hill Avenue and was waiting in the line of cars to turn right from the off-ramp, she called the number he'd given her. It picked up on the second ring.

"Rosemary?"

There was a faintly questioning tone to his voice, as if he'd guessed it must be her because he didn't recognize the number but wasn't sure. "Yes, it's me," she said. "The house is at 1295 East Mountain Street. I should be there in just a couple of minutes."

"Probably at least ten or fifteen for me," he told her, eliciting a vague feeling of relief. At least he wouldn't be waiting on the front porch as she drove up. "I'm in Old Town right now."

"No problem. I'll see you when you get there."

"Sounds good…and thanks."

She made a noncommittal noise, since she didn't know quite what else to do. Then it was her turn to go right on Hill and head up to the neighborhood of lovingly restored houses where Michael's home was located. She dropped her cell phone back in her purse and bit her lip, knowing that she needed to call Audrey and let her know what she was up to. In fact, several times during the course of the afternoon she'd picked up the phone at the store, thinking she'd better make the call sooner or later, but she'd been interrupted on each of those occasions and had decided it could wait until after she was off work. Now, though, she was starting to wonder if she really needed to say anything at all, since it was very likely that she and Caleb wouldn't find anything worth mentioning. Besides, Audrey had already hinted that Rosemary was free to have any company over that she liked, that she and Michael didn't want to think their friend had any restrictions just because she was acting basically as a glorified house-sitter.

However, asking a date over wasn't exactly the same thing as inviting some random stranger to the house to paw through a dead man's belongings.

By that point, she was almost to the house, so she waited until she'd pulled into the garage and gotten out of the car before she grabbed her phone and forced herself to make the call. Rosemary hoped her friend would be available; it was almost six-thirty, a little early for dinner but not by much. And she really didn't know much about the details of Audrey's schedule, although it seemed that she was usually around whenever Rosemary called her after she got off work.

Luck seemed to be with her, because Audrey picked up just as Rosemary had finished unlocking the back door to the house. "Hey, Rosemary. Everything okay?"

The question wasn't that strange—they hadn't

talked much for the past couple weeks, except the one time she'd called Audrey to see if it was okay to have a plumber come over to look at the slow drain in one of the upstairs bathrooms. Rosemary knew her friend was buried in her post-grad work and didn't have a lot of time for chitchat. "No, it's all fine," she said hastily as she paused at the alarm panel next to the door and entered the code so it wouldn't go off. "I mean, the house is fine. But I had this guy come in the store today asking about *Project Demon Hunters* and Colin, and the footage he'd shot but which never got aired, and I wanted to know if it was okay if we took a quick look in the boxes in the garage."

These were probably questions she should have asked before she told Caleb to go ahead and come over, but Rosemary figured better late than never. Maybe his appearance had flustered her more than she'd thought.

"What guy?" Audrey asked, her voice sharpening. Clearly, she hadn't been fooled by Rosemary's overly casual tone.

"His name is Caleb Dixon. He says he's an amateur filmmaker or something."

"Hang on."

A pause while Audrey called out to Michael, repeating Caleb's name. There came a muffled reply of some sort, one that Rosemary couldn't really hear clearly. Then Audrey came back on the phone, saying, "Michael hasn't heard of him, but he admits that doesn't mean much. He doesn't pretend to keep up with all the people out there producing documentaries and short subjects, even the ones in his field. But he suggested that maybe you should check IMDB to see if this guy's legit. If he is, well, Michael says it's fine to look through Colin's stuff. There's really nothing there, though —just some of his books and folders from his file cabinet, that kind of thing. Stuff that didn't have any sentimental value and was too heavy to ship to the U.K."

"I figured," Rosemary said. "But Caleb still seems interested. Maybe he's trying to get some ideas for his next video or something."

"I suppose." Another pause, one where Audrey let out the faintest of sighs. "If he finds something he can use, more power to him. That stuff sure isn't doing anyone else any good."

That comment definitely sounded like permission to Rosemary. Or at least, she thought she could convince herself that Audrey had signed off on the whole thing. No harm, no foul.

It wasn't as if she and Caleb were going to find anything anyway.

"Great, thanks," Rosemary said. "How's Tucson?"

"Pretty amazing, actually," Audrey replied. "My coursework is really interesting, and the house is wonderful. I'm going to miss the swimming pool when we're done here."

Well, there was definitely enough room in the backyard here to install a pool at the Pasadena house, if she and Michael so desired, but maybe he wasn't all that amenable to tearing up his nicely landscaped yard. Either way, that was their problem, not Rosemary's. She'd asked the question out of politeness, but she realized she didn't have much time to look up Caleb online before he got to the house.

"Sounds great," she said. She was about to say, *I'll let you go,* but then Audrey spoke again.

"Hang on—Michael wants to talk to you for a minute."

He did? A small trickle of apprehension worked its way down the back of her neck. She sincerely hoped he wasn't about to tell her that he'd decided he didn't want her poking around in Colin's stuff. If she had to call Caleb and let him know he couldn't come over after all, she was going to feel like a real idiot.

"Hi, Rosemary," came Michael's voice.

"Hey, Michael," she responded, trying to sound perky and not terribly concerned about the way he'd inserted himself into the conversation. "How are you?"

"I'm fine," he said. "But that's not what I wanted to talk to you about."

"Oh?"

"I'm a little concerned about you pursuing anything *Project Demon Hunters*–related without assistance. Professional assistance, I mean," Michael added, as though guessing she might be offended that he didn't consider her own family— or possibly Caleb—to be any kind of useful help in this situation. "And while I know I could be in Southern California in a couple of hours if I had to, that still might not be enough if a real emergency comes up. That's why I think you should get in touch with someone I've worked with on a couple of cases. His name is William Gordon, and he's a minister at All Saints Church in Pasadena."

Seriously? she thought. *You want me to work with a minister? What part of the New Age Wicca stuff did you not get?*

However, she didn't have much time to indulge her irritation, since he kept going without giving her a chance to interject. "I know you're probably raising your eyebrows right now. But Will knows what he's doing, and you don't have to worry about him trying to convert you or anything. He's not the proselytizing sort. I'd just feel better knowing he's there in a pinch."

Since he paused to take a breath there, Rosemary said tartly, "Honestly, Michael?"

He chuckled. "Honestly."

"There's not going to be a 'pinch,'" she told

him. "You banished the demons. All's quiet on the western front. Right?"

"Audrey and I banished *a* demon," he replied. "That doesn't mean there aren't plenty more where he came from. And if you and this Caleb Dixon start poking around, trying to find Colin's lost footage...well, it just has me a little worried."

"That's because you're a worrier, Michael," Rosemary said, and he chuckled again.

"True. But it's saved my ass a few times, so I'm going to keep on worrying. Just please...let me give you Will Gordon's number."

Since he couldn't see her, she figured it was safe to roll her eyes. However, she knew it was probably better to have him give her the contact information for this Will Gordon—some crusty old minister who'd probably shoot her the side-eye as soon as he found out she was a practicing pagan —and get it over with. That didn't mean she had to call him. Like, ever.

"Sure," she said as she headed over to the drawer where Michael kept his old take-out menus and a couple of pens. She got out one of each item and added, "Go ahead."

Relief clear in his voice, Michael said, "Will's number is 626-555-9478. I already told him I was giving you his contact info, so he won't be too surprised to hear from you if it becomes necessary."

"Okay," she replied, knowing she was rapidly running out of time. Caleb would be here at any moment, and she still hadn't had a chance to look him up on IMDB. "I've gotta go."

"Take care," Michael told her, then ended the call.

Scowling, Rosemary laid her phone on the kitchen counter and hurried off toward the library, where she'd left her laptop the night before. As she went, she tried to tell herself Michael meant well. That wasn't the point. It was more the insinuation that she couldn't handle things on her own. Hadn't she already proved she was able to handle a crisis just fine? After all, she'd flown to Tucson to help him find Audrey, had gone with him into a snowy, nearly trackless wilderness in Colorado to get her friend away from the old mansion where the demon Belial had been hiding her. Those weren't exactly the actions of a woman who had to call in the meta-physical cavalry every time the damn house creaked.

Besides, this particular house was warded against demons, so she really didn't have anything to worry about.

Her laptop was sitting in the library on a small table next to an armchair, which was where she'd been using it before she left for work that morn-ing. In her haste, she'd forgotten to plug it into its charger, but the MacBook Air still had more than half its battery left.

Hurriedly, she logged in and navigated to IMDB, then typed in Caleb's name, halfway expecting him not to have any sort of profile at all. But no, there he was, with an actual picture, albeit one where he looked kind of grim-faced and out of focus. Not the world's best selfie, but at least it was recognizably him. She guessed that he hadn't wanted to waste the funds on a real head shot when he wouldn't be working in front of the cameras anyway.

And yes, he had a credit as an assistant director on some low-budget direct-to-streaming horror movie, and another credit as co-screen-writer on another bargain-basement flick, that one some kind of alien-invasion thriller she guessed wasn't very thrilling. Not the most impressive of resumés, but it did seem to prove that he was who he said he was.

The doorbell rang then, and she startled and shut the laptop. A pause to smooth her skirt and run her hands over her unruly curls—after several decades of fighting with her hair, she knew better than to attempt much more beyond pushing the craziest of her wayward strands in place—and then she hastened to the door.

Standing on the doorstep, Caleb Dixon looked even more impressive than he had when confronting her in the store, although Rosemary honestly hadn't thought such a thing was possible. She swallowed and assumed what she hoped was a careless smile.

"Hi, Caleb. Come on in."

She stepped aside so he could enter, noticing the way he allowed himself a quick glance around before he returned his attention to her. Although the friendly expression he wore didn't really change, she thought she could sense he was impressed with the place.

As he should be. Even though Audrey had once confessed that Michael had bought the house at a ridiculously low price because of all the work it needed, his home had to be worth almost a million now, if not more, thanks to the numerous improvements and upgrades he'd made during the time he was living there. It definitely didn't look like the kind of house someone who co-owned a small independent bookstore in the San Gabriel Valley would live in.

However, she didn't see the need to explain any of that to Caleb. He already knew this was Michael's house, but there was no use in going into lengthy explanations. Best thing to do was go out to the garage and get this over with. Even though Caleb seemed friendly enough, the whole situation was still strange, and she didn't see the point in stretching it out any longer than necessary.

"Do you want a glass of water?" she asked. "You might want to hydrate before we go out to the garage—it's pretty hot in there."

"Sure," he said.

She motioned for him to follow her into the kitchen, where she poured both of them some cold water out of the Brita pitcher in the fridge. "I talked to Audrey," she said casually, figuring it was probably better not to mention the way Michael had offered her the assistance of an Episcopal priest, of all people. "She and Michael are okay with us looking at Colin's stuff—but they also warned me that there isn't much to see."

Caleb seemed to take this advisory in stride. If he was at all surprised by the way she'd asked for permission after the fact, he didn't show it. "They're probably right, but I figure it couldn't hurt to look."

A sip of water, and Rosemary asked, "And if we do find something?"

"That depends."

"On?"

"What it is." He hesitated for a moment before going on, tone earnest, "If it's really the missing footage, then I feel like we have a duty to get it out there. I mean, this sort of thing is the holy grail of the paranormal research world, you know? Actual video evidence of demonic infestation and possession, something that will be easy to authenticate. It'll turn the world upside down."

Personally, Rosemary already thought the world was upside down in a variety of not-so-pleasant ways, but she knew that wasn't what Caleb had meant. Before *Project Demon Hunters* —before Colin and Michael and Audrey had captured actual images of demons on tape—what evidence existed for a world beyond this one had been flimsy at best. She was no demonologist, still had a hard time believing there really were creatures who'd once been angels and had been cast out of Heaven into Hell, but she knew what her friends had encountered was real. Once the footage was proved to be authentic, there probably wouldn't be many atheists left. For herself, she'd always believed in some kind of power behind the workings on the universe, but God? The Devil? Not really.

Except if you believed in demons, then you kind of had to believe in the rest of it.

Pushing those troubling thoughts aside, she asked, "So, you'd upload it to YouTube or whatever, like Colin was planning?"

"Well, unless Michael wants to do the honors. It sounds like he's kind of backed off from the whole thing, though."

That was true. She could see why he would

prefer to have someone else do the uploading, if for no other reason than it would give him some plausible deniability in case the studio tried to take legal action for the data leak.

Caleb drank some of his water, then went on, "I would never blast it out there without making sure Michael and Audrey were okay with the whole thing."

Well, that was something, Rosemary supposed. She wondered if Colin would have bothered to get permission if their roles had been reversed. Somehow, she had the feeling he probably wouldn't. He'd definitely seemed like someone who had "better to ask forgiveness than permission" as one of his mantras.

"Okay," she said. "Let's go see if there's anything worth finding."

She put her glass down on the counter, and Caleb did the same before following her out the kitchen door and down the short walkway that connected the house to the garage. It wasn't all that far, but she could still feel the hot breeze tug at her hair, could tell that if it was still this warm outside where she could actually feel the wind, it was probably going to be ten times worse in the garage, especially with her car still venting heat from its trip back here.

Since she'd left the side door to the garage unlocked, they didn't even have to pause before entering. As she'd feared, the air was stifling inside, and she hurriedly went over and pressed the button for the garage door opener, figuring she could at least get something of a breeze inside. Only partway, though; she really didn't want the neighbors lingering on their evening dog walks to catch a peek at what she and Caleb were doing inside the garage.

"Those boxes there," she said, pointing toward the group of small and medium-sized boxes from Lowe's that occupied part of the space. Michael had left a lot of his own stuff here as well, but most of his belongings were neatly stacked in the built-in cupboards or stored in plastic bins that had been placed under the workbench. Colin's leftover possessions, on the other hand, occupied a couple of messy piles in the space where a second car should have been parked, as if Michael had shoved everything in there after clearing out his producer's rented home and then had forgotten about it.

Or, more likely, had gotten distracted by his and Audrey's move. It wasn't as though they'd needed the space in the garage, since Audrey's old car had been out of commission during the few months she lived here, and she'd only bought her new CR-V a week or so before they left for Tucson.

Caleb nodded. "Okay. I'll start with the smaller boxes, since they're on top."

He fished his keys out of the pocket of his jeans and opened up the Swiss Army knife he was using as a keychain. Armed with the knife's scissors, he made short work of the packing tape that held the first box closed and opened it up. Inside appeared to be stacks of folders, all of them filled with text printouts from various websites, or full-page images printed off the internet, or bits of paper in various sizes covered in sprawling, heavy handwriting Rosemary guessed had to be Colin's.

"Some of this might be useful to someone at some point," Caleb said as he quickly rifled through the contents of the various folders. "It looks like a lot of notes and ideas for various shows or documentaries. But I don't see anything specific to *Project Demon Hunters.*"

"Michael said you could have some of those materials, if you wanted," Rosemary offered, and he sent her a surprised glance. "I think this stuff has been sitting here because he really didn't know what to do with it. Sounds like Colin's sister Emma didn't want it shipped to her."

Caleb still looked as though he wasn't quite sure that she was serious. "I can have it? You're sure?"

"Yes," she replied. "I guess Michael figured someone might as well make use of this stuff. I know he doesn't have any plans to do any more television work. Or at least, that's what Audrey told me. From what I can tell, he really wasn't that big on *Project Demon Hunters* anyway. Colin sort of talked him into it."

"Good to know." Now apparently finished with that one box, Caleb lifted it from where it had been resting on a larger one beneath, then set it aside. Once again deploying the scissors on his Swiss Army knife, he cut the second box open, then almost immediately set it aside. "Just clothes," he said, sounding disappointed.

Sure enough, the box was filled with neatly folded shirts and jeans, with a dark sport coat on top. Looking at those items sent a wave of sadness through Rosemary. No, she hadn't been a big fan of Colin Turner's, but for some reason, seeing the clothes he'd left behind made her think once again of how his life had been cut so brutally short, how he probably hadn't even been able to fight back against the thing that had killed him. She hadn't asked for a lot of details, but it sounded as if there hadn't been any sign of a struggle.

I'll ask Audrey if I can donate those, she thought. *They might as well go to someone who could use them, instead of sitting here in a box.*

Caleb had moved on to another small box, this one also sitting on top of a medium-sized box. It appeared to hold a jumble of books and

DVDs, all of them piled in together because there hadn't been enough of each type of media for them to require a box of their own. Watching him, Rosemary could feel a trickle of perspiration inch its way down her back, and she reached back surreptitiously to press her tank top against the moisture to blot it away. Her companion, on the other hand, didn't even appear to have broken a sweat.

Of course not. Greek gods don't perspire, silly.

She supposed she should be glad that he was working fairly quickly, and hadn't even paused to look at the books and DVDs, instead setting that box aside as well so he could get at the box underneath. Same drill—he used the scissors on his knife to cut open the tape, then pushed back the folded box top so he could look inside. From what she could tell, this box seemed to have been a catch-all for the items that hadn't been packed in the others. She saw a small space heater, one of those air popcorn-popper gadgets, a small aluminum trashcan, the kind you stepped on to get the lid to open.

And finally, a plain metal cash box, the sort of thing Rosemary herself used when she worked psychic fairs or New Age conventions or any other sort of event where she was away from the store. True, these days most people used plastic, which she ran through the Square app on her phone, but there were always enough customers who paid cash that she brought the cash box along as well.

As Caleb lifted it, she thought she could hear something clank inside.

He tried to open the box, but then he shook his head and said, "It's locked."

"Is there a key?"

"I didn't see one. But let me check again."

After setting the cash box down on top of the cardboard box filled with clothes, he started rummaging around, taking everything out of the container where he'd first found it, even turning the box upside down once it was empty on the off chance that maybe the key had gotten caught in the gap at the bottom where the edges were taped together. At last, though, he set it down, his expression disappointed.

"Nothing," he told her.

"Well, bring it inside," Rosemary said, trying to sound encouraging. "I've got one that's similar, so I know those locks are pretty flimsy. We can try picking it."

To her relief, Caleb didn't argue, only hurriedly put everything back in the box before picking up the one thing they'd found that looked remotely promising. She closed the garage door all the way, then led him back to the house and let out a quick sigh of relief as soon as she was back inside in the blessed air conditioning.

"Let's take the cash box to the family room," she suggested. It was a bit friendlier than the living room, and had a nice big coffee table that would give them a place to set the cash box while they messed with it.

"Sure," he said, and waited while she grabbed the two water glasses they'd left behind so she could bring them with her before following him in there.

They both drank some much-needed water, and then Caleb lifted the cash box and gave it another shake. Once again, she thought she heard something rattle inside.

"Do you think he left some money in there?" she asked.

Caleb's brows pulled together briefly as he appeared to consider her question. "I don't think so. It feels to me like there's one metal object rattling around in there. Could be just a quarter or something else he left behind." After he put the cash box back down on the coffee table, he sent her a sideways glance. "Do you even know why Colin Turner would have something like this?"

"Your guess is as good as mine," she said. "Did he ever have a table at horror or sci-fi or comic conventions, something like that?"

"I doubt it." Caleb crossed his arms and stared at the innocuous-looking cash box, clearly flummoxed. "I mean, I know he attended those kinds of events because that was where I met him, but he was a guest of the con and was on a couple of panels. I don't think he had any reason to sell anything at those conventions."

"Not even DVDs of shows he produced, anything like that?"

"I don't think so." A quick flash of a grin, one that made a little thrill work its way down her spine. Damn, she really needed to get it together. She didn't care how good-looking Caleb was; she shouldn't be reacting to him like she was still back in high school and crushing on the lead in the school play. Apparently, he couldn't tell that her hormones were playing havoc with her brain, because he went on to say, still smiling, "I mean, can you imagine Colin Turner trying to hand-sell DVDs at a science fiction convention? When I met him in person at that one convention a while back, he was doing everything he could to avoid talking to the fans so he could run off to the bar."

Well, that definitely sounded like Colin. She supposed maybe he could turn on the charm when he was trying to get funding for a project, but even then, Rosemary wondered whether he was effective mostly because of his British accent. It had been pretty charming, even though the man himself was an ass.

She returned Caleb's smile. "I see your point. Well, let me run upstairs and get a bobby pin. I've used one before when I had to jigger the lock open on my own cash box. Give me a sec."

As Caleb nodded, she rose from the sofa—a little relieved to put some distance between the two of them so she wouldn't make an idiot of herself—and went upstairs to the master bedroom. Although most of the time, she let her hair go wild because fussing with it took too much work, she did have a small container of bobby pins in the bathroom for those rare times when she wanted to tuck a few strands out of the way. She grabbed two and then headed back down to the living room.

"Okay, let's see what we've got here," she said.

After setting the second bobby pin aside in case she messed up the first one beyond repair, she straightened the first pin, pulled off the little blob of plastic that protected the metal on one end, and then inserted it in the lock. As Caleb watched, she twisted it this way and that, hoping to catch the tumblers. There wasn't any real art to what she was doing; it wasn't as though she actually knew how to pick locks. However, this same method had worked for her in the past, and she didn't know what else to try.

Out of the corner of her eye, she saw the way his fingers tightened on the knees of his jeans, as if he itched to take the bobby pin from her and give it a try himself, but she had to give him credit for remaining silent, for not doing anything so obviously rude. His forbearance was rewarded, too, because in the next moment, she felt something go *click,* and the lock slipped open.

"There you go," she said magnanimously, handing the cash box to him. She figured he might as well have the honor of opening it.

Which he did, lifting the lid so he could peer inside. At first glance, it appeared completely empty. But then he lifted out the cash tray to look under it…and there it was.

A medium-sized brass key, bigger than the one that would have come with the cash box.

A faint smile touched Caleb's mouth as he held up the key, eyeing it closely. "It's marked 'do not duplicate,' but I don't see anything else on it to say where it came from."

"Can I look?"

He handed it over immediately, which relieved Rosemary for some reason. She wasn't sure what she'd been expecting him to do—bolt as soon as he had the key in his possession?—but he didn't seem at all reluctant to let her inspect the thing.

As he'd said, the key had the standard warning against duplication on it. On the reverse side was engraved a five-digit number. "What do you think the number is for?" she asked before giving it back to him.

"I don't know," he replied. "It seems too short

for a serial number, but it's got to be some kind of I.D. I just don't know what kind."

Neither did Rosemary. The thought flitted through her mind that maybe it had been a spare key to Colin's rental house, but she dismissed that possibility almost immediately. House keys generally weren't marked "do not duplicate." No, that was the sort of thing you might get from a place where you worked—except that Colin had been a freelance producer and probably hadn't had a "real" job in years...if ever. When she was ten and her father took off, she and her sister Celeste and their mother had lived in an apartment complex briefly before they moved in with Grandma. The key to the gated swimming pool at the complex had also been marked "do not duplicate"—except Colin hadn't lived in an apartment, but a rented house that was a lot more than he could really afford, according to Audrey.

"Can I see it again?" Rosemary asked, and Caleb obligingly handed it over, although she could tell from his expression that he didn't quite understand why she needed to take a second look at the thing.

She stared down at the key, turning it over and over in her hand. Surely, she'd seen something like this before, but she couldn't think where. The thought nagged at the edges of her memory, and she frowned. Where...where...?

Of course.

Her fingers clenched around the key, and she shot a look of triumph at a somewhat startled Caleb. "I know what it is," she announced.

"This key goes to some kind of storage facility."

Chapter 3

CALEB STARED AT HER. "HOW CAN YOU KNOW that?"

She shrugged. "Okay, I don't know for absolutely certain, but my sisters and I shared a storage unit for a while when we were first putting together our inventory for the store. The key looked a lot like the one that you got for the gate to the property—not exactly, but close enough."

This response earned her a considering nod. "Can I take another look?"

"Sure."

He took the key from her. As he did so, his fingers brushed against hers. Just for the barest bit of a second, nothing that she guessed had been deliberate, but even so, a thrill shivered its way through her body.

Get a grip, she told herself. *This isn't high school.*

No, it wasn't. In a way, she wanted to mock herself for being so bowled over by Caleb Dixon just because he was unbelievably good-looking. Hadn't she evolved beyond that sort of behavior? It was what was inside that mattered, right?

Well, her brain might believe that kind of thing, but her body was telling her something very different.

Luckily, he didn't seem to have noticed her discomfiture. Instead, he was turning the key over in his hand again, dark brows drawn together as he stared down at it. "I wonder if there's any way to figure out which storage facility this came from based on the number engraved on it."

"Probably not," Rosemary told him. "I mean, if it were that easy, then it would be kind of dangerous to lose the key to your storage place, since someone could just look on the internet to figure out where the key goes. They'd still have to get inside your individual unit, but it would get them past the first hurdle."

He didn't look exactly crestfallen, but she got the impression that he was inwardly berating himself for not thinking of that himself. Not for the first time, she wished she could actually read minds instead of getting impressions and flashes of people and events, or—a little more rarely—feelings from her surroundings. She couldn't get much from Caleb, which didn't tell her anything at all. Oh, sure, there had been more than one occasion when she'd met a person and knew somehow in their bones that they were up to no good, but she didn't get that kind of feeling from him. She really didn't get anything at all.

Well, except possibly a strange desire to jump his bones. She tried to excuse her reaction by reminding herself that it had been a while. All right, a lot more than just a while.

And whose fault is that? she thought, although she wouldn't allow herself to linger on the answer.

"But," she went on, thinking that maybe if she acted brisk and businesslike, her overactive hormones would get the message, "possibly there's some paperwork from the storage company in all those files we left out in the garage."

"Right," Caleb said. The disappointment was gone from his expression, and he now looked excited and eager again. "I guess we should go get the box of files and take a closer look. I didn't see anything like that, but I wasn't really looking for it, either."

The thought of going back out to the hot garage wasn't all that appealing, but she realized they only had to grab the box and bring it back into the house so they could inspect its contents here. "Okay. Let's get it."

They both rose from the couch and headed out to the garage, where Caleb hefted the box with ease and brought it back inside. "Where should we put this?" he asked as she shut the kitchen door behind them.

"Probably the dining room table," Rosemary replied. "That'll give us more room to spread out. This way."

She loved almost everything about Michael's house, but one of her favorite spaces was the dining room, probably because of the stained glass window set high in the eastern wall. The window had stylized flowers in warm shades of yellow and gold and copper, tones that were echoed in the bronze chandelier that hung above the large Mission-style table, as well as in the landscape paintings that adorned the walls.

Whether Caleb was impressed by the room was difficult to tell; he set the box of files on the table and almost immediately began pulling out loose papers and file folders, doing his best to make neat stacks even though not everything wanted to cooperate. Once he was done, he glanced over at Rosemary. "I'm not sure of the best way to go about this."

"I doubt there is one," she said, tucking a loose tendril of curly hair back behind one ear as she leaned down to take a closer look at the files he'd set out. "I mean, it seems as though Michael just sort of tossed stuff in the box, so even if there was once some kind of filing system going on here, it's pretty much gone now."

"True." Caleb pushed one stack toward her. "I guess you can start with these, and I'll go through this one." A finger tapped against the pile of folders immediately in front of him.

"Okay." She hesitated as she sent a quick sideways glance at her watch. Now it was almost seven. Dinnertime, but she didn't know whether she dared suggest ordering something to fortify them while they went through Colin's papers. Then again, the worst Caleb could say was no. And she realized she was hungry and had no idea how long this was going to take. "Um…did you want to get a pizza or something? This might keep us busy for a while."

He looked surprised. "Is it that late?"

"Well, not *late* late or anything, but it's almost seven."

"Oh, well, sure. Pizza's a good idea. Pepperoni?"

A few years ago, she would have said that sounded great. Now, though, she could only shake her head and reply, "How about just on half the pizza? I try not to eat red meat too often."

To her relief, he didn't look at all taken aback. "Half is fine."

"I'll call it in." Another pause, during which she wondered whether to go for broke. Nothing ventured, she supposed. "You want a beer? I've got some in the fridge."

That offer made him smile once again. "A beer sounds awesome."

Okay, so obviously, he didn't have a problem drinking with her. She gave him a nod and headed into the kitchen, where she got her phone out of her purse and then rummaged through the drawer where Michael kept his take-out menus. They were all pretty well-worn, some of them with grease stains. Obviously, he'd ordered a lot of take-out in his day.

After calling in the order for the pizza—half pepperoni, half veggie—she got two bottles of Anchor Steam out of the fridge, popped off the caps, and took them with her back into the dining room. Caleb was leafing through a stack of papers, one file folder set off to one side, which meant he'd probably already looked through it and found nothing.

"Thanks," he said as she handed him a beer.

"Any luck?" she asked, even though she probably already knew the answer.

He took a swig of beer and replied, "Not in looking for a storage unit contract. But I did find some notes and research that might be useful—if you don't mind me taking them."

"I already said you could."

"True, but—"

She tilted her head at him, then swallowed some of her own beer as she waited for him to explain.

His next words surprised her, though. "This feels weird, doesn't it?"

If she'd wanted to be self-conscious, she could have guessed that he was asking about the two of them standing here and drinking beer when they'd only just met barely an hour earlier, but Rosemary knew that wasn't what he'd meant. "A little," she admitted. "But, on the other hand, I'd like to think that Colin would want someone to continue his work, wouldn't want all that to go to waste." She gestured with her free hand toward the file folder Caleb had set aside. Since he only nodded, looking thoughtful, she went on, "How did you get into all this, anyway?"

"Filmmaking?"

"Well, that and the occult. It's kind of niche, isn't it?"

"Says the woman who owns a metaphysical bookstore."

That comment made her chuckle. "Okay, you got me. Being psychic runs in my family, though, so it's not really that strange where I ended up."

Even as she said the words, though, she could feel herself tense, wondering how he was going to react to that revelation. Long ago, she'd decided to get the whole psychic thing over with early on when she met someone, just because it was emotionally easier to have a guy run for the hills when she barely knew him, rather than waiting for a connection to form and then have him decide that he really wasn't in the market for a psychic girlfriend.

Not that Caleb Dixon appeared to be looking for one, either. However, they'd formed some kind of tentative partnership already, so it still seemed safer to get the truth about herself out of the way.

He didn't seem put off, though…more intrigued than anything else. "Really? You're psychic?"

"Yes. Me and my two sisters. We co-own the bookstore—that's why it's called 'Sisters We.'"

"So, it runs in the family?"

She nodded. "My grandmother was psychic, my mother is psychic—my sister Celeste is the only one with any kids, and she has just the one boy right now, so we don't know whether her daughters will be psychic, too. Assuming she has any," Rosemary added, thinking that two-year-old Tyler was enough to handle at the moment. But with Isabel divorced and definitely not planning to start a family any time soon, there didn't seem to be many more prospects for adding to the younger generation of McGuires. All right, Rosemary knew she had plenty of time, but since her last date had been almost a year ago and she had absolutely no desire to do the whole single-mother thing, she doubted she'd be popping out any psychic daughters any time soon.

Caleb's eyes were full of questions, but she guessed from the way he paused that he didn't want to ask anything that might offend her. "So... how psychic are you?"

"I don't read minds, if that's what you're asking."

"I suppose I should be relieved."

"I don't know," she returned. "I guess it depends on whether you're hiding something."

Her remark only made him grin. "Not that I know of. Well, except that my electric bill is overdue because I was waiting to get paid on Thursday, and I figured if it was already late, I could take care of it then."

This confession actually made him that much more appealing to her. She could identify with someone who was trying to achieve his dream while barely scraping by. Okay, she hadn't done much "scraping" over the past six years, thanks to the money she'd inherited when her grandmother passed away, but at least she now realized Caleb wasn't some dilettante rich boy playing filmmaker because it amused him. When she opened the front door to let him in, she'd noticed an older-model Nissan pickup truck parked out front, and the modest vehicle he drove seemed to support his story about waiting to pay the electric bill.

Since it didn't seem like a very good idea to tell him anything of what she'd actually been thinking, she only nodded.

After a somewhat awkward pause, he asked, "So, if you don't read minds, what do you do?"

"I get feelings about things," she replied, knowing how vague that sounded. The technical term for what she did was "clairsentience," but it sounded horribly pedantic to introduce that word in casual conversation. "And I can sense other people's feelings, can sometimes pick up psychic residue in a location, if you know what I mean."

"Clairvoyance?" Caleb asked. That eager expression had returned to his handsome features, as if what he actually wanted to do was film her while she was having a psychic episode or something.

It really didn't work that way, though.

"Like visions?" Rosemary shook her head. "Not exactly. I'll get flashes of things sometimes, but it's not like I can sit down and get clear images of something that's happening across town...or across the country. My feelings generally are pretty accurate, though."

His mouth opened, as if he was about to ask another question, but the doorbell rang right then.

"Pizza," she announced, quite unnecessarily. After all, she wasn't expecting any visitors. Izzy and CeeCee had visited a couple of times, but they would never drop by unannounced. They had too much respect for Michael and his house to do that. In fact, CeeCee had actually gotten a babysitter for Tyler when she made those visits, as if even her motherly indulgence didn't extend to letting her two-year-old son run loose in this carefully preserved Craftsman sanctum.

Rosemary went to the door and handed over some cash, then brought the pizza into the kitchen. No way would she set a hot pizza box down on any of Michael's furniture, but the tile counters in the kitchen should be safe enough.

Caleb followed her, beer still in hand. "I should have helped you pay for that."

"And take that money away from SoCal Edison?" she joked. "It's fine."

"Then next time."

Had he really meant that there might be a next time, that this little fact-finding mission wasn't a one-off? She certainly hoped so, but she knew better than to respond with anything more than a casual, "Sure."

Getting out plates and grabbing some paper

towels for napkins helped her to cover up some of her discomfiture. Once they had everything they needed, they went back out to the dining room. Silence for a few minutes after that as they ate pizza and drank beer, and did their best to do some one-handed sorting of the papers in front of them.

After she'd finished her first piece of veggie pizza, though, Rosemary asked, "What about you?"

"What about me?" Caleb responded as he set yet another file folder off to one side.

"You and filmmaking. The occult. Whatever."

He picked up his bottle of Anchor Steam and drank, then said, "Oh, I was one of those kids who borrowed his parents' video camera and tried to remake *Star Wars* in his backyard."

"No prequels?" she asked. After all, the original *Star Wars* had been around for almost two decades by the time either of them was born.

A chuckle. "I prefer the classics. Anyway, I just thought it was cool that you could make something so much bigger than yourself, could tell a story with actors and props and scenery. Of course, my little sister didn't like getting drafted to play Princess Leia every weekend, but she went along with it…mostly."

Rosemary had to grin. "I thought everyone wanted to be Princess Leia."

"Did you?"

"Hell, yeah. Princess Leia doesn't take crap from anybody."

"True."

They both sobered after that exchange, though, maybe because they were both thinking of Carrie Fisher, whose own life hadn't exactly had a fairy tale ending. Then again, neither had Princess Leia's, come to think of it.

"Anyway," Caleb went on, "film school was kind of out of reach, so I've just done what I could by working on low-budget stuff, picking up non-union gigs here and there."

"But you're on IMDB," Rosemary said. "That's more than a lot of people can say."

Almost as soon as the words left her mouth, she realized she'd kind of screwed up. Did she really want Caleb to know she'd been checking up on him?

However, he didn't seem annoyed. In fact, a corner of his mouth lifted in a twitch that wasn't quite a smile. "Doing your research, I see."

Since she'd already put her foot in it, she figured she might as well go for broke. "Well, I wanted to make sure I wasn't inviting a serial killer back to my house."

That comment actually made him laugh out loud. "Yeah, I suppose that would be a good idea.

I guess you could tell I don't have the world's most impressive filmmaking resumé."

"At least you have one," she pointed out.

"I suppose." He was quiet for a few seconds as he lifted his bottle of beer and eyed it, probably trying to determine how much was left. Rosemary was almost done with hers, but she didn't know whether she should offer to get a second round or not. That might be pushing things. "As far as the occult stuff goes...." Caleb shrugged. "I don't know...I've just always been fascinated by the supernatural. My mom is into it, actually. I suppose that's where it started—she always had books about ghosts and UFOs and psychics and all kinds of stuff lying around the house. My dad would tease her about it all the time."

That all sounded so...normal. Rosemary tried to think if she could even recall her father teasing her mother about anything. Maybe he had, back before things started to go sour between the two of them, although he'd always seemed too serious to engage in that sort of behavior. At any rate, so many of her early memories of her father were overlaid by the things he did and said when she was older, it was now hard to remember the good times. Tone light, she said, "I guess his teasing wasn't enough to put you off."

"I guess not." Caleb drank the last swallow of beer in his bottle, then set it down before he reached for yet another file folder and began leafing through it.

That seemed to be her signal to get some work done as well. At some point, she figured she'd go back into the kitchen to fetch another piece of pizza, but her hunger had been assuaged enough that she could wait another five or ten minutes. At the moment, it was probably a good idea to look as if she was contributing something worthwhile to their search.

The folder she picked up next didn't appear to be one of Colin's research binders. No, it was a clutter of random papers—take-out menus, the instruction manual for a paper shredder, receipts from the grocery store and various restaurants and liquor stores and gas stations. Just the everyday sort of crap that accumulated unchecked unless you threw everything out as it came in or were one of those anal-retentive types who scanned all their receipts and kept a tidy household ledger on your computer. Rosemary knew all about it, mostly because she had a similar pile accumulating in a basket in the office upstairs.

But then she came across a full-page receipt that had obviously been produced by someone's laser printer...from a place called Storage Etc.

She drew it out, then scanned the paperwork. Yes, Colin Turner had rented a storage unit at the facility, which—according to the small map printed on the reverse side of the paper—looked like it was right off Los Feliz Boulevard on the east side of the 5 Freeway, a few blocks away from San Fernando Road. He'd paid last December for a year in advance, which meant that technically, the unit was still in his name and shouldn't have been disturbed. Since the paperwork listed the unit number, it would be easy to find, and because they already had the key to get them onto the property, they shouldn't have any problem getting access. And there on the back, scribbled in Colin's heavy black handwriting, was a set of three numbers, probably the combination for the padlock on the unit itself.

"I think I found it," she said, then handed the piece of paper to Caleb.

He took it from her, dark eyes quickly scanning the sheet. "He paid in advance."

"Good news, right?"

"Very."

Their gazes met, and she made herself look back at him steadily, hoping he didn't see anything except excitement that they'd actually managed to find the one piece of information they needed. "So…what next?" she asked.

He glanced toward the window, where the sky was finally darkening toward twilight. "Well, it's probably too late to head over there now. Most of those places close at around six, maybe seven o'clock at the most. But we should go tomorrow."

"We should?" she said, not sure why she should be so surprised that he'd want to include her.

"Well, of course," he replied. "I wouldn't know anything about the storage unit—or where it's located—if it weren't for you. Why do you think I wouldn't want you to come along?"

Good question. Put that way, the proposition sounded pretty reasonable. And Wednesday was her day off this week—the shop was closed on Sundays, so the three sisters each got their other day off on a rotating basis so no one would be stuck always having to work on a Saturday. She could go with Caleb to check the storage unit without being forced to explain to Isabel or Celeste why she couldn't possibly come in to work that day.

"I don't know," she said. "But you're right. Besides, if I come with you, then I can let Audrey and Michael know right away if we've actually found the backup files for the video Colin shot."

"Exactly." His dark eyes glinted at her, the corners crinkling a little with amusement. "Is there more beer? Because this calls for a celebration, don't you think?"

"Plenty more," she responded. "I'll go get us a couple more bottles. Back in a sec."

She headed into the kitchen, smiling to herself as she went. Who knew that her day would end up with her sharing beer and pizza with the hottest guy she'd ever met, and getting to play Nancy Drew at the same time?

Right then, she didn't need to be psychic to know that her future was definitely looking up.

Chapter 4

HE LEFT AROUND NINE O'CLOCK AFTER THEY spent a little more time going through Colin's papers—more to put things in order than because they were looking for anything else. In fact, Caleb departed with several folders' worth of material tucked under one arm, and thanked her again for letting him have the research. No romantic overtures or anything like that, but he was acting pretty darn friendly.

Rosemary chose to take that as a good sign.

They decided to meet at ten o'clock in order to let the worst of the rush hour traffic get cleared out. He told her that he lived in Eagle Rock and so he didn't have quite as far to drive as she did, but it was still better to give it a little time in order to be safe. Besides, that storage unit wasn't going anywhere.

Because she didn't know how much digging through stuff they'd have to do in Colin's storage space—or how hot it was going to be—Rosemary put on a pair of well-worn skinny jeans and a green sleeveless top with some fun tone-on-tone embroidery around the neckline. A pair of newish beaded sandals—thank God she'd gotten a pedicure just last Friday—and some big silver hoops, and she thought she looked pretty good. Not dressed up or anything, but also not completely sloppy, either.

Traffic on the 210 westbound was still pretty thick, but she soldiered her way through it until she could cut south on the 2, which would bring her to the San Fernando Road exit and a jump of only a couple of blocks to get to the Storage Etc. facility. Once she'd gotten off the 210, she was able to go a little faster, but still not the full speed limit. Impatiently, she drummed her fingers on the steering wheel. She thought she'd given herself plenty of time, but it looked as though she was going to be at least five minutes late no matter what she did.

Oh, well. Being late was almost a given in Southern California. It was only when you were heinously late—like twenty minutes or even a half hour—that the person who was meeting you would generally give you the side-eye.

The storage place turned out to be located on

a little carve-out of a street just off Los Feliz, with modest one-story homes across the way. There wasn't a lot of parking, but at that time of day, it wasn't so crowded that she couldn't pull her Fiat up to the curb right behind Caleb's truck. He got out as soon as she parked and came over while she was locking the vehicle. Since she'd kept the paperwork and the key, he couldn't have gotten inside without her.

"Ready?" he asked, again with that eager little-boy expression on his face. Or at least, as much of it as she could see; the sunglasses he was wearing hid his eyes.

"Yes," she said, then reached into her purse and pulled out the contract with the padlock combination written on the reverse side. "This says it was a ten by twelve unit, so it should be one of the ones you drive up to and not any of the smaller ones inside the building."

"Should we drive in?"

Good question. Normally, that was what you did when accessing those sorts of storage units, but since they were already standing here and talking, it might look strange for them to get in one of their cars just to go a couple of hundred feet. Besides, even though she couldn't see anyone through the plate-glass windows that framed the front entrance where the office was located, that didn't mean they weren't watching on security cameras or something.

"No, let's just walk," she replied. "I mean, once we use the key to get in the gate, it's going to be obvious that we're not trying to break in or anything."

"True."

They headed over to the gate, Rosemary doing her best not to take sideways glances up at Caleb while she walked. He seemed very tall as he strode along next to her. Had she just not noticed the difference in their heights the day before, or did it feel more obvious now when they were walking side by side?

It probably didn't matter all that much. She'd come to terms with her lack of height a while back, even though she still wished from time to time that she could be statuesque like Izzy, who was nearly five foot ten, or even slightly above average like CeeCee, who was a couple of inches shorter than their oldest sister. At barely five four, Rosemary had always felt like the runt of the litter.

Caleb wasn't quite a foot taller than she was, but even so, she'd have to stand on her tiptoes to—

Don't you even, she told herself. *Pay attention.*

She got out the key and inserted it in the lock on the gate, wondering what she would do if she'd miscalculated and it was for something else completely. But the gate swung inward without any trouble, and she and Caleb slipped in, then paused.

"B-222," she said, scanning the information on the paperwork.

"That way, I think." He pointed to the aisle on their right. "Probably at the end of the row, judging by the way the numbers are going up."

Of course, the unit they were looking for was located at the far end of the row where they stood. Well, at least at barely ten o'clock, the sun hadn't gotten quite hot enough yet to make it too uncomfortable out here. Rosemary guessed that a few hours from now, the reflected heat from the metal storage units and the blacktop beneath their feet would make the spot where they stood nearly unbearable.

She only nodded, though, and they set out for the unit in question. As Caleb had predicted, it sat in a prime spot at the end of its row, which meant it could have been accessed by either the narrow lane they'd just traversed, or the one that came from the other side, meeting it at right angles. She turned the paper over, to get the combination for the padlock securing the door.

And thank God Colin had used a combination lock and not one with a key. That would have made this outing a lot more difficult. She supposed they could have used something to break the lock, but that sort of activity definitely would have attracted some very unwelcome attention.

"How about you read the numbers, and I enter them?" Caleb asked, obviously noting the way she'd awkwardly shuffled the paper to her other hand in preparation to work with the padlock.

"Perfect," she said, relieved…and a little surprised by his thoughtfulness.

Nice and divinely gorgeous? That was a very dangerous combination….

Clearing her throat, she went on, "Seventeen, twenty-two, eight."

The lock clicked open. Caleb pulled it off and shoved in his jeans pocket, where it rattled against his keys. His hand rested on the latch. "Do you want me to do the honors, or should you?"

"Go ahead," Rosemary replied. "It'll probably be easier for you."

Which turned out to be only the truth, since he slid up the roll-up door with one casually graceful push. The bright early morning sunlight glared inside, revealing the contents of the storage unit.

"Wow," Caleb said after a long pause. "This could take us a while."

There was an understatement. The unit was

one of the bigger spaces the facility offered—at least, according to what she'd read on the Storage Etc. website the night before—but it was packed almost from floor to ceiling with boxes and furniture, including a queen-size mattress wrapped in plastic. They'd definitely have to haul that out of the way before they could really get a good look at anything.

"It looks like he has a whole apartment's worth of stuff in here," Caleb remarked. "I wonder why he wasn't using any of it."

Good question, although Rosemary thought she had an answer. "I remember Audrey saying that Colin was renting a furnished house. I suppose he just decided to put everything in storage for whenever his lease was up."

"I guess so." Caleb still looked dubious. Even so, he grabbed one end of the mattress and dragged it a few feet out of the way, biceps bulging impressively the whole time. It was hard not to stare, but she did her best. Panting a little, he added, "Although I wonder why he'd go to the extra expense of renting someplace furnished when he already had all this stuff."

Colin Turner's thought processes were not anything Rosemary had much desire to analyze, but she could guess at some of his motivations... especially now that she was able to get a better look at what the mattress had been hiding. The furniture in the storage unit looked like a collection of garage sale finds—pieces that were chipped and scratched or badly painted. Nothing seemed to match, and they didn't go together in a quirky and fun way, either, unlike the eclectic pieces she'd assembled for her own house in Glendora.

"This was probably his fallback furniture," Rosemary said. "I was never at the house he was renting, but it sounded pretty high-end. I have a feeling he wanted to project an image of doing well, even if that maybe wasn't his reality. He was probably riding high on the *Project Demon Hunters* money but kept this stuff in storage… just in case."

Caleb looked around again, a faint frown touching his brows. Then his expression cleared, and he gave a philosophical lift of the shoulders. "I guess I can see that. Anyway, this is a lot of stuff to go through. Any ideas?"

"Start at the outside and work in?" she suggested. Organization wasn't exactly her forté—this task was something Isabel probably could have tackled with the brute force and efficiency of a field marshal, but unfortunately, she wasn't here. "Or vice versa?"

"Probably vice versa," he said after a considering pause. "At least that way, we'll be finishing up just as we're reaching the entrance to the storage unit, instead of having to burrow our way out."

That made sense. "Sounds like a plan."

"You can go through the furniture," Caleb offered. "It might be kind of hard for you to reach some of those boxes."

Which was only the truth, but she still slanted a sideways look up at him through her lashes. "Are you saying I'm short?"

"Well—"

She chuckled and decided she'd better let him off the hook, he looked so awkward, gaze moving around the interior of the storage unit so it wouldn't have to fix on her. "It's okay. I am short. So thanks for letting me tackle the furniture."

Her response earned her another one of those flashing grins. "Not a problem."

He headed toward the back of the space, where there was just barely enough room for him to grab a box and lower it to the floor. The top had only been folded in, not taped shut, so he didn't have to spend any time digging out his Swiss Army knife to cut it open.

"Bedding," he said after peering inside. "Don't think that's going to help us much."

"Unless he shoved a couple of disk drives in there." After all, they were talking about Colin. Rosemary hadn't known the guy well at all, but even she had been able to tell that he had something of a paranoid streak.

"True."

While Caleb was digging through the folded sheets and blankets, she turned toward the battered dresser immediately to her right. Methodically opening all the drawers and looking inside didn't turn up anything, though, except a few loose pennies and some old movie ticket stubs. If there had been someplace where she could have discarded the trash, she would have, but since she didn't spot anything she could use, she only closed the drawers again, leaving their little bits of rubbish in place.

Next up was a nightstand. Same thing there, except that one contained an old Ace bandage, its edges frayed and worn. Rosemary wondered why Colin had needed it. Had he wrenched an ankle or wrist while filming one of his shows? Someone who lived on the edge the way he had probably didn't have any health insurance. That thought saddened her for some reason, and she put the bandage away while holding back a small sigh. Actually, it felt kind of terrible to be here, pawing through the things he'd tried to keep hidden from the world. Sure, she could rationalize their search by telling herself that Colin would have wanted the footage released, and since this kind of search was the only way they could possibly find it, there wasn't anything wrong with what she and Caleb were doing.

It sure felt wrong, though.

If her companion was having any kind of reservations about their current activity, he didn't show it. Apparently done looking through the box that contained the sheets and blankets, he'd set it aside and was already searching through another smaller one filled with a miscellaneous assortment of kitchen gadgets and odds and ends.

Clearly, she needed to be more efficient, although she didn't have nearly as many items to go through as Caleb did. After closing the bottom drawer of the nightstand she'd been inspecting, she straightened up and dusted her hands on the knees of her jeans, glad that she'd put on a well-worn pair and not the new dark ones that would have shown up every speck of the light-colored dust that even now floated through the air of the storage unit, dancing in the sunlight like motes of pure gold.

Hands on her hips, she surveyed the other pieces of furniture, taking note of what seemed most promising. No point in looking at the small dining table and matching chairs—it wasn't as if they had drawers that could hold anything. There was a low entertainment unit with storage space at the bottom, a side table with a single drawer, and then a big oak desk and file cabinet...and a footlocker.

For some reason, she felt drawn to that footlocker. Was that her psychic sense finally waking up and kicking in to provide her with some guidance?

Maybe. Or maybe it just seemed like a footlocker would be a good place to hide some disk drives.

As she crouched down next to it, though, she realized she might have run into a small snag. Just like the storage unit itself, the footlocker was secured with a padlock with a combination lock. Unlike the lock they'd opened just a few minutes earlier, however, she didn't have the combination to this one.

Still, she knew she'd have to give it a try. Maybe Colin had made things easy for himself and had used the same combination for both locks.

Two tries were enough to tell her that no, of course Colin couldn't have made things that simple.

Caleb glanced over at her as he set aside the box of kitchen gadgets. "Did you find something?"

She gave an exasperated shrug. "Who knows? The fact that this thing is locked tells me Colin probably had something important inside, but we don't have the combination."

"The one we used already?" he suggested, but she shook her head.

"That's what I just tried. It didn't work."

His mouth tightened, but then he shrugged, expression resigned. "Well, maybe look through something else for now, and then we can circle back to that."

Caleb's suggestion sounded like the best thing to do, and yet Rosemary wasn't sure whether she was willing to let it go. Even as he turned back toward the stack of boxes he'd been working on, she stood there in front of the footlocker, arms crossed. So frustrating to have their efforts stymied by something that seemed so small and insignificant. Just a round piece of metal that needed to have a sequence of a few numbers entered to make it work.

She saw it as a glimmer on the air, almost as if the dust motes had coalesced in that instant, forming a hazy, blurred numeral before it disappeared once more.

Five.

No…she had to have imagined it. But what if she hadn't? What if her psychic senses had somehow reached out and plucked that number from the ether?

Might as well try, she told herself. *It's not a*

bomb or something—it's not going to explode if you enter the wrong combination.

Or at least, she hoped it wouldn't. For all she knew, Colin Turner had been the sort of guy who liked to leave booby traps for unwary intruders.

But if that were the case, either she or Caleb probably would have already gotten zapped. She squatted down and held the padlock in her left hand while she turned the dial with her right, pausing at the number five.

Fine. Unfortunately, a single number did not a combination make.

The second one blazed bright in her mind, maybe because it was part of the street number of the house where she'd grown up.

Twenty-two.

She rotated the dial, resting on the little mark indicating the number she'd wanted. No explosions or anything, but of course, she was going to need more than those two numbers. Sometimes locks like this had three-number combinations, sometimes four. About all she could do was keep going and see what happened.

But to keep going, she needed another prompt, and right then, her mind was awfully blank. Neither did the dust motes appear inclined to form another numeral like they had the first time. A few feet away, Caleb paused and stared down at her, obviously confused as to why she'd be squatting there beside the footlocker when there was clearly nothing she could do with it. He held a box that had an address written on one side—35 Louise Street, probably an old rental property where Colin had once lived.

That was it. She knew it with as much certainty as the color of her hair—chestnut brown —or her eyes—blue.

Thirty-five.

The lock clicked open. Caleb's eyes widened.

"How the hell did you do that?"

She grinned up at him. "I told you I was psychic."

That reply earned her a shake of the head, but she wouldn't let herself get distracted by her companion's obvious befuddlement. Instead, she slipped the padlock out of the latch, then lifted the lid of the footlocker to see what was inside.

Rosemary had been expecting to see portable hard drives, or at least DVD-ROMs. Reel-to-reel tapes. Something that would obviously be the footage she and Caleb were looking for.

What she saw, however, were several photo albums, a few items of women's clothing, a stuffed panda that looked like the sort of thing you might win at the county fair. The collection of odds and ends was so completely out of left field that about all she could do was say, "What the hell?"

Caleb came over and stared down into the footlocker. "What is that stuff?"

"I have no idea."

"Was Colin Turner into cross-dressing or something?"

The mental image of Colin in a pink mohair sweater à la Ed Wood was so incongruous, Rosemary couldn't help but laugh. "I don't think so," she said as she lifted up a sweatshirt with a Universal Studios logo printed on it. "This stuff doesn't look very fluffy. Also, it's way too small for him." She set down the sweatshirt, then reached for one of the photo albums and opened it. Inside were picture after picture of an extremely pretty woman who looked to be in her mid-twenties, with long dark hair and big brown eyes. Had Colin been obsessed with her or something?

If he had, it seemed the obsession had been mutual, because there were also plenty of shots of the unknown woman with Colin—laughing into the camera with what looked like the Santa Monica pier in the background, or someplace she thought was The Grove shopping center in the Fairfax District, or another one with the unmistakable outlines of Griffith Observatory behind them. In fact, as Rosemary flipped through the rest of the first photo album and then went on to the next, it looked as if the couple had managed to photograph themselves in pretty much every popular tourist destination in Southern California.

Looking over her shoulder, Caleb asked, "Is there anything that says who she was?"

"I don't think so." None of the photos were annotated, as if Colin had known the details of every photograph so well that he hadn't seen any need to make a written record. Just to be sure, though, she went through each album page by page, inwardly surprised that the man she'd met briefly in Tucson could have ever looked so happy, so at ease. It was hard to say for sure, but she guessed that these photos had probably been taken a while back, maybe as much as ten years. He certainly appeared younger and far more relaxed. Not bothering to keep the disappoint- ment out of her tone, she added, "I can't find anything at all."

"Well, look through the clothes. Maybe you'll find something there."

Rosemary sort of doubted that. What had been packed in the footlocker were obviously souvenir sweatshirts and T-shirts, not the kind of thing that had pockets where you'd stow a ticket stub or a receipt. However, as she unfolded the tee at the bottom of the pile—one that had a "Venice Beach" logo screen-printed on the front—a piece of paper came fluttering out. Or rather, it was two pieces of paper stapled together, the kind of handwritten sales ticket you might get at a boutique somewhere, along with a more formal receipt from a credit card machine. She'd expected to have it say "Colin Turner," but no, that wasn't his signature, nor his name.

No, it had been signed by someone named Madeline Nash.

A surge of excitement went through Rosemary, even though all they had was a name—and one that wasn't unusual enough to make tracking the mystery woman down all that easy. Still, it was something.

She handed the receipt to Caleb, who stared at it and frowned.

Rosemary wasn't frowning, however. This was quite possibly the clue they'd been looking for.

"I don't know who Madeline Nash was to Colin…but I think we need to find out."

Chapter 5

EVEN THOUGH GOING THROUGH THE REST OF the storage unit felt anticlimactic after that discovery, Rosemary and Caleb dutifully searched the rest of the boxes and the few remaining pieces of furniture. As she'd halfway expected, they didn't find a damn thing. Maybe this all had been a wild goose chase after all. Really, they didn't know for sure that Colin had made backups of his footage. He could have been planning to and never gotten around to it. Things had gotten kind of crazy with *Project Demon Hunters* toward the end, at least as far as Audrey had described the situation. By that point, Rosemary had, thankfully, been back home in Glendora and safely away from the worst of the action.

Once they were done with their search, Caleb locked the storage unit back up, and the two of them walked out the spot to where they'd left their cars. "Buy you lunch?" he asked, his tone almost too casual.

A happy little thrill went through Rosemary, even as she tried to tell herself that he was probably only trying to be nice and was simply returning the favor for the pizza and beer she'd provided the previous evening. Also, they'd just spent the better part of three hours rummaging through the storage unit, and she guessed he was probably just as hungry as she was. "Sure," she said, then added, "but I'm not dressed for anything fancy."

"No worries. There's a place not too far from here that's good for lunch. They have a patio, so we can sit outside if you want."

She wasn't so sure about that, since it was a pretty warm day and air conditioning sounded good after mucking around in that storage unit for the last couple of hours. But she could cool down in her car on the drive over. Anyway, just because there was outdoor seating didn't mean there wouldn't also be shade.

"Sounds great. Should I follow you?"

"Yes. It's only about a mile from here."

Rosemary nodded and got into her Fiat, while Caleb unlocked his truck and climbed into the driver's seat. A minute later, they were turning left on San Fernando Road and heading up into Glendale. She didn't know this area all that well, but she supposed if she lost track of him, she'd just call.

However, those emergency measures weren't necessary. Traffic was a little thick, but not so heavy that she couldn't keep an eye on his black Nissan truck, or the way it turned into the parking lot of a place called Foxy's. Thoughtfully, he'd turned on his signal when they were still a hundred feet away from the entrance, so she had no problem figuring out where they were going.

Foxy's? she thought with an inner lift of her eyebrow. *Is he trying to tell me something?*

Hard to say, but they were here, and actually managed to find parking. The receipt with Madeline Nash's signature was tucked into Rosemary's purse, along with one photo of her, just for extra insurance. They hadn't really discussed yet how to track her down, but she had a few ideas.

Since it was now past one o'clock—and because it was a Wednesday—they didn't have to wait for a table, but were immediately guided out to a cute little table for two on the patio, next to a planter filled with cheery vinca and petunias, and with plenty of overhang to shield them from the midday sun. The hostess, a pretty blonde girl who didn't look old enough to be out of high school but obviously had to be over eighteen, told them their waiter would be out in a few minutes.

Rosemary picked up the menu and gave it a quick scan. Plenty of stuff she'd need to avoid, but she figured she couldn't really go wrong with a grilled chicken sandwich. The restaurant served alcohol, although she knew she'd only order an iced tea. It was one thing to share a couple of beers out of her fridge; she wasn't going to make Caleb spring for some overpriced chardonnay.

He set down his menu just a few seconds after she did. Those warm brown eyes met hers, and she found herself looking for some reason to glance away. Putting her napkin in her lap seemed like a good excuse, so she busied herself with that for a few seconds.

"Who do you think she was?" he asked. Most likely, he'd noticed the awkward pause before he spoke and decided the best thing to do was ignore it.

"Madeline Nash?"

He nodded.

About all Rosemary could do was lift her shoulders. "Old girlfriend?"

"That was my first thought, except Colin Turner didn't seem like the sentimental type."

No, he didn't. Then again, people could hide all sorts of things about themselves, could present a very different front to the world than who they truly were deep inside. Yes, Colin had acted like a jerk, but maybe he'd behaved that way as a reaction to long-buried wounds he'd never allowed to heal.

Or he could have been a raging asshole and nothing more, and had kept the photo albums as a way to remind himself of all the ways Madeline had wronged him. Since Rosemary hadn't been there to witness their relationship for herself, it was impossible to say.

"True," she allowed.

The waiter came by then, and since they'd both already made their selections, it only took a minute for them to place their orders. As soon as they were alone again, Rosemary reached in her purse and pulled out the photo of Madeline she'd brought with her. This one showed the woman posed against an arbor covered in bougainvillea, the shocking pink of its blooms creating a bright halo around her head. She definitely was beautiful, whoever she'd been to Colin.

"I thought I'd take a picture of this with my phone and send it and her name to Audrey, and then she can pass it on to Michael," Rosemary said.

"What about Colin's sister?" Caleb asked. "You could check with her."

The thought had crossed her mind, but then Rosemary shook her head. "I'd rather not bother Emma. She's still grieving…at least, that's the impression I got from Michael. It's probably better to let him handle this without involving her. He's really good at tracking people down—or at least, he knows someone who's good at it, which I guess amounts to about the same thing."

"Someone in the FBI?" Caleb asked, although she guessed from the glint in his eyes that he was teasing her.

"I doubt it," she replied. To show him she knew he was pulling her leg, she raised an eyebrow slightly as she went on, "No, I got the impression that the guy is just good at hacking databases. Or maybe he has a P.I. license or something—I know a private investigator can get into DMV records, things like that. Anyway, it'll probably be a lot more efficient than us trying to track her down online and getting bombarded with ads from those places that try to get you to sign up for their stupid identity-tracing services."

He nodded knowingly, as if he'd gotten sucked into one of those misleading links in the past as well. Really, it was almost impossible to avoid them. Knowing the new address of one of your exes really wasn't worth $49.95—or at least, Rosemary didn't think it was. Actually, the only real reason she'd want to know something like that was to find out whether they'd moved safely out of state.

She set the photo down on the tabletop, then got out her phone and took a quick snap of it.

After that, it was the work of less than a minute to attach it to a text message.

Hey, Audrey, this woman might be a possible lead. Her name is Madeline Nash. Can you have Michael check into it, maybe get me a current address?

And off it went into the ether. To Rosemary's relief, it looked as if the message was delivered almost immediately. Just a few seconds later, Audrey's reply came back.

Sure. I'll let you know as soon as I do.

Thanks.

That done, Rosemary tucked her phone back inside her purse. "Okay, they're on it. About all we can do now is wait."

Caleb sent her an approving look. "Very efficient. Do you guys have your own detective agency or something?"

She chuckled. "Nope. Let's just say that Michael has more practice with this sort of thing than you might think."

"I guess so. He sounds like kind of an impressive character—I've read a couple of his books, but I've never been to any of his lectures or anything."

Actually, Rosemary had, although she decided it was probably better not to mention any of their past history. Back in the day, she and Michael hadn't exactly seen eye to eye on a variety of topics, and her impression of him hadn't been at all favorable. Once she'd gotten to know him, however, she realized she'd probably been judging him unfairly. His knowledge of the supernatural and the occult was vast, and he was immensely capable. More than that, though, she'd seen how he'd fallen for Audrey, how he'd put any concern for his own safety aside to rescue her from the demon who'd been holding her captive.

Having someone love you like that had to be life-changing. Maybe someday, Rosemary thought, she'd get to learn how it felt.

With Caleb? She honestly didn't know. After the way her father had walked out on her family, she'd learned to be careful with her heart. Being so cautious had shielded her from any serious heartache, but at the same time, she didn't think she'd ever experienced true love. Not like what Michael and Audrey had, anyway.

"He is impressive," she agreed, hoping Caleb hadn't noticed the pause before she made that remark. "Both of them are, really."

"Him and Audrey Barrett, you mean."

"Yes. Once she's done with school and out working in the field, the two of them just might become the new Ed and Lorraine Warren."

Most people probably wouldn't have known who she was talking about, despite the popularity of the *Conjuring* movies. However, Caleb nodded at once, even as he looked slightly puzzled. "'School'?" he repeated.

"Audrey went back to school to get her Ph.D.," Rosemary explained. "Over in Arizona. You can still get a doctorate in parapsychology at U of A in Tucson."

"Good for her."

Yes, good for Audrey. Everything had worked out great for her, despite the hell she'd gone through. Hopefully, she wouldn't mind that Rosemary was now digging through the mess she and Michael had done their best to leave behind. Not that Audrey had probably shed too many bitter tears over Colin Turner, but still....

No response felt exactly right, so about all Rosemary could do was shrug. Once again, she wondered if she and Caleb were doing the right thing. Maybe it would be smarter to just let all this go.

Well, if you were going to do that, you're a day late and a dollar short, she thought. *The time to put the kibosh on all this was yesterday when Caleb first came into the store. But you took one look at him and decided to go with it, no matter what happened.*

All right, maybe she was being a little hard on herself. She actually did agree with him that it was wrong for the show's footage to be buried where no one could ever see it. Maybe he'd been able to convince her a little more quickly than he might have if he weren't quite so handsome, but she had never been a fan of hiding knowledge, no matter how difficult or unpleasant it might be. In a way, it would have been easier for her to deny everything that had happened to Audrey and Michael, to pretend that demons and devils didn't exist. But she couldn't do that. She'd seen the evidence with her own eyes, had felt the truth ringing in everything they'd told her.

"So," Rosemary said, "are you a native of Eagle Rock?"

Ouch—that sounded so hackneyed and awkward. But she thought it was probably better to get the conversation on a semi-normal track, since she had no idea when the waiter would be back with their drinks. It did seem as if he was taking an awfully long time to get a couple of iced teas.

A corner of Caleb's mouth lifted slightly. Obviously, he'd seen the question for exactly what it was. To her relief, however, he seemed willing to go along, because he said, "No. I've lived here for a couple of years. But I grew up in Indiana. My whole family is still back there—and thinking I'm crazy for moving to L.A. You can't start a film career in Indiana, though."

No, she supposed that would be difficult. Not that it was a picnic even when you were out here, considering how cutthroat the business was and how stiff the competition for every single job. Which made her wonder why he was available to come out on a Wednesday during work hours and go prospecting in Colin's storage unit. His comment about getting paid on Thursday had made it sound as if he had a regular job of some sort.

Well, she'd already stuck her foot in it, so she figured she might as well soldier on. "So…what are you doing now? For work, I mean."

He grinned, settling back in his chair. "I just finished up doing some P.A. work on a new Netflix series. Only ten episodes, but it's something to add to the resumé. Which is why I'm fancy free right now."

"Was I that obvious?"

"Sort of, yeah." Before she could say anything else, he added, "But it's okay. I suppose it's natural to wonder why an able-bodied twenty-nine-year-old guy is available to go dig through a storage unit on a Wednesday morning."

Twenty-nine. Not quite two years older than she was. Rosemary didn't know why that information should make her feel relieved, but it did.

"It really isn't any of my business—" she began, but he cut her off.

"No, I kind of dragged you into this thing, so I can see why you would have questions." He looked as if he was about to say more, but at that moment, their waiter finally reappeared, carrying not just their MIA iced teas, but also the food they'd ordered. After offering apologies for the delay in getting their drinks out—and asking if there was anything else they needed—he took off, and they were left mercifully alone again.

"Still," she said, even as she picked up her sandwich, "I'm generally not a nosy person."

Caleb took a bite of his turkey club. "It's okay," he said after he finished chewing. "I am."

That comment made her lift an eyebrow at him again. "Excuse me?"

"I always want to know why people do what they do, why things happen the way they do. The only reason I haven't been picking your brain about being a psychic is that I didn't want to scare you off."

All right, now she knew this guy was too good to be true. Her strange powers were generally something that most men didn't want to deal with. It wasn't as if she didn't have sad experience to back up that assertion—both of her long-term boyfriends had bailed after they'd decided they'd had enough of the strange dreams and the odd feelings and the crystals and the sage and all the rest of it. She didn't know all the reasons behind her parents' breakup, but she'd heard them arguing several times on one of the

98

rare occasions when he was home between business trips, had once heard her father say that her mother needed to stop making major life decisions based on feelings and premonitions and not much more.

And even though Izzie never talked about her divorce, Rosemary couldn't help thinking that much the same dynamic might have been in play. Isabel's ex was a very down-to-earth, no-nonsense kind of guy—a former Marine—and he'd probably gotten tired of the woo-woo as well.

Honestly, with a family history like that, she wondered why she hadn't given up on men a long time ago. All right, CeeCee's husband Kevin was an exception to the family rule, but Kevin was kind of a saint. Too bad there wasn't a way to clone him.

Then again, Rosemary thought, looking across the table at her current companion, maybe there were better options available than a clone of her brother-in-law.

"Pick away," she said cheerfully, and took a bite of her chicken sandwich. It was good, better than she'd been expecting. Maybe their waiter wasn't so great, but the food here seemed to be excellent. "I really don't mind."

He leaned forward slightly, brown eyes warm with interest. "You're sure? You're not just saying that?"

"No. It's the sort of thing people tend to be curious about."

A pause as he sipped some of his iced tea, and then he asked, "When did you first know you were psychic?"

"Always, really," she replied. "For one thing, it kind of runs in my family, so no one was that surprised when I started to show signs of having the same abilities my sisters have. I'd dream things, and they'd come true. I knew that our missing cat Sheba was actually down the street at the neighbor's house because the little boy who lived there was hiding her in his bedroom. Things like that."

Was that a flicker of envy she saw in Caleb's expression? Maybe. Rosemary wouldn't hold something like that against him, especially since she'd encountered that reaction in other people before then. It was natural to want to feel special, to think you had some kind of gift or power that made you stand out from the crowd. Of course, his model-worthy good looks were enough to make him stand out pretty much anywhere, even a town as over-populated by attractive people as L.A. "That sounds amazing."

"It's not as amazing as you might think," she remarked, then drank some of her own iced tea. "I didn't talk about it much, but people still knew, probably because my older sisters both had the same sort of talents. In a way, it was kind of a relief when my parents split up and I had to go to a different school and could start over with a new batch of kids who didn't know anything about my history."

Now all Rosemary could see was sympathy in his face. "How old were you?"

"Ten," she said, as casually as she could. After all, divorce wasn't that big a deal. Close to half of the kids she'd gone to school with had parents who were divorced, or going through the process. Besides, her parents' breakup meant that she and CeeCee and their mother—Isabel had just started college that year—eventually had moved into Grandma's big old house in Sierra Madre, where the true magic had begun. That was when Rosemary began to really develop her powers, to learn about the old ways her grandmother had followed. If her parents had stayed together, she doubted her father would have been quite so accepting of the smudging and the incense and the rites of blessing performed at the four corners of the year. Since Caleb was still looking at her with concern, she added, "Really, it was okay. Like I was saying, it was good that I got a chance to start over in a place where the teachers wouldn't give me and my sister the side-eye because they thought we were going to reach into their brains and get the answers to the spelling test, or whatever."

"Could you?"

"No," she said. "I already told you, I don't read minds. I just get…impressions. Feelings. Sometimes dreams that come true, or flashes of scenes that don't seem to make sense at the time but I figure out later once I have the context."

"It's still pretty incredible." Caleb took a few more bites of his club sandwich and washed them down with some iced tea. "So, why the bookstore instead of being a full-time psychic?"

Rosemary swirled the straw in her own glass of tea. The paper felt rough and strange under her fingertips; she supposed at some point she'd get used to paper straws, but they still jarred her every time she touched one. "That was something my sisters and I decided on. When my grandmother passed away, she left us some money and said we should do something worthwhile with it. None of us were exactly what you could call corporate types, and we'd already talked about starting some kind of business together…creating our own jobs, so to speak. The bookstore made the most sense to us. We ended up in Glendora because we got a deal on the building, and so it just sort of followed that we'd all buy houses there, too."

A flicker of confusion crossed over Caleb's face. Frowning slightly, he pointed out, "Why are you staying in Michael's house if you have a place of your own?"

She'd been wondering when he was going to ask that question. "Actually, I'm housesitting for Michael and Audrey while they're in Tucson," she explained. "The place next door to my house in Glendora is getting completely rebuilt, so I'm staying in Pasadena to avoid the mess. And since they wanted someone to watch their home while they were gone, it sort of worked out best for everyone involved."

"Ah. That makes sense. Construction noise is no fun."

No, it wasn't. She'd gone back over to Glendora the weekend before to check on her place and fetch a couple of things, and even though it was Saturday, the construction crew was hard at work next door, knocking out walls or whatever the hell it was that they were doing. All Rosemary knew was that they made a hideous amount of noise. In addition to the sound pollution, a huge dumpster had been left in the driveway to collect the demolition debris, making the situation even less appealing. She'd been glad to see that her own modest home was intact, if in need of a good rain shower to wash away the construction dust, and then tossed the shoes she'd been looking for into the trunk of her car and sped away.

She shrugged. "Anyway, co-owning a store is a

little more stable than being a freelance psychic. I do some stuff on the side, mostly at psychic fairs, that kind of thing. To be honest, I wouldn't want to do readings full-time. They can be draining."

"I never thought of it that way." Caleb gave her a considering look. "I suppose it must be hard to give people bad news."

Yes, it was, although she'd always done her best to phrase things as gently as she could, to say that the Tarot cards were only giving an interpretation of what was yet to come, rather than being the ultimate authority. Still, there were times when she'd done readings for people and had known death and disaster waited for them, no matter what she said.

It was a lot easier to sell books and incense and local hand-crafted jewelry and leather book covers.

She shrugged and took another bite of her sandwich, even though she wasn't quite as hungry as she'd been a few minutes earlier. "It's not fun, that's for sure."

Apparently sensing something of her mood, Caleb went quiet then and returned to his own food, making short work of the second half of his club sandwich and the fries that had accompanied it. Rosemary had gotten a salad rather than fries, but the honey mustard dressing tasted bitter on her tongue. What had been a fun lunchtime conversation had taken a turn for the worse, and yet she wasn't quite sure how to steer the discussion in another direction.

Her phone beeped from within her purse, and she set down her fork. Caleb looked at her, expression a bit livelier now.

"Maybe that's Audrey getting back to you."

"I don't know—I'm not sure they would get the information we needed quite that fast." Still, Rosemary's heart beat sped up a little as she scrabbled through the interior of her voluminous bag until her fingers closed on the wallet case that protected her iPhone. She unfastened the case and entered the code to unlock the screen, then went to her messages.

Yes, there was a text from Audrey. A horrible tightness took hold of Rosemary's throat as she read the brief message.

Michael found Madeline Nash.
She died seven years ago.

Chapter 6

"I guess that explains why Colin kept all those photographs of her," Caleb said. He looked stunned, strong, sun-browned fingers playing with the unused fork at his place setting. The nervous movements seemed out of character, based on what little Rosemary knew of him, but she could see why he was fiddling with the utensil, not sure what else he should do.

"Now I feel bad for thinking he was such a jerk." Once again, the words slipped out before she could stop them, but in this particular case, she didn't think her companion would find anything strange about what she'd said. "He probably never got over her death."

Michael's source hadn't been able to locate too much more information, although it seemed as though the couple had been together for several years. Enough time for Colin to be devastated by her death. No wonder he'd seemed so focused on his work. He'd wanted to do whatever he could to distract him from the loss that obviously would haunt him until his own untimely passing.

"No, I guess not." For a moment, Caleb was silent.

During that lull, the waiter came by and asked if they were still working on their meals. Rosemary usually hated that expression, but in this case, she was only too glad to have the remnants of her lunch cleared away. Caleb also said he was done, and the waiter picked up their plates and departed.

"So…why did you see the numbers, then?"

Rosemary stared at Caleb, perplexed. "What do you mean?"

He straightened in his chair and folded his hands on top of the table in front of him. "I mean, why would you have a vision of the numbers to open the lock on the footlocker if what we found there was only going to lead us to a dead end?"

Although she could see why he might think such a thing, she knew matters weren't quite so cut and dried when it came to the world of the psychic. "Because it's possible that there aren't any real clues to find. Maybe…maybe the universe just thought we needed to find those photo albums so we'd have a different opinion of Colin going forward. That's all."

While such an explanation made total sense to her, she could tell that Caleb wasn't quite so convinced. He gave the slightest lift of his shoulders, then said, "Maybe. Or maybe there's something else we're overlooking."

"Like what?"

"I don't know."

Any speculations were delayed at that point, since the waiter came back with the check. Caleb dug out his credit card and handed it over without even looking at the total, which was probably an indication of his current unsettled state. Most guys Rosemary knew would have eyeballed the thing to make sure there weren't any hidden charges, nothing that might balloon the total into something much less affordable than they'd planned.

"Well, we don't have to figure it out right now," she said. "At least we know the storage unit wasn't hiding the missing footage, so that's something you can scratch off your list."

"I don't really have a list," Caleb responded, now looking somewhat sheepish. Maybe he was comparing his scattershot approach to the problem with the efficient way Michael Covenant had handled the mystery of Madeline Nash's identity. "I just thought I'd try to reach out to some people who might have some information."

Which made Rosemary ask the question that had been nagging at the back of her mind all day. "Speaking of which, how did you even know to come talk to me? It's not like I worked on the show or anything."

He didn't seem surprised by the question. "Oh, I talked to Daniela Rodriguez, and she mentioned you."

Daniela had been the hair and makeup person on *Project Demon Hunters*. Rosemary met her briefly during the show's shoot in Tucson and thought she seemed nice enough—probably too nice to be tangled up with Colin, since the two of them had been seeing each other while the show was shooting. However, she'd also gotten the impression that the makeup artist wasn't the world's most discreet person, so it made sense that she wouldn't have tried to keep Rosemary's somewhat nebulous connection to the show a secret.

"You know her?"

"Not really," Caleb responded. "I just saw that Daniela had been attached to the show, so I got in contact with her via her website. That was when she told me you were a friend of Audrey's and maybe someone I should get in touch with, since she really didn't have much information to give me."

Once he had a name, it had probably been pretty easy for him to track her down. Rosemary knew that all you had to do was Google her name, and the store was one of the first hits you got. No doubt Caleb had been glad to discover that she worked someplace fairly public, giving him an easy way to approach her. It would have been more difficult if she worked in a cube farm somewhere.

Well, mystery solved. She couldn't really be annoyed, since she was glad he'd come into her life. Too bad that their search didn't seem to be netting them any useful information.

"Did Audrey say anything about what happened to Madeline?" he asked then. "How she died?"

Rosemary had noted the omission, but maybe all Audrey—or hers and Michael's source, to be more precise—had to go on so far was a brief mention in an obituary. They didn't always list cause of death. If Madeline had died of natural causes, there wouldn't necessarily have been any mentions in a newspaper the way there might have been if she'd been the victim of a homicide. True, perfectly healthy-looking women in their twenties didn't generally drop dead for no reason, but....

"No. I guess I can get back to Audrey on that

if we need to, but I'm not sure it makes any difference either way."

"Probably not." Caleb folded up the customer copy of the receipt for their lunch and tucked it into his wallet. "Well…."

This was the awkward moment where they parted company. After all, Rosemary knew she hadn't been that much help. Yes, they'd found the storage unit, but since it hadn't yielded anything to assist them with their search, there wasn't much point in the two of them continuing to work together. She pushed away the inevitable feeling of disappointment, telling herself that it didn't really matter. Sure, Caleb was friendly and smart and drop-dead gorgeous, but they really didn't have anything in common.

He went on, "I want to keep looking…if you're willing to help me."

Startled, she gazed across the table at him, wondering if she'd heard him correctly. "What?"

"Maybe it's crazy, but I still feel as if there's something we're missing. Something we've overlooked. So, I want to keep trying. If that's okay."

If that's okay? Of course, it was okay. Never mind that she had no idea what they could do to find the elusive footage. She was willing to grasp at straws if it meant spending more time in Caleb Dixon's company. He was strangely easy to be around…and also awfully easy on the eyes.

"Um...sure," she responded. However, reality inserted itself, reminding her that, unlike him, she wasn't between jobs and didn't have unlimited time on her hands. Sure, the sisters spelled each other at the store if something unexpected—and urgent—came up, but Rosemary doubted either Isabel or Celeste would be too thrilled about giving her an extra day off to go chasing all over L.A. on the hunt for some video files that might or might not exist. "But I won't have another day off until Sunday."

"That's all right," he said at once. "It'll give us both some time to mull things over, start figuring out other avenues we can try. Also, you might see if Audrey and Michael's source can give us any more information about Madeline Nash. Then, when Sunday rolls around, we'll be better prepared to keep going."

Caleb's plan sounded reasonable enough. There wasn't any point in going off half-cocked, so to speak. This way, they could be more methodical. If nothing else, that way they'd know they'd done their best.

"Sounds like a plan," she said.

"Great." He glanced over toward the parking lot, where far fewer vehicles surrounded their two cars than had been there half an hour ago. "Ready?"

She nodded, and they rose from their table

and headed out to the lot. Experience had taught Rosemary to already have her car keys in hand, just to avoid any awkwardness as they said their goodbyes. True, he hadn't given her the slightest hint that he intended to lean in and kiss her or even give her a hug, but better to avoid one of those uncomfortable moments in the first place.

Just as she pressed the button on her fob to unlock the car door, Caleb spoke again.

"Maybe," he began, then paused.

"'Maybe'?" she echoed, wondering if he'd forgotten something.

"I know we said we'd get together on Sunday to do the Scooby Doo thing or whatever, but maybe you'd want to go out on Friday? To a movie or something?"

A movie or something. He looked so adorable right then, expression earnest as he gazed down into her face, like he was some high school kid worried that the popular girl was going to snub him in front of the whole cafeteria. Of course, she had no intention of snubbing him. She'd been secretly hoping he'd want to make their relationship a little more than just business, although she honestly hadn't expected him to ask her out on a normal, garden-variety date.

"That sounds like fun," she replied. "But maybe not a movie. Do you know Monrovia?"

Looking a little mystified, he nodded. "I've

been there a couple of times. What's in Monrovia?"

"They have a street fair every Friday night. Food, live music, that sort of thing. The weather's so nice and warm, it might be more fun to do something outdoors instead of going to a movie."

This description obviously intrigued him, because he replied at once, "You're right—that does sound like fun. Monrovia, then. What time?"

"Six-thirty? We can meet in front of the movie theater on Myrtle Street. There's free parking everywhere, so hopefully, that won't be too much of a problem."

"Six-thirty, then." He paused, warm brown eyes fixed on her face. "If I get any more information on the footage, I'll let you know. But otherwise, I'll see you Friday night."

And before she could even begin to react, he bent and gave her a very quick, very chaste kiss on the cheek before he hurried over to the spot where he'd parked his truck. About all Rosemary could do was stare after him, expression wondering.

She might be psychic, but she sure hadn't seen that one coming.

By the time she got back to Pasadena, it was nearly two o'clock. Usually on her days off,

CHRISTINE POPE

she did laundry, ran errands, took care of whatever minutiae couldn't be managed on the days when she put in nine hours or more at the shop. That afternoon, though, Rosemary was having a difficult time trying to focus on anything except that kiss Caleb had given her. No, it hadn't been an impassioned embrace for the ages or anything like that, but she knew he must have done it because he wanted her to know where he wanted things to go on Friday night. He didn't want them to be investigative buddies and nothing more, which meant he must be as attracted to her as she was to him. That realization made a happy little thrill go through her.

For probably the first time in her life, she wished she had some housework to do. Michael had kept his same cleaning crew, same team of gardeners, probably because he wanted to make sure everything would be in tip-top shape when he and Audrey returned to California. But at least if she'd had some dusting or vacuuming to take care of, it would have helped take her mind off the lingering sensation of Caleb's lips against her cheek, the way his eyes had caught hers and held. Because she'd been expending so much effort to act casual—and because she'd made herself think that a guy like Caleb Dixon couldn't possibly be interested in her—she hadn't picked up on any of his cues.

Well, she knew where things stood now. Or at least, where they were about to start heading, if that kiss was any indication.

Restless, she went to the library and retrieved her laptop from where she'd left it charging on a side table, then carried it into the family room. With a glass of ice water within easy reach on the coffee table and her feet up on the couch, she thought she was ready to do a little investigating of her own.

Unfortunately, Googling "Madeline Nash" brought up a long list of candidates. Even narrowing it down by entering "Madeline Nash Los Angeles" didn't really help all that much. Rosemary didn't have a scanner here at Michael's house—he'd taken all his office equipment with him—or otherwise, she would have scanned in the photo of Madeline she'd brought home with her, just to see if that might fetch a more targeted result.

Time to try something else. She typed in, "Madeline Nash Colin Turner," but that only returned a bunch of hits that definitely didn't have anything to do with either of the people she was looking for.

No wonder people in the internet age still paid for private detectives.

Of course, Rosemary had resources of her own that no P.I. could offer. She couldn't force a vision to come, but often, if she sat and meditated on a problem or a question, the answer would come to her. Or some kind of answer, anyway. Maybe not always the one she'd been looking for, but....

She lifted the laptop and set it down on the coffee table, then drank some ice water. As she was wondering whether to try her meditation session here on the couch or whether to get down on the floor and go into a true lotus position, her phone rang.

Almost at once, her heart began to beat a little faster, even as she told herself not to be an idiot, that she doubted Caleb would be calling her again this soon. When she looked down at the screen, she saw her sister's number and was glad that she hadn't set herself up for disappointment.

"Hi, Izzie," she said, tone casual, although she had to wonder why Isabel would be calling in the middle of the afternoon on her day off. "Is everything okay at the store?"

"Yes, it's fine," her sister responded, sounding tense. "Is everything okay with you?"

Mystified, Rosemary returned, "Why wouldn't it be?"

"I don't know...I started to get a weird feeling, and so I thought I'd better call you and see if you were all right."

Usually, Isabel's "weird feelings" were nothing to be ignored. Now, though, Rosemary couldn't help but experience a stab of irritation. The last thing she wanted was for her sister's second sight to be interfering with the afterglow of Caleb's quick little kiss. "What kind of feeling?"

A pause. Then Isabel said, "I'm not sure. Just a sensation of something dark out there on the horizon. It feels as if it's somewhere around you, but I can't get much more sense of it than that."

No, that really wasn't the sort of thing she wanted to hear. Although a cold little tendril of fear trailed its way down her neck, Rosemary forced herself to sound casual. "Is this going to be one of those 'girl, you're in danger' conversations?"

"I'm not joking, Rose."

Isabel sounded so serious that Rosemary said at once, "Sorry. It's just…can you be more specific than 'something dark'?"

"If I knew anything else, I would have told you." Her sister paused again, although this time to say to someone, obviously a customer, "That would be shelved next to Eckhardt Tolle. T-O-L-L-E. Right." Then she went on, "Sorry about that. Anyway, you know I wouldn't have said something if the feeling wasn't pretty strong. Is there something you haven't told me?"

Oh, a whole lot of somethings. But Rosemary hesitated, not sure how much she wanted to take her older sister into her confidence. If she told Isabel that she'd met a handsome stranger who wanted to go in pursuit of Colin Turner's missing *Project Demon Hunters* footage, she could only imagine how she would react. It had been pretty clear that Izzie was very relieved to learn that her sister was only very peripherally involved in the project—mostly through her friendship with Audrey—and so there wasn't much chance of any wayward demons deciding to make her their target. But this? This was like daring them to come after her.

Or not. The new owners had moved into the previously haunted—and demon-infested—Whitcomb mansion in Glendora, and everything appeared to be calm and quiet on that particular front. There definitely hadn't been any activity here at Michael's house, but that could be because of the wards he'd put in place. More to the point, the lot where Audrey's former home had stood—before the demons had burned it down—had been sold and new construction already begun there, and that all seemed quiescent as well. Wherever the demons had gone, it didn't seem as if they had continued to hang around the foothills of the San Gabriel Valley.

"I met someone," she said, figuring it would be easy enough to tell Isabel about Caleb without going into too much detail as to why he'd come into Sisters We. "He came into the shop yesterday."

"Really? Who is he?"

The concern in Isabel's voice was clear and sharp. Rosemary knew it was only her sister's worry that the man in question was also the source of the darkness she'd sensed, but she found that very difficult to believe. While each sister's psychic ability was slightly different from the other's, they all tended to have good instincts about people. If there had been anything off about Caleb, she knew she would have sensed it.

"Just a guy," she said gently. "His name is Caleb, and he works in the film industry. And before you ask, he really does—he has an IMDB page and everything. Anyway, he was over here yesterday, and you know if there was something strange about him, the wards Michael put all over this house would have kept him out."

"Oh." That seemed to be Isabel's only response, probably because she was admitting to herself that Rosemary had just shot down most of her intended arguments about this apparent stranger. "Well, you still need to be careful."

"I am being careful. We have a date Friday night, but we're meeting at the Monrovia street fair. Nice public place, hundreds of people everywhere. Totally safe."

Isabel hesitated, then said, "That sounds good. And I'm sorry if I'm being over-protective, but this feeling—it's strong. So...just keep an eye out."

"I will." That wasn't an empty promise. Rosemary knew she would take care, not just when meeting Caleb, but also while driving or going about her daily routine. After all, the sensation of foreboding her sister had experienced could just as easily mean an impending car accident as anything to do with the man who'd walked into the store yesterday afternoon. Sometimes Izzy's feelings didn't have anything to do with much that was personal—she'd had a "bad feeling" back in college, and the stock market had crashed the next day. No one in their family played the market, and their grandmother's house had been paid for, so the McGuires had weathered the storm a lot better than many other people they knew. Even so, better to be careful.

"Okay," Isabel said. "I have to go—more customers coming in. But we'll talk soon."

That seemed more like a threat than a promise. Rosemary made a noncommittal sound and ended the call, then set the phone down on the coffee table next to her laptop. As much as she wished she could brush aside Isabel's warning, she knew that probably wouldn't be very wise.

Well, she'd already promised herself she would keep a weather eye out for anything that seemed out of the ordinary. There wasn't much else she could do. She couldn't hide here in the house forever, and she sure as hell wasn't going to cancel her date with Caleb.

As she reached for her glass to take a drink of water, Rosemary's gaze fell on the photograph of Madeline Nash, which she'd left lying on the table. The other woman's smile blazed out of the picture, bright as the sunlight that made the bougainvillea behind her almost incandescent. She didn't look like someone who'd been ill, someone who had only a very short time left to live.

What happened to you? Rosemary thought. *Why is it important for me to know who you were?*

But Madeline was gone, and couldn't give Rosemary the answers she needed.

No, she'd have to discover those for herself.

Chapter 7

No dreams or visions provided any illumination that night. Neither did Rosemary's day at the store, which felt as though it dragged interminably. And she still had another whole day of work to get through before she could see Caleb. At least he'd sent her a brief text, letting her know that he was still poking around but hadn't found anything. The message probably wasn't all that necessary, but she was glad for it anyhow. It meant he was thinking about her, hadn't wanted to pretend to act aloof until they saw each other the following evening.

She'd messaged Audrey, asking if she could find out anything more about Madeline Nash. Luckily, Audrey had only said she'd pass on the request and hadn't asked why Rosemary thought Madeline was so important. To be honest, she didn't think she had a real answer to that question. Maybe it was nothing more than a need to understand why Colin had been such an ass. After all, lots of people suffered terrible losses every day and didn't turn into insufferable jerks.

Because she didn't feel like cooking and felt even less like going back out, she ordered Thai delivery. Now she sat on the couch in the family room, bingeing the latest season of *Nailed It* on Netflix because she needed something mindless and silly and relentlessly normal to watch. Maybe watching people fail to make fondant-covered dinosaur cakes and molded chocolate monsters wasn't the best use of her time, but she knew she wouldn't have been able to concentrate on anything more mentally challenging.

The image on the screen shivered, turned to snowy flecks. Annoyed, Rosemary set down her plate of cashew chicken and glared at the TV. It was a fairly new high-definition LED screen, so she doubted the problem lay with the television. No, probably Time-Warner cable was acting up again.

As she sat there and wondered whether it was worth the effort to get on the phone with customer service to find out what was going on, the snowy image on the television flickered again, showing a close-up of a green-frosted dinosaur for just a second before the snow returned.

Only now it seemed to be resolving itself into an entirely different image, this one of a woman's face.

No…it couldn't be.

But it was.

The image was grainy, but identifiably Madeline Nash's face. Her dark eyes were wide, fixed on Rosemary where she sat frozen on the couch. Cold fear flooded her body, and she didn't think she could have moved even if she wanted to.

Madeline's lips were moving, but no sound emerged. In a way, that was probably a good thing. Rosemary wasn't sure how she would have reacted to hearing the dead woman speak.

However, it was still easy enough to make out what she was saying. Back in grade school, she and CeeCee had spent a year teaching themselves how to read lips, and although she'd had no reason to use that skill for more years than she wanted to count, apparently some of what she'd learned still lingered in her memory.

Help.

The cashew chicken felt as if it had congealed into a cold, hard lump in her stomach. Still, Rosemary made herself get up from the couch and move closer to the television…although not so close that anything inside could reach out and touch her. Or at least, she hoped not.

"You need me to help you?" she asked.

Help, the vision mouthed.

"I see you, Madeline," she said quietly. "But you need to tell me how I can help you."

A shake of the head. *No.*

"No what?"

No...I'll help you.

Her fingers were like ice. Rosemary clenched them, doing her best to hold back the shivers that wanted to wrack her body. Was she really having a conversation with a dead woman inside Michael's TV?

Apparently so. Maybe this was the darkness Isabel had warned her about, the looming sensation of something heavy and cold. That was the way her body felt...chill with dread, although she knew that the dead weren't necessarily anything to be feared. Still, even an encounter with a benign spirit could shake you to the core...no matter how many psychic experiences you might have had in your lifetime.

"Help me do what, Madeline?"

Find.

"Find the tapes?"

Colin wants you to find them.

Now that icy feeling had moved to the pit of her stomach, down to her bare toes in their flip-flops. It would have been easier to blame the sensation on the house's air conditioning, which she'd turned on because the day was still extremely warm, but Rosemary knew that probably wasn't the real reason.

"Is Colin there with you?" She could only hope she was asking the right questions. Her psychic powers dwelled in the realm of dreams and visions, not communicating with the dead. She'd never even attended a séance, had never had any desire to. Her belief was that souls moved on to a different world, a different plane, after they'd learned the lessons of this one. She'd certainly never envisioned them living inside a TV set, no matter what those old *Poltergeist* movies might have had to say on the subject.

No. A pause, and then the fuzzy image on the screen shifted, as if the ghostly Madeline had just looked over her shoulder. *He's gone.*

"Gone where?"

Gone. But he wants you to have the tapes. Go to the house.

"'The house'?" Rosemary repeated, hoping she was reading the ghost-image's lips correctly. She was definitely rusty at this. "What house? The house he was renting in Los Feliz is already occupied by someone else."

Go to the house, the ghost-Madeline repeated, and then she was gone, the blurred grayscale image of her face replaced by the bright colors and noise and chaos of the episode of *Nailed It!* Rosemary had been watching.

Hand shaking, she reached out and touched the TV to turn it off.

SHE BURNED SAGE AFTER THAT, CLEANSING the house as best she could, uttering invocations to bring light and peace to Michael's home. Afterward, she sat in the library, phone in her hand, not sure what to do next. Her first impulse had been to call Caleb, but for some reason, that didn't feel right. Logically, she knew she was safe; yes, she'd had a visit from a spirit, and yet she'd survived the encounter just fine. Then she'd thought maybe she should reach out to Audrey and let her know what had happened, but, as Michael himself had pointed out just the day before, they were hundreds of miles away. What could they do to help?

Not much. Which led her to a place she really didn't want to be.

She needed to call Will Gordon, Michael's minister friend. He was the only person who might be able to offer any assistance. At the same time, she really, really didn't want to call him.

What else are you going to do? she asked herself. *Sit awake all night with the lights on?*

Probably not.

She allowed herself a sigh, then went to her

contacts list and found the number, which she'd programmed in just the day before, transferring it from the Chinese take-out menu where she'd first written it down. Her gaze strayed to the small clock that sat on top of one of the bookcases. Only ten minutes after eight, a perfectly normal time to call. Or maybe not so normal; she didn't know what kind of hours ministers even kept. Were they on call all the time, sort of like doctors? She honestly had no idea.

Before her courage could desert her, she touched the phone's screen to make the call. It rang several times, and she found herself hoping it would go to voicemail. That might be easier—she could leave a message and feel as though she'd done her due diligence...although she wasn't sure if leaving a message would really help all that much.

But then the phone picked up, and a man's voice said, "Hello, this is Will Gordon."

His was a nice, deep voice, with possibly the faintest hint of a Boston accent, although one clearly rounded down by spending years here in California. Kind of sexy.

She wouldn't stop to think about why she'd let such a random thought cross her mind. "Um...hi, Will. My name is Rosemary McGuire. I'm a friend of Michael Covenant's."

At once, Will Gordon's tone sharpened. "Is everything all right?"

"I—" She faltered, wishing she'd never made this call. "I'm really sorry to bother you, but Michael gave me your number and told me to call you if…well, if anything happened."

He didn't bother to ask what she meant by "anything." "Are you someplace safe now?"

"I'm at Michael's house." Voice a little plaintive, she added, "I thought it was safe here."

"Something got past his wards?"

So Will Gordon knew about those. Rosemary wondered how much else he knew. "I—I'm not sure that's what's going on. This wasn't a demon… it was a ghost."

"I wasn't aware Michael's house is haunted."

"I don't think it is. This spirit…this woman… she's connected to Colin Turner, Michael's producer on *Project Demon Hunters*. I think that's why she appeared to me. And honestly, she didn't do anything except try to communicate. It just—" She paused there. If she admitted how freaked out she'd been, wouldn't that make her sound like a complete coward? She gathered a breath and went on. "It startled me. And since Michael wanted me to get in touch with you if anything strange happened, well…here we are."

A pause, and then Will Gordon said, "Do you want me to come over there?"

Oh, hell no. While being alone here was mildly freaky, she could only imagine how awkward it would be to have a complete stranger show up on her doorstep. "No. I mean. I'm okay. I just thought I should call you and let you know what was going on."

"You're sure."

"Yes."

He hesitated again. Rosemary guessed that he was probably arguing with himself as to whether he should press the issue or let it go. Then he said, "All right. But you call me if anything else happens. It doesn't matter what time it is. And I think it might be a good idea if I came by tomorrow, just to check on things."

"I have to be at work—" she began, but he cut her off.

"So do I," he said. "But I can come over before you leave. What time do you have to start work?"

"Nine-thirty," she replied, knowing how resigned she sounded. Obviously, he didn't want anything on his conscience if something happened to her. At least if he checked in on his way to the church, he wouldn't linger. Just a quick visit to make sure she hadn't been spirited away by ghostly visitors or had a hellmouth open in the basement, or whatever.

"I'll see you then," Will said. "But call me if anything changes."

"I will," she promised. "See you tomorrow."

The call ended, she set down her phone and wondered what the hell she'd just gotten herself into.

AT PROMPTLY 9:30, THE DOORBELL RANG. Rosemary took a quick gulp of air, smoothed her skirt, and went to open the front door.

A man she guessed must be Will Gordon stood on the front porch. He wasn't wearing a clerical collar, but the dark shirt and trousers he wore still gave off a priestly impression, even though she knew that technically he was an Episcopalian minister...although they called their ministers priests. At least, that was how they were referred to on All Saints' website, which she'd looked at the evening before, hoping to get some info on Father Gordon. Unfortunately, the website didn't have any pictures of its clergy, so she'd had no idea what to expect.

What she definitely hadn't been expecting was that Will Gordon would be good-looking. Maybe not model-pretty like Caleb, and quite obviously older, probably in his middle thirties, but still. His hair was very dark, almost black, and he had piercing gray eyes that for some reason made a sudden flush rise in her cheeks.

"Rosemary McGuire?" he asked.

"Yes, I'm Rosemary," she replied, recovering herself enough to move forward into the doorway, hand outstretched. "You're Father Gordon?"

"Just call me Will," he said, then gave her hand a brief shake. His fingers were warm and strong.

"Come on in," she told him, releasing his hand and stepping aside so he could enter the foyer. "I hope it wasn't too far out of your way to come over this morning."

He shook his head. "No, my house is less than half a mile from here. It was no problem at all." Pausing there, he let his keen gray gaze sweep the interior of the house. "So...where did it happen?"

"The TV in the family room," she replied. "This way."

She led him out of the entry and into the family room, which definitely looked prosaic enough in the early morning light, with its nicely worn leather sofa and Mission-style furniture. Standing off to one side, she was uncomfortably aware of his presence, of how tall Will Gordon was, even taller than Caleb. His profile was to her as he stared at the television set, and she could clearly see the strong outlines of his forehead and nose and chin, the way his near-black hair waved back from his brow.

Stop looking, she told herself. *He's...he's a minister. And you're dating someone.*

All right, "dating" was probably a stretch to describe hers and Caleb's relationship, but still, she already had someone in her life, however casual their relationship might currently be. Despite the internal admonition, she couldn't quite prevent her gaze from slipping downward to Will's left hand, noticeably bare of a wedding ring.

Okay, stop. Just stop.

He didn't appear to notice anything strange about her behavior, because he asked, "The ghost appeared in the TV?" To her surprise, he looked almost amused. "Like in *Poltergeist?*"

"Those spirits came *out* of the TV," she responded, knowing how sharp her voice sounded. "This ghost just sort of stayed in there."

"Did she try to communicate with you?"

"Her mouth moved, but I couldn't hear her say anything out loud."

"Could you understand anything of what she was trying to convey?"

Rosemary wondered if she should explain where she'd gotten her lip-reading abilities from, then decided Will Gordon really didn't need to know that much. "I think so," she replied. "She kept telling me to go to the house."

"Which house?"

"I don't know for sure." She made herself step closer to the television, even though that meant she was now standing next to Will. This close, he seemed even taller. She forced herself to focus on what had happened in this room the night before, what Madeline had said. "I recognized her—she was Colin Turner's girlfriend or something. Colin was—"

"I know who Colin is," Will said. His tone was so gentle that Rosemary couldn't be too annoyed with him for the interruption. Expression now somewhat sad, he asked, "Do you think she was talking about Colin's house?"

About all she could do was give a helpless lift of her shoulders. "I suppose so. But Audrey told me it was already rented out, so I'm not sure what I'm supposed to find there."

"I don't think you should go and find anything," Will said then, and she sent him a surprised look.

"But Madeline told me to look there."

For a few seconds, he paused, his expression troubled as he continued to gaze at the TV. "I can't tell you what to do," he said at last. "That's your decision. But this doesn't sound like the sort of thing you should just jump into, either."

"I won't," Rosemary replied, a little surprised that she hadn't shot back with a quick retort of, *I do what I want!* That wouldn't have been a very mature response, though, especially when she could tell Will was only trying to help her. And he was probably right—going off without much of a plan was generally not a good idea, especially when it involved ghostly advice that might or might not be steering her in the wrong direction. However, as frightening as the experience had been, she hadn't sensed anything evil about Madeline's presence. Rosemary didn't think the ghost was the "darkness" her sister had mentioned. Since Will was still watching her carefully, she added, "Or at least, I'll think about it."

Something about his posture seemed to relax a little at her response. "I suppose that's all I can ask for." He went over to the television and laid a hand on top of it, being careful not to let his fingers touch the screen and possibly smudge it. "I don't feel anything evil here."

"You're psychic, too?" she asked, and then wondered, with an inner wince, if she should have left off the "too." After all, she had no idea how much Michael had told Will. He might not know that her background included a lot more than helping to run a small indie bookstore.

However, he only gave her a rueful smile—the sort of smile she guessed might make some of his parishioners a bit weak in the knees—and shook his head. "No. At least, not in the way that

Michael is, or the way you are. But when it comes to demonic presences, I can sometimes pick up something. A little bit of their dark residue, so to speak."

"Well, there wouldn't be any demons here," Rosemary said. "Michael's got this house locked up pretty tight."

"So he told me. But it never hurts to check." Will turned away from the television and surveyed the room, his gaze moving to the kitchen beyond. Good thing she'd made an extra effort to tidy up the breakfast dishes before he came over. "Anything else happen here?"

At least that was one thing she could be sure of. "No. I've been here for a little over two months now, and this is the first time anything like this has ever happened."

That answer seemed to reassure him, because he nodded and said, "Well, it's obvious that this spirit is trying to reach out to you, but she seems benign enough. Still, if she appears again—or if any other phenomena occur—don't hesitate to call. The number Michael gave you is my private cell, and you can reach me there any time of day or night."

From someone else, such a remark might have sounded slightly suggestive, but Rosemary could tell that Will was only letting her know in order to reassure her. It was pretty obvious that he didn't have anything on his mind besides helping out a friend of a friend.

As to what was in her own mind…she honestly wasn't quite sure about that.

"Thanks," she said, since his words required some kind of a response. "For all I know, this was a one-time occurrence. But since this is Michael's house and he told me I should get in contact with you if anything strange happened, I figured I shouldn't let it go."

"You did the right thing." For a second or two, his gaze met hers, and another of those strange little thrills worked its way down her spine. Had she ever met anyone else with such clear gray eyes, like crystalline quartz? "And call if you need to. It's fine. But I need to get to my office now."

"I need to head out, too." She walked him to the door and opened it. "Thanks again for coming over."

"It's no problem. Have a good day."

He descended the front steps and strode down the path that led to the sidewalk. Parked at the curb was a gleaming black vintage car, something from the late '60s or early '70s probably, although Rosemary didn't know enough about cars to hazard a guess as to what it might be. The vehicle definitely didn't look like the sort of a thing a clergyman might drive, and she found herself watching with slightly raised eyebrows as Will got in and drove off, the throaty rumble of the engine telling her that it could do a lot more than the sedate thirty miles an hour the neighborhood speed limit required.

Interesting.

Maybe too interesting. She knew she shouldn't be thinking about those piercing gray eyes meeting hers, or the strength in the broad shoulders beneath the dark shirt he wore. What she should be thinking about was her date with Caleb that night.

Still, as she closed the front door and headed back toward the kitchen to retrieve her purse so she could head out as well, she couldn't quite prevent herself from wondering if she'd be seeing Will Gordon again any time soon.

Chapter 8

THAT FRIDAY AT WORK FELT EVEN LONGER than she'd been afraid it would, but at last Rosemary was able to make her escape, glad that she'd be going the opposite direction of the rush-hour traffic and therefore shouldn't have much more than a fifteen-minute drive ahead of her. The streets around Monrovia's old town district were packed, but she found parking in a structure just a block west from the movie theater where she was meeting Caleb, so that wasn't so bad.

And there he was, standing out in front, the sleeves of his button-down white shirt rolled up in a concession to the warm October weather, looking casually gorgeous—and completely oblivious to the admiring stares a group of giggling high school girls gave him as they passed by before disappearing into the theater's lobby.

And yes, he is *gorgeous,* she reminded herself. Not that she'd forgotten what he looked like, but more than once during the day, she'd found herself thinking about Will Gordon rather than the man she was meeting here tonight. And that was just ridiculous. She needed to focus on the guy who was obviously interested in her, rather than the one who was only helping her out because Michael had asked him to.

Caleb smiled as soon as he caught sight of her, and, despite her muddled thoughts, Rosemary could feel a happy little flush move through her body. Today, she'd worn one of her long sequin-spangled skirts from India, along with a sleeveless wrap top and some sandals, figuring she might as well let him see her in all her boho-chick psychic glory and let him decide for himself whether he was cool with it. She knew she wasn't going to change who she was just because her dress code didn't fit the norm.

"Hi," he said as soon as she got close enough. "This thing is kind of a big deal, isn't it? I wasn't expecting this many people."

The street fairs generally were popular, but she had a feeling that this one was a little more crowded than most that were held in October, probably because it was still early in the month and the day had felt like a leftover from the tail end of August rather than the beginning of autumn. California autumn, but still.

"It can get a little crowded," she allowed. "Did you find parking okay?"

He nodded. "I'm in the structure up the street."

Which meant he'd parked the same place she had. She hadn't seen him or his truck, so he must have gotten here some time before she had. While she'd been running a few minutes late, she hadn't expected to be that far behind him.

Possibly an expression of dismay at her tardiness passed over her face, because he quickly added, "I actually got here about ten minutes early, just because I'd never been here before and I didn't know what the parking would be like. You're right on time."

Rosemary offered him a grateful smile. Actually, he was being generous, because she had been a few minutes late, but she wouldn't argue the point. It was probably better to move on to something else. "Do you want to wander first, or get something to eat? There are a lot of good places around here."

"I could wander a bit—unless you're hungry and need to eat now."

She reassured him that she was fine and could definitely wait, and so they began meandering along Myrtle Avenue, the main street in

Monrovia's old town, which had been closed down for several blocks to accommodate the street fair. Down at one end, a fairly decent bluesy rock band was covering an old Rolling Stones song, and everyone seemed to be in a good mood, laughing and talking, sharing bags of kettle corn purchased from one of the vendors, or eating hot dogs and burgers.

Surrounded by such a crowd, Rosemary could almost forget what had happened to her the night before, could almost put aside her meeting with Will Gordon earlier that day…the operative word being "almost." She knew she should probably tell Caleb what had happened with Madeline's ghost, but she was glad he'd opted for checking out the street fair before they settled down at a table at one of the restaurants that were located in the immediate area. At least this way, she would have a little more time to organize her thoughts, try to figure out how to handle the situation if he started pressing hard for them to visit Colin's former home as soon as they could.

Or so she'd hoped. In actuality, though, she found herself so focused on her current interactions with him as they looked at hand-dipped candles and artisan pottery and goat's milk soap and all the other myriad items on display at the street fair, she didn't have much mental space left over to rehearse what she was going to say. Also, she could tell she was making herself keep all her attention on him so her mind wouldn't wander. Was that a good thing, or was she just trying desperately to ignore the way she'd reacted when she first met Will Gordon?

Eventually, she and Caleb managed to walk all the way down to the bottom of the street, dodging the kids playing in the bouncy house at that end of the street fair, then back up the other side. As they made the circuit, he bought a hand-tooled leather journal, a purchase that surprised her a little. It had been fairly expensive as such things went, and he hadn't impressed her as the sort of person who had a lot of disposable income. But maybe he was feeling flush because he'd just gotten paid, and anyway, it wasn't really her place to question his expenditures.

Because he'd bought the journal, though, she decided to go ahead and make a purchase of her own—a necklace of pure sky-blue Arizona turquoise and clear crystal quartz, a piece she'd seen on several earlier visits and had promised herself she would finally make her own if it was still available the next time she went to the street fair.

"Do you want to wear it?" Caleb asked her as they walked away from the jeweler's booth and she began to stuff the small paper bag with her purchase into her purse. "Your skirt has some of that same color in it."

She glanced up at him, a little surprised. Most of the guys she'd known hadn't paid much attention to what she was wearing, especially not the colors included in those ensembles.

Maybe he's gay, she thought, even as she chided herself for subscribing to the stereotype that all gay men were into fashion and color and style. However, she kind of doubted he would have kissed her—even just on the cheek—if he wasn't interested in something a little more happening between them.

"Um, sure," she said, and paused behind a bench on the sidewalk. Of course, there was no chance of actually sitting down, since a family of four currently occupied that spot, but at least the bench provided a little shelter from the crowds that filled the street and overflowed onto the walkways.

She reached up to undo the necklace she currently wore, a simple silver chain with a plain silver ankh hanging from it, then slipped it into an interior pocket of her purse. As she got out her new purchase and unfastened the clasp, Caleb asked, "Do you want me to help you with that?"

What a question. Or at least, she thought she wanted him to help her...even as she wondered once again if he was just trying to be friendly, or whether he'd detected an opportunity for some more intimate contact and had decided to go for it.

"Thanks," she said, hoping she hadn't hesitated too long. "The clasp is a little small."

He extended a hand and she laid the necklace in it, then reached up to push her hair away from the back of her neck so he wouldn't have to fight the curly mass as he fastened the clasp. Hoping she looked casual and unconcerned, she stood there as he laid the necklace against her throat and then worked the lobster-claw closure to secure it. Maybe there had been the faintest brush of his fingers against her neck as he settled it in place, but that was all. And she hadn't reacted, not even a little bit. Did her lack of a response even mean much, except that they were in a public place, so of course she wouldn't allow herself to do anything?

He looked down at her, smiling a little. "I like it," he said. "It suits you."

About all she could do was repeat, "Thanks," and then hurriedly move on to a topic that was a little less awkward. "If we go up another block, there's a new gastropub I've been wanting to try. Sound good?"

"Sure. Lead on."

Rosemary began walking in the direction she'd indicated, glad that she could concentrate on looking at the storefronts so they wouldn't pass their new destination by accident. While she was glad to be here with Caleb, she wished she could relax and allow herself to enjoy her evening a little bit more. It figured, though; her first date in months, and she was letting herself get distracted by someone who probably hadn't spared a second thought for her.

The restaurant wasn't as busy as she'd feared, possibly because most of the people with families were buying their dinners on the street and eating as they walked, or maybe taking their food to be eaten in the large park that surrounded the library across the street. Whatever the reason, she and Caleb got a prize table by one of the windows where they could sit and watch the world pass by.

He picked up one of the menus, and she said, "This is my treat, since I suggested the place."

That comment made him raise an eyebrow. "I'm the one who asked you out."

"True, but—"

"Rosemary."

She stopped then, allowing herself to meet his gaze. His dark eyes were fixed on hers, earnest, but also a little amused.

"It's okay," he went on. "Eating here isn't going to break the bank, if that's what you're worried about."

A flush touched her cheeks. Had she really

been that transparent? Probably. She knew she would have made a crappy poker player.

"All right," she said. "If you're sure."

"I am."

After that, they were both silent for a moment as they studied the menu. Actually, the prices weren't as high as she'd feared they might be. Of course, it was the drinks that could really set you back, but since she had to drive home after this, she wasn't planning on having anything more than a single glass of wine anyway.

She debated with herself as the waitress came by and took their drink and food orders—chicken tacos and a glass of chardonnay for her, a burger and a beer for Caleb. Should she keep her mouth shut about her visit from Madeline Nash, or should she tell him the truth? Hiding something of such importance felt wrong, especially since she wouldn't have even found out about Madeline at all if he hadn't gone looking for Colin's missing footage in the first place.

Oh, the hell with it. "Something kind of weird happened to me last night."

At once, his gaze sharpened. "Weird how?"

Even though she'd made the decision to let him know about her strange experience, now that the time had come, she wondered if she was making a mistake. But she'd already started down this path, so there wasn't much she could do except keep going.

After taking a sip from her water glass to fortify herself, Rosemary launched into a brief description of her exchange with Madeline's spirit —or whatever it had been. Although she tried to be as factual and no-nonsense as she could in her retelling, she knew how crazy the whole thing must sound. For some reason, though, she decided against mentioning Will Gordon. What would be the point? Nothing much had come from their meeting, and she didn't want Caleb to think that she'd reached out to someone else because she didn't believe he would be of much help.

As she spoke, she could see his eyes widening. However, he was prevented from replying right away by the waitress returning with their drinks. She put them down on the table, told them their food would be out shortly, and headed back to the kitchen.

Still looking bemused, Caleb picked up his Guinness and stared at her. "Why didn't you call me?"

"What could you have done?"

Faced by such a practical reply, he only blinked. "I don't know. Maybe nothing. But you were okay with being in the house alone after that?"

Well, not really. Or at least, not at first. But after she'd gotten out her smudge stick and done a quick cleanse, she'd felt a bit better. She'd also felt better after she spoke to Will, although she didn't bother to mention that little fact, either. Anyway, whatever might be going on with the spirit who had spoken through the television set, Rosemary hadn't felt any ill intentions from her, nothing that made her think Madeline's ghost had meant her any harm. Actually, just the opposite. Her own feelings of unease stemmed from the overall weirdness of the experience and nothing else.

She tried to explain as much to Caleb, adding, "Honestly, if I'd really started to feel hinky, then I would have called one of my sisters, or even gone over to one of their houses to stay the night. But I didn't get a sense of any kind of threat."

Whether this reply mollified him was difficult to tell. He drank another mouthful of stout but didn't set down his glass this time. Instead, he stared into it, as if the dark, heavy liquid was a sort of black mirror that might reveal something of what Madeline Nash's spirit had truly intended. "But it—she—wanted you to go to the house."

"Supposedly," Rosemary replied, knowing she needed to tread cautiously here. Will's warning was all too clear in her mind. "But I don't see how that's going to help us at all. Audrey and Michael went through the place and cleared out all of Colin's belongings—that's what's in the garage right now. As far as I know, the house he was living in has already been rented."

"Still, we should try," Caleb told her. "I don't know—we could tell the people living there now that we think he left something behind. Maybe Michael and Audrey overlooked something in the garage."

That sounded highly unlikely, but Rosemary didn't feel like arguing the point. Both of her friends were detail-oriented, conscientious people; she couldn't picture them leaving anything of Colin's behind. Also, she knew that they'd paid out of their own pocket to have the house professionally cleaned, just so the entire security deposit could be sent back to Colin's sister in Manchester. There really shouldn't be anything that could have been overlooked.

Unfortunately, she and Caleb really didn't have any other leads. And Madeline had said that Colin wanted them to go to the house. Yes, Will had advised her to be careful, but if she and Caleb went together, how dangerous could it be? After all, Colin's house hadn't been haunted. Whatever had attacked him was long gone.

"Do you know where the house is located?" Caleb asked then, and she shook her head.

"Not exactly. I mean, I know it's in Los Feliz

somewhere, but I'll have to get the exact address from Audrey."

"Won't she wonder why you need it?"

Of course, she would. But Audrey knew she and Caleb were trying to track down the missing footage and besides, she'd probably be happy to hear that they had a lead worth following.

"Yes," she said. "And I'll tell her what I'm doing. I have a feeling the current residents won't be all that happy to have us come invade their space, but we shouldn't be springing any huge surprises on them. I'm pretty sure the management company had to disclose that a murder happened on the property."

"Is that a California thing?" Caleb asked, looking surprised.

She didn't know for sure, but she gave a hesitant nod. "Maybe. I just remember reading it somewhere. Makes sense—a lot of people are put off by that kind of stuff, especially if it wasn't a death by natural causes." Mouth curling slightly, she added, "Although I have a feeling its history probably wouldn't deter anyone who wanted to rent that particular house. The real estate market in L.A. is just way too tight."

Her wry smile was echoed in Caleb's expression. "You're probably right. The only reason I can afford the house I'm in is that it's owned by my roommate's parents."

Of course, he had a roommate. There was no way a guy of his modest means could have managed to rent a house by himself. Actually, Rosemary knew she couldn't really have afforded her own home, either, except that she'd inherited enough money when her grandmother passed away that she'd bought her house in Glendora for cash and therefore didn't have any real housing costs beyond the property tax and utilities. So what if she barely cleared 40K a year working at the store? She still had plenty to live a comfortable lifestyle. However, she knew her situation was far from the norm for someone in their mid-twenties.

"That sounds like a good deal for you," she said.

"I suppose so. Luckily, Nick works crazy hours and is on location half the time—he's a grip—and so I have the house to myself a lot."

Was that Caleb's way of hinting that they wouldn't be hampered by a roommate if they went back to his house at some point? Maybe. She wasn't sure how she felt about that. Right then, she honestly wasn't sure how she felt about much of anything.

"That must be convenient," Rosemary replied, since she felt like she needed to say something.

His smoky brown eyes glinted at her. "It can be."

She was saved from having to make a response

by the arrival of the waitress with their meals. For a few minutes after that, they were both quiet as they got to work on their food. The chicken molé street tacos were excellent, and, judging by the way Caleb plowed into his oversized burger, his dinner seemed to be just as good.

But after a few minutes, he said, "Does it feel weird?"

"Does what feel weird?"

"To be living in Michael and Audrey's house."

Rosemary wiped her fingers on the napkin in her lap, then reached for her glass of wine. "At first, it was a little strange. But the bedroom I'm staying in was the guest room, so it doesn't feel as if I'm really intruding on their space too much. Plus, Michael took his most valuable books and other things with him. I'm just…care-taking."

"It's a pretty amazing house, that's for sure." He paused, head tilted slightly to one side. "What's yours like?"

"My what?"

"Your house."

She shrugged. "It's a lot smaller, that's for sure." Then, relenting as Caleb lifted an eyebrow at her, she went on, "It's a little English-style cottage that was built in the late 1920s. The people I bought it from had already done a lot of the updating, though—they remodeled the kitchen and added a second bathroom—so I didn't have to do much more than move in, which was convenient."

"It sounds nice."

It was. Right then, she found herself missing the place, despite having a lot more room to spread out in Michael and Audrey's house. But that seemed to be how life worked—you thought you had everything set up nice and comfortable in your world, and then the people next door decided to sell their property to some house flippers who wanted to tear it all down. Not that she knew for sure the new owners were actually flipping the house, but she liked to think that about them because that scenario made it easier for her to dislike the people involved.

"Maybe you can come by and see it sometime," Rosemary said casually. Was she making a mistake? Maybe, but she knew she needed to stop being so wishy-washy if she wanted to see how things might progress with him. "The construction crew next door usually knocks off around six."

"You'll have to give me a tour." His expression sobered. "After we go look at Colin's house in Los Feliz."

That was a field trip she would prefer to avoid, but the spirit-Madeline's instructions had been pretty clear. "I'll call Audrey tomorrow and get the address, and then we can go on Sunday on my next day off. Sound good?"

"Sounds great."

After that, their conversation moved on to another Netflix pilot Caleb had applied for—he figured since he'd already worked on one, he might have a better chance at getting hired by the streaming service again—and a discussion of restaurants in Pasadena and Eagle Rock. Just ordinary stuff, which Rosemary was all too ready for. None of the topics they'd discussed before then was anything that would have sounded too strange to someone listening in, but they might as well be discreet.

The sun had set by the time they emerged from the restaurant, but the street was still brightly lit, although the throngs from an hour earlier had begun to thin out a little. They didn't have to fight the crowds as much to walk back to the parking structure where they'd both left their cars.

Caleb followed her to the space where she'd parked her little green Fiat, explaining that his truck was on the next level up. "I want to make sure you get in safely," he said soberly.

"Monrovia is very safe," she said, slightly amused by his concern.

However, his expression was serious enough as he paused a few feet away from her vehicle.

"Maybe it is. But after what happened to you last night...." The words trailed off; Rosemary wasn't sure what he'd intended to say, but he left it there. Instead, he asked, "Are you sure you're okay with being by yourself?"

"I'm fine," she told him, even as she hoped she actually was fine. What if she went back to the house and found...what? The ghost of Madeline Nash still haunting her television? A horde of demons lurking in the shrubbery in the backyard?

Well, if nothing else, she knew she didn't have to worry about the demons. The wards Michael had set protected both the house and the property itself, including the front and back yards and the detached garage.

She opened her mouth, intending to tell Caleb that this time she'd call if anything strange happened. However, she didn't get the chance to say a single word, because right then, he bent and kissed her.

It was a gentle kiss with closed lips, almost as chaste as the one he'd placed on her cheek the day before. As she stood there, halfway shocked, halfway interested, he moved closer to her and his arms went around her waist.

Then his lips parted, and she couldn't help smiling inwardly, thinking he should taste like beer and burger but somehow didn't. She made herself focus on the moment, on nothing except the kiss—which was a good one, she had to admit. A moment or two later, he lifted his mouth from hers and stared down at her, gaze intent.

"Was that too soon?"

Oh, you could take the boy out of Indiana, but apparently, you couldn't take the Indiana out of the boy. She looked up into his face and smiled. "No, it was great."

And she told herself it was, even though she honestly wasn't sure how she felt about the situation. Deep down, wasn't this how she'd wanted the evening to end? Why was she feeling so ambivalent now that he'd actually kissed her?

A relieved smile tugged at his lips. "Good. Although really, I meant our first kiss to be someplace a little more romantic than a parking garage."

Where should that first kiss have happened—in the park down the street, which was still busy with families with kids and people walking their dogs? At least in this particular location, it was a little more private, since the spaces to either side of her car were vacant and no one had driven by while they were standing there.

She shrugged. "I think things are about as romantic as we want to make them."

Again, he bent and kissed her. Nothing too long or too drawn out, but enough to tell her that he thought their current location was romantic enough for their purposes.

When the kiss ended, he reached over and touched a tendril of her hair, winding the curl around his fingers before he let go so it could spring back into its usual spiral coil. "Your hair is amazing."

"Really?"

"You sound surprised."

"Well, having crazy curly hair really isn't in style right now."

"Who cares about that?" Caleb shook his head, as if incredulous that such a thing might matter to her. "It's gorgeous, just like you are."

He thought she was gorgeous? A flush touched her cheeks, and she glanced away from him, a bit unsettled. She'd been called pretty often enough in her life, beautiful by people she thought might have been overestimating her appearance just a little a bit, but no one had ever referred to her as gorgeous before that moment. Not sure how she should react, she settled for giving a shrug as she said, "It's not so gorgeous when you're fighting with it to do something besides be curly."

"Then don't fight it."

Rosemary gazed up at him. His expression was completely serious, and there was a warmth in his eyes that hadn't been there earlier this evening.

Right then, she wondered if she should take his advice. All evening she'd been fighting with herself, and for what? She should let things progress and see how it went.

After all, what was the worst that could happen?

Chapter 9

ALTHOUGH IT HAD BEEN HARDER THAN SHE'D thought to say goodbye to Caleb on Friday night —they'd shared two more increasingly passionate kisses before she finally got into her Fiat and shut the door—at least Rosemary was able to tell herself that she'd see him again on Sunday. And since Saturday tended to be the busiest day at the store, she hoped the time would pass quickly enough. In fact, she and her sisters always made sure to have at least two of them working at Sisters We on Saturdays, since one person trying to handle everything tended to get overwhelming.

Most of the time, Rosemary was glad to work with one of her sisters. That day, though, she wished that sister had been Celeste and not Isabel. Celeste was generally so wrapped up in her family's doings that she didn't pay a lot of attention to what her younger sister was up to, whereas Isabel didn't have nearly as much to distract her.

"How was your date?" she asked during one of the rare lulls when there weren't any customers in the store.

"Great," Rosemary replied. At least she could be honest about that. Everything had gone just about perfect with Caleb, so there was no reason to answer with anything except the truth. And there definitely was no reason to mention the strange ambivalence she'd felt during the time they'd spent together. Most likely, she was trying to self-sabotage because that way she wouldn't be as upset when the inevitable breakup occurred. "We're seeing each other again on Sunday."

This comment elicited a raised eyebrow, as if Isabel was surprised they'd have a follow-up date so soon after the first one. True, Caleb wasn't acting like your standard-issue L.A. guy, the type who tended to behave as though he didn't care one way or another whether he ever saw you again, but Rosemary was just fine with that. She liked that he was sweet and kind of old-fashioned. He represented a refreshing change, something she thought she could probably use in her life.

But at least Isabel only said, "That sounds wonderful. I'm glad you two have hit it off." A pause as she glanced toward the storefront, toward a couple in their forties who'd paused to look in the window before continuing on their way. Apparently judging it safe to change the subject, she went on, "And there's nothing else?"

Rosemary supposed it was too much to hope that her sister wouldn't have picked up on any of the weirdness from her ghostly guest on Thursday night. She held back an inner sigh as she said, "I had a visit from a spirit on Thursday."

"What?" Isabel asked, looking genuinely shocked. Her blue eyes—a darker, truer shade than Rosemary's own crystal gray-blue—widened, and she reached up to tuck a strand of curly brown hair behind one ear. "I thought you said Michael's house was warded."

"It is…but not against ordinary ghosts and spirits. Audrey saw the ghost of her own great-grandfather there a couple of times."

This revelation did not seem to reassure her older sister very much. "If I'd known that place had ghosts coming and going—"

"You'd what?" Rosemary asked, more amused than irritated by her big sister's overprotective stance. "Tell me to stop staying there?"

"No," Isabel replied, her expression somewhat wounded, as though she couldn't believe Rosemary would even think she'd try to lay down the law in such a way. "You're an adult. I can't tell you what to do. But I at least would have advised caution."

"You already did that when you called to warn me that you'd sensed something wrong. I didn't feel anything evil from this spirit…just sadness."

"Who was it?"

Rosemary hesitated. So far, she'd managed to avoid telling her sister the actual reason why Caleb had come to the store in the first place. Although he certainly hadn't discouraged her from talking about what they were up to, she also didn't want to provide Isabel with too many details. As soon as the subject of the doomed *Project Demon Hunters* venture came up, all of her big sister's protective instincts would engage full throttle. Besides, Michael and Audrey knew what was going on, and they were the only ones who might actually be affected by anything she and Caleb discovered. If they weren't worried, then Isabel shouldn't be.

"I don't know," she said, hating herself for lying to her sister. Had she ever done such a thing before in her life? Oh, maybe about something inconsequential, like saying she hadn't borrowed Celeste's favorite barrette back in fifth grade and accidentally broken it, but nothing important. Nothing that really mattered. This felt wrong… but blurting out the whole story about the missing footage and Colin Turner's lost love Madeline somehow felt even worse. "She didn't say."

For a long moment, Isabel was silent, staring down at Rosemary. Not for the first time, she keenly felt the difference in height between the two of them. Izzie could be intimidating enough without using those five inches of additional height to her advantage.

Eventually, though, all she said was, "'She'?"

"The spirit was definitely a woman," Rosemary responded, glad she could focus on something fairly innocuous. "I got the feeling she was probably around my age when she died. But she didn't speak."

Which was true enough. Madeline's spirit hadn't uttered any actual words, had only mouthed her instructions to Rosemary.

Since Isabel didn't reply immediately, Rosemary went on, "I thought I'd call Audrey and let her know what I saw. Maybe she and Michael can tell me who the woman was, or why she'd be reaching out in such a way. I don't know for sure, though—I honestly have no idea how much Michael knows about the history of the house. Still, it's old enough to have collected its share of ghosts over the years."

Isabel nodded, but since the front door to the shop opened then, and the same couple who'd been looking in the window a few minutes earlier entered, she apparently decided not to continue the discussion. Only a single look, one that seemed to tell Rosemary they'd pick this up at a later time.

About all she could do was hope the store would be busy enough for the rest of the afternoon that her sister would drop the subject permanently.

THE CALL TO AUDREY HADN'T BEEN A fabrication; Rosemary had already planned to swing by her house here in Glendora on her lunch break and make the call there where she knew she wouldn't be disturbed. Next door, the construction crew was going full swing despite it being a Saturday, and she shot them a baleful look as she parked her Fiat in the driveway and went inside.

It was warm in the house, but not so hot that it was worth turning on the A/C for the short amount of time she'd be here. She settled for switching on the ceiling fan in the dining room, then sat down at the table and unwrapped her chicken salad sandwich and took a few bites.

Although she came by at least once a week to check on the house—mainly to make sure the gardeners hadn't missed anything in the yard and the irrigation system was still doing its job—Rosemary didn't tend to spend a lot of time on those visits, only making a quick pass of the inside and the exterior to assure herself there hadn't been a massive ant invasion or something else that might require her immediate attention. She couldn't remember the last time she'd sat down at the table and allowed herself to simply be in the space, even though once upon a time, she'd loved this little house, loved that it was hers and that no one could take it away from her.

Now, it felt cramped and just a little bit off, like a pair of shoes she'd outgrown. Maybe that sensation came from having spent so much time in Michael and Audrey's much larger house, although she told herself not to get too used to living in such splendor, that eventually they'd come back to California and she'd need to get used to living in twelve hundred square feet all over again.

Rosemary made herself focus on all the things in here she loved—her outrageous purple velvet couch, the painting of Quan Yin that hung above the small but functional fireplace, the antique armchair that had belonged to her grandmother and which occupied an honored place in one corner of the living room. Her plants she'd brought with her to the Pasadena house, since they couldn't have survived in here with the drapes closed for days on end. Everything else, though, looked the same, although she realized as she looked around that she needed to come back some time the following week and do some serious dusting.

Once she was done eating her sandwich, she folded up the paper wrapper it had come in and put it back inside the bag from the deli. A few swallows of iced green tea, and then it was time to make her phone call. One forty-five, which meant she had fifteen minutes before she was due back at the store. Rosemary hoped Audrey would pick up, because otherwise, she'd have to try again after she was done with work for the day…and that might be cutting it a little too close, considering Caleb was relying on her to have the address to Colin's house for their expedition the next day.

However, Audrey answered on the second ring, thus assuaging Rosemary's fears that the two of them might have gone out shopping or to the movies or whatever else they did with their free time. "Hi, Rosemary. What's up?"

"A lot of things, actually," she replied. "But first, I was wondering if you had the address to the house Colin was renting in Los Feliz."

That request elicited a small pause, followed by, "Yes, I have it—it's in the address book on this phone. But why do you need that? Everything that was left in the house is now in our garage."

Rosemary expelled a breath, then made herself repeat to Audrey the tale of the ghostly visitation she'd experienced on Thursday night, along with

Madeline's request that she go to the house. She finished by saying, "I don't know why she'd want me to go there, but obviously, I need to check it out."

Judging by the long silence that followed Rosemary's story, Audrey was genuinely flummoxed. But at last she said, "Hang on a sec."

At first, Rosemary thought her friend had taken the phone away from her ear so she could look up the address to the Los Feliz house, but then she heard muffled voices and realized Audrey and Michael were having some kind of convo. Not that surprising, she supposed; it was natural that she'd want him to know what was going on. What surprised Rosemary, however, was that when the phone picked up again, it was Michael on the line, not Audrey.

"Hi, Rosemary," he said, and although he sounded casual enough at first, she thought she could detect an edge to his voice. "Audrey told me about what happened."

"It's not that big a deal."

"I'm not so sure about that. Usually, a spirit won't come to deliver such a specific message unless the matter is very urgent." He hesitated, then went on, "I'm worried that you're getting in over your head."

"I'm fine," she returned, doing her best to curb the irritation in her tone. "I even called your friend Will Gordon and had him come over to take a look. He didn't sense anything off, so I think it's fine. Really, Madeline's spirit appearing should be a sign that I'm on the right track."

"Maybe. If it was even Madeline's spirit at all."

The room where she sat might have been stuffy and warm, but an uneasy little chill threaded its way along her spine. "What do you mean?"

He let out a breath that wasn't exactly a sigh. "I mean that we're dealing with demons here, Rosemary. They can take on whatever form they want in order to trick you into doing their bidding."

"I suppose," she said reluctantly. There was no point in arguing with him, not when she knew Belial had done that very thing, assuming the form of Jeffrey Whitcomb in order to do his dirty work. "But wouldn't the wards on your house have kept out a demonic presence?"

"They should have. But...."

"But nothing," Rosemary told him. Exasperation creeping into her voice, she added, "Either they work or they don't. Which is it?"

"They work," Michael said. Now his voice sounded firmer, although she could tell he was still worried. "They kept Audrey and me safe when the demons were wreaking havoc elsewhere. But even if it wasn't a demon—even if it really was

Madeline Nash's ghost trying to communicate with you—you have to understand that sometimes a spirit's meaning doesn't come through clearly. You need to be careful."

"I will be careful," she replied. "Caleb is coming with me."

Obviously, Michael wasn't too impressed by that particular piece of information, because he said, again with that sharp note in his voice, "The guy who's looking for Colin's missing footage."

Rosemary found herself frowning at his tone. "Yes, that guy. He's harmless."

The comment sounded horribly dismissive, but she couldn't take it back now. Besides, she wanted Michael to think of Caleb as a complete non-threat. That way, he wouldn't take it into his head to tell her they needed to back off on their little investigation. Or at least, she hoped he wouldn't.

Clearly, Michael wasn't buying it. "If he's as harmless as you say, then I'm sure you won't mind if I check his background, see what I can find."

Was that a threat? "Michael, I already looked Caleb up on IMDB. He's who he says he is."

"I'm sure you're right. But it couldn't hurt to look into it further."

Obviously, Michael was going to do what he was going to do, and she couldn't really stop him. He knew Caleb's full name because she'd already given it to Audrey on Wednesday. Well, fine. Let him investigate and discover there wasn't anything to find. "Sure," she said, her tone indifferent. "Speaking of looking into things, did you find out anything else about Madeline Nash?"

"She died in her sleep. Undiagnosed epilepsy."

Oh, damn. While there were probably far more terrible ways to leave this life, it was horrible to think that she'd suffered a seizure while she slept, that Colin had probably been blissfully asleep next to her and had no idea what had happened…until he woke up the next morning.

No wonder he couldn't let go of her memory…and no wonder he'd wrapped himself in emotional armor that made him prickly and unpleasant to everyone around him. Just thinking about the loss he'd suffered made Rosemary wish she'd offered him a kind word when she met him. For all her psychic abilities, she'd had no inkling at all of the wound he carried deep inside. Some people were like that, though. Their barriers were far too thick for even a person with her abilities to penetrate.

"That's terrible," she whispered.

"Yes. Poor Colin. He never said anything about her to me." A long pause, and then Michael added, "My source is still trying to figure out something of his history with Madeline Nash. There's this period of about three years where he can't find any rental records for either one of them. But he'll keep working at it. Something's got to turn up."

Or so they all hoped. It was a little strange that the couple had gone off the grid, so to speak, for a few years, but maybe they'd rented a place with utilities included and so wouldn't have any record of an account with the gas company or the power company. Colin was definitely the sort of person to use a mail drop for everything, which meant it might be even more difficult than usual to figure out where his actual residence had been.

"Okay," Rosemary said. She glanced over at the clock on the mantel; five minutes until two. The store was only about three or four minutes away, but she still needed to get going. "Hey, Michael—I have to run. My lunch break is almost over."

"I'll let you go, then." A pause, and then he added, "Be careful."

What was with everyone telling her to be careful? Did they always wonder how she'd managed to get to the ripe old age of twenty-seven without seriously injuring herself? She bit back the sharp reply she'd intended to make, mostly because she knew that Michael—and, by extension, Audrey—was only concerned about her.

"I always am," she said blithely, and ended the call.

AT LEAST THE REST OF THE DAY WAS uneventful, as was the evening that followed. No sign of Madeline's ghost, even though Rosemary had been halfway hoping the spirit would reappear and possibly offer some guidance for the next day's visit to the Los Feliz house. But nothing interrupted her viewing of *Wine Country* on Netflix, and her sleep afterward was a deep and dreamless one.

She'd agreed to meet Caleb at his house in Eagle Rock, since it was on the way to their destination and it seemed silly to take two cars. Besides, she knew she was curious to see where he lived.

And because they didn't want to show up on the doorstep of Colin's former rental too early, they'd decided to leave from Caleb's house around eleven. Rosemary's conversation with Michael had gone in a direction she really hadn't expected, but Audrey had dutifully texted the address to her later that same afternoon, so at least they knew where they needed to go.

Not quite ten minutes before eleven, she pulled up in front of Caleb's place, a modest-looking single-story house that was probably still worth an obscene amount simply because of its hillside location. She'd passed quite a few BMWs and Mercedes and Lexuses—or was that Lexi? she could never be sure—as she drove slowly down the street, looking for the address he'd given her.

When he opened the door, she blurted out, "You sure about that whole 'struggling filmmaker' thing? Because this neighborhood sure doesn't fit the profile."

Caleb grinned even as he stepped aside so she could enter the house. "Like I said, the place belongs to my roommate's parents. They've owned it for twenty years, but they don't want to sell yet because the market keeps going up."

"So, where are they now?" As she asked the question, she couldn't help taking a surreptitious look around. The living room was quite large, with hardwood floors and French doors that opened out onto a large brick patio complete with an eye-popping view of downtown Los Angeles. Despite the million-dollar view, the room itself was a hodgepodge of mismatched furniture, probably hand-me-downs and garage sale finds.

"Nick's parents? They're retired. They live somewhere in the Phoenix area…Tempe, I think."

What Rosemary knew about Phoenix could probably fit in the palm of one hand, but she gave what she hoped was a knowing nod. "That seems to have worked out well for you."

"That's for sure. I kind of lucked into this place—Nick's former roommate bailed on him to move in with his girlfriend, and a friend of a friend introduced us. Otherwise, I'd probably be living in a crappy studio apartment in Glassell Park." Caleb fished his keys out of the pocket of his jeans. "Do you want a drink of water or anything before we go?"

"No," she said hastily. Clearly, he wanted to get on with this, and she was just fine with that. "I've got some bottled water in my car."

"Maybe you should grab it before we leave," he suggested.

Which meant he wanted to drive. She'd been inclined to offer, mostly because she guessed that her little Fiat got much better gas mileage than his truck, but she decided against it. If he wanted to drive, then she'd let him.

"Sure."

He let her out the front door so she could retrieve her water bottle, then locked it behind her and disappeared into the house, presumably to head over to the attached garage. Sure enough, the garage door began to roll up as she was walking back from her car, water bottle in hand. He'd already started the engine, so she went ahead and climbed into the truck's passenger seat.

The interior of the truck was in much better shape than the oxidized black paint on the outside promised, and it was neat as well—no discarded soda cans or fast food wrappers to be seen, unlike the vehicles of several of the guys Rosemary had dated. She deposited her bottle in the cupholder and fastened her seatbelt, then set her purse on her lap.

"Do you want me to use my phone to navigate?" she asked. A single glance had told her the truck was too old to have a built-in navigation system.

"Thanks," Caleb responded, pausing at the bottom of the driveway to let a Mercedes SUV drive past. "I put the address in my phone, too, but it's always easier if I have a navigator."

Those words were delivered with a smile that told her he was very happy to have her in the passenger seat. She was glad to be there, too. It had been so long since she'd been with someone that she'd forgotten what it was like to simply go along for the ride.

Of course, she might be jumping the gun to say that she was "with" Caleb. The early stages of a relationship were always fraught, one way or another. He seemed to enjoy being with her—and his kisses had proved he wasn't exactly indifferent to her physically, either—but maybe he was just caught up in the excitement of their search and would lose interest as soon as they found the missing footage. Rosemary didn't really want to think that about him because it sounded so calculating, and yet she realized she needed to steel herself in case that eventuality presented itself.

For now, though, she would just focus on the drive, on the beautiful mild, sunny day. The temperatures had dropped since their high on Friday, and this Sunday promised to stay in the middle or upper seventies at the most. Not exactly a crisp fall morning, but gorgeous nonetheless.

Caleb followed her instructions, getting off the freeway at Los Feliz Boulevard and heading west, climbing as they followed the wide street—crowded even at this hour on a weekend—and then turned off into an upscale neighborhood on the south side of the main drag.

"Right on Gainsborough," she said. "It should be on the right side of the street—number 1933."

"I see it." He slowed down and then passed their destination, since there was already a car parked in that spot. Actually, the narrow residential street was so crowded that they had to drive past three more houses before an open space presented itself. He pulled up to the curb and parked, then looked over at her. "So, what's our story?"

"The truth," Rosemary replied. She'd thought about the situation as she was heading over to Caleb's house, and had decided there wasn't any real need for them to lie. Not that she planned to tell the current occupants of the house about the footage itself, only that they were friends of Colin's and wanted a chance to make sure he hadn't left anything behind, since they were packing the rest of his belongings to send to his sister in England. She hoped that no one would be hard-hearted enough to refuse such a request, but she knew it was a possibility. In that case, she just prayed that her own powers or instincts or whatever you wanted to call them would be enough to point her in the right direction. "Or at least, enough of the truth for us to sound plausible. I can do most of the talking, if you want."

"That's probably a good idea." Caleb ran a hand through his hair, mussing it in an adorable sort of way. Frankly, Rosemary guessed that if the current occupant of the house was female and straight, she'd probably have a hard time sending him packing. Maybe she should reconsider her plan to be the one who was doing the talking.

Well, they'd just go with the flow and see what happened. That was the most she could do in any situation anyway.

"Ready?" she asked.

"As I'll ever be, I suppose."

Maybe not the most ringing endorsement, but Rosemary could see why he might be feeling reluctant. It was one thing to make a plan in the comfort of your own home, but quite another to walk up to a stranger's house and ask if they'll let you poke around to see if you can find anything that belonged to a former resident who was murdered in a gruesome way.

At least, she assumed the manner of Colin's death had been gruesome. Audrey hadn't provided any details, and Rosemary had known better than to ask.

She and Caleb got out of the truck and walked down to the house in question, then headed up the gently curved path out front. The yard looked good, the grass green and thick despite the hot, dry weather they'd been having lately, but probably landscaping was included as part of the rent. On the front porch, warm-toned chrysanthemums bloomed in pots, looking cheerful and happy.

Somehow, she doubted Colin had kept flowers in pots during his tenure here.

Caleb sent her a questioning look, and she nodded. With a fatalistic shrug, he leaned forward slightly and pressed the button for the doorbell.

Although Rosemary had been halfway expecting to get no answer at all, since so many people used their Sundays to run errands, the door opened almost at once. A thin, intense-looking woman with an immaculate silver-gray bob stared out at them.

"Can I help you?" she asked, looking a little confused.

Well, her confusion wasn't that misplaced. Although Rosemary had pulled some of her wild hair back in a barrette and had dressed a little more simply than usual, in a dark green draped sleeveless top and jeans and flat sandals, she still doubted that she and Caleb looked like a couple of missionaries going door to door.

"Hi," she said. "My name is Rosemary, and this is Caleb. This might sound kind of strange, but we were friends of the man who used to live here, Colin Turner."

"Oh, I'm so sorry," the woman replied at once, indicating that she knew enough of the story to understand this wasn't a simple social call.

Her obvious sympathy made Rosemary's next words that much more difficult to say. Yes, she didn't plan on lying outright, but still, they wouldn't be telling the exact truth, either. "It's okay," she replied, and hoped she didn't sound too dismissive. "Normally, we would never have bothered you, but we're in the process of boxing up the last of Colin's things to send to his sister in England, and we just wanted to make sure nothing had been overlooked."

"Come in," the woman said, stepping aside so the two of them could enter—an invitation that surprised Rosemary, since she wasn't sure she would have so easily invited a couple of strangers into her home.

Then again, she hadn't really hesitated to let Caleb in....

"Thank you," he said with a smile, and moved into the small entry that faced the front door. Since he'd taken the first step, Rosemary had no choice but to follow him.

"I'm Analise Becker," the woman went on. "My husband and I are renting the house while our own place is being remodeled."

Which meant they must have a lot of disposable income. Although Rosemary didn't consider herself much of an expert, she knew that the rock on Ms. Becker's ring finger and the matching diamond studs in her ears had to have cost a lot. Her clothes were the kind of quietly elegant pieces that looked dead simple but were probably equally expensive.

Before either she or Caleb could speak, Analise went on, "I'm not sure I can help you, though. This house was completely empty when we moved in."

"It was?" Caleb asked.

The older woman gave him a quick, appraising glance. Not in a sexual way, but more as though she was taking note of every detail of his appearance. "Are you an actor, Caleb?"

"No," he said, sounding almost horrified. Or maybe it was only he'd been asked the question enough times that he was pretty sick of it by that point.

"Surprising. Anyway," she went on, "there was absolutely nothing in the house except some spare bulbs for the vanity lights in the guest bath."

Damn. Rosemary had been expecting as much, but she'd still allowed herself to hope there might have been something that was overlooked.

"What about the garage?" Caleb asked then.

Analise Becker's unnaturally smooth brow creased ever so slightly. "Now that you mention it, I think Henry did say something about a box of odds and ends he found in the garage. I think he left it sitting on the workbench. You're welcome to look."

Trying not to sound too eager, Rosemary said, "Do you mind?"

"Not at all. I'll show you."

She led them through the house and out the kitchen door, which opened onto a backyard with a large swimming pool that sparkled almost neon blue-green in the bright morning sun. A man in a pair of loud hibiscus-patterned swim trunks and a white T-shirt lay on one of the chaise longues by the pool, but he had a floppy canvas hat covering half his face and didn't stir as they went by.

"That's my husband Henry," Analise said. "He does like his poolside naps. Anyway, the garage is unlocked. If the box has your friend's things in it, then feel free to take them with you."

"Thanks," both Caleb and Rosemary responded, almost in unison.

"Not a problem. Henry and I were wondering what to do with that box. We decided to hand it off to the management company, but we hadn't gotten around to it yet. Just come back up to the house when you're done. I'll be in the kitchen."

After delivering that particular instruction, she turned away and headed back to house, leaving Rosemary and Caleb to look at each other in some bewilderment.

"She's being awfully casual for someone who just let a couple of strangers into her house," he said in a murmur, to which Rosemary could only shrug.

"Maybe she thinks there isn't much trouble we can get into out here," she suggested. "Or maybe we're just that trustworthy-looking."

"I suppose so. Anyway, let's take a look."

They went into the garage, which was nearly as neat as the house. A sleek black Mercedes roadster was parked nearest them, while a Porsche Cayenne occupied the other space. Looking at it, Rosemary couldn't quite keep herself from shivering. Colin had driven one just like it, although his had been black and this one was a dark silvery gray.

But because the garage was so tidy, the small cardboard box sitting on the workbench was almost painfully obvious. They went up to it and saw that it was taped shut.

"You do the honors," Rosemary said, and Caleb nodded and got out his Swiss Army knife so he could cut open the box.

This would have felt like *déjà vu,* except this garage was not nearly as cluttered—or as hot—as the garage back at the Pasadena house. She stood next to Caleb, trying not to allow herself to be overly affected by his proximity…and failing miserably. Although they'd both been all business so far today, she couldn't help but remember how he'd kissed her on Friday night, the way his arms had gone around her. She wanted to think about those things, because maybe if she focused on the intimacies they'd already shared, she could force Will Gordon to stop taking up space in her head.

"Well, that's a whole lot of nothing," Caleb said, his tone disgusted.

"What?" she asked, blinking as she brought herself back to the here and now, to the almost painfully neat garage where they currently stood.

In answer, Caleb opened the box a little wider so she could look inside. It contained stacks of DVDs, all of which showed the same illustration of a foggy graveyard and a drippy red font that proclaimed, *America's Top 10 Most Haunted Cemeteries!*

Disappointed flared. "Is that all that's in the box?"

He scooped out several stacks of the DVDs and set them aside, then lifted the empty box and tapped on the bottom, as if he somehow hoped a flash drive or an SD card might magically come flying out. But no, there was nothing else inside, no missing footage, not even a spare piece of change. From what she could tell, the box had never even been opened before now; the DVD manufacturer had probably sent the disks to Colin as promotional items, and he'd shoved them into a corner of the garage and forgotten about them.

"Nothing to see here," Caleb said, sounding annoyed as he picked up the DVDs and set them back inside their box. "But I suppose we'll have to take these with us, even though they're of absolutely no use."

"Yes, I think we'd better." And do what with them, she had no idea. Maybe stick them in the garage at Michael's house and figure it out later. But if they left the box behind, Analise Becker would be forced to wonder why they'd abandoned something that had obviously belonged to their friend.

Sighing a little, Caleb began to lift the box from the workbench, then paused and looked around the garage. "Do you want to check to make sure there's nothing else here?"

"Analise said there was only the one box."

"Maybe, but it couldn't hurt to look."

Rosemary supposed he had a point. Dutifully, she turned around and began making a circuit of the garage's interior, looking for anything that appeared out of place. That was easy enough to do, since it was so neat in here.

But there wasn't anything to see. One wall had a cabinet that appeared to be full of cleaning supplies, and that was it. No unmarked boxes, no miscellaneous little bibs and bobs lying around, nothing that shouldn't be where it was.

A whole lot of nothing, basically.

She turned back toward Caleb, shoulders lifting in a helpless shrug. "There's nothing here."

He frowned, brows furrowed. It was the first time she'd seen him appear truly irritated. "Then why would Madeline Nash tell you to look in this house?"

"I have no idea." Since Rosemary was feeling as annoyed as he looked, she added sourly, "I'm not a medium. I'm not someone who routinely talks to dead people. So how the hell would I know why she sent us on this wild goose chase?"

Almost at once, his expression turned contrite, and he stepped away from the workbench and came over so he could pull her into his arms and give her a hug. "I'm sorry," he said. "I didn't mean to bite your head off. I'm just disappointed."

"So am I." She allowed herself to remain in his embrace for a few seconds more, breathing in a clean scent that might have been aftershave or just the fabric softener he used on his clothes, then pulled away and gazed up at him. "And we'll figure something else out. For now, though, we should probably just leave. Analise was nice enough to let us poke around in here, but if we take too much time…."

Rosemary let the words trail off, but Caleb appeared to get the point. It wouldn't do to overstay their welcome, especially when there wasn't any reason to linger here.

In fact, he grinned and said, "Yeah we'd better get going. We wouldn't want Analise to sic the fearsome Henry on us."

Despite the disappointment she was feeling, a giggle escaped her lips. "No, probably not."

Caleb went over and picked up the box of DVDs, and Rosemary followed him out of the garage. As she closed the door behind her, she looked upward, as though directing her thoughts there would somehow allow them to reach the woman who'd been dead for the past seven years.

Why here, Madeline? What are we missing?

Of course, there was no answer.

Chapter 10

Since they had the box with them, Analise didn't seem all that surprised when the two of them peeked into the kitchen and said they'd found what they needed and would be on their way. She had been in the middle of doing something with a collection of herbs and decorative glass jars—Rosemary thought Annalise might be making some kind of infused vinegar, although she couldn't be sure—and gave them an off-hand thank-you and told them she hoped they would have a nice rest of their day.

And that seemed to be that.

Now they were driving back to Caleb's house, the box riding on the cramped back seat in his truck's extra cab. It was almost one o'clock, and Rosemary wondered if he was going to ask if she wanted to grab lunch or something. That seemed the natural thing to do, and yet he hadn't mentioned anything about getting some food or even if he planned for them to do anything at all after they got back to his place.

Maybe he didn't have any plans. Maybe he was so frustrated by the way things had turned out that he just wanted her to go on her way so he could blow off some steam by playing *World of Warcraft* or *Skyrim* or something equally mindless for the rest of the afternoon.

She realized then how little she actually knew about him, about how he liked to spend his time. Yes, she knew he was a transplant from the Midwest, that he was interested in the occult and maybe one day wanted to be an independent film-maker and producer like Colin had been, but that was about it. She didn't know what kind of music he liked, whether he was an indoor gaming kind of guy or whether he preferred to go hiking when he had the free time.

And she told herself that was okay, because they'd only just met less than a week ago. They'd have plenty of opportunities to get to know each other a little better.

Or…would they?

She realized how ambivalent she felt as she tried to answer that question. And she shouldn't be ambivalent. She should want to know everything about him.

Maybe she just had low blood sugar.

As they pulled up into the driveway of his house, Caleb finally spoke. "Sorry I'm being a grouch. I guess I just hoped that would have turned out a little better."

"That makes two of us." Rosemary paused and allowed herself a quick sideways glance in his direction. "I guess I'll just have to try to reach out to the spirit world and see if I can get Madeline to cough up something a little more valuable. I'll let you know."

He pushed the button on the garage remote clipped to the sun visor above his head, then looked over at her, obviously puzzled. "You'll let…." The sentence sort of died there as comprehension apparently dawned. "Oh, hell. You didn't think I wanted you to go straight home, did you?"

She shrugged. "Well, I did sort of get that impression."

"Because I'm a dumbass. No, I don't want you to go home. Let's order in some lunch. We can sit out on the back patio and enjoy the sunshine."

That actually sounded great, definitely better than going back to the house in Pasadena and brooding over what Madeline had really been trying to tell them. However, since she didn't want to seem too eager, Rosemary said, "If you're sure—"

"I'm sure. Really. There's a great Italian place just down the hill that delivers. Sound okay?"

Now she allowed herself a smile. "Sounds more than okay."

He parked in the garage, and they went inside and headed back toward the kitchen, which had a few dishes drying in the sink but otherwise looked pretty clean for a couple of guys in their twenties. Then again, Caleb had mentioned that his roommate was off shooting on location somewhere.

"Water?" he asked.

"Sure."

After pouring some for the both of them, he got his phone out of his pocket. "This place has a great antipasto salad," he said, tapping the screen so he could navigate to the restaurant's website. But then his face fell. "Oh, you don't eat red meat."

"It's okay," Rosemary said. She tried to be careful about what she ate, just because she figured that an efficient body meant an efficient mind, but she allowed herself to cheat every once in a while. "A few pieces of salami aren't going to kill me."

"We can get something else—"

"It's fine," she assured him. "Antipasto and….?"

"Chicken pesto pasta?" he suggested. "It's also really good."

"Sounds great."

Looking relieved, he entered the number for the restaurant and made the call. As he was placing the order, Rosemary wandered over to the window so she could look outside. Because of the house's location, you could see the back side of the Hollywood Hills—although not the Griffith Observatory—and past the hills all the way into downtown. Since the wind was blowing from offshore, pushing Southern California's natural fog and clouds far out to sea, everything looked crisp and hard and diamond-bright.

"About twenty minutes," he said, coming over to stand next to her. "I hope that's okay."

"It's fine." And it was; she'd eaten some muesli with her yogurt and fruit at breakfast that morning, just because she hadn't been sure how late she'd be having lunch. After releasing a small breath, she said, "Do you ever get tired of this view?"

A quick flash of a smile. "Not really. It's going to suck whenever I have to move out of here, but I guess I'll enjoy it while I can. We can head on out there—I should still be able to hear the doorbell since the windows are all open."

That sounded like a good idea. Some fresh air might help to clear the cobwebs from her mind, might allow her to figure out what they should do next.

She waited as he unlocked the French doors that led onto the patio, then followed him out there, glass of water in one hand. The sun was bright, but Caleb hoisted the umbrella above the table and chairs where they'd been sitting, and it did a good job of blocking a lot of the glare.

They both took their seats, and Rosemary drank some of the water he'd gotten for her, glad of its coolness against her throat. She'd finished the bottle she'd brought with her as they were driving back from Los Feliz and was already feeling thirsty again.

Caleb stared out at the distant skyline for a minute, then shook his head. "It's kind of hard to believe in a world with spirits and demons on a day like this, isn't it?"

She had to admit to herself that he had a point. However, since she'd experienced such phenomena for herself—or at least knew people who'd been impacted directly by such supernatural beings—she couldn't deny that they existed. "It is. But just because we can't see them doesn't mean they aren't there."

Without replying right away, he lifted his own glass of water and drank from it. "I know. Still…." The word trailed off, and he gave the slightest shake of his head. "Are we crazy for doing this?"

"Define 'crazy.'"

He chuckled. "I don't know. It's just…ever

since I saw Colin's posts in that forum, promising something big, I had to know what it was. What he'd seen, and whether he was just blowing a lot of hot air. But he wasn't, was he?"

It would have been nice if Colin had been making things up, trying to make his show seem more dramatic than it really was. However, Rosemary knew the exact opposite was true. The images he'd captured with his camera would shake a lot of people's worlds to their foundations...if she and Caleb could only figure out what had happened to the damn footage.

"No, he wasn't blowing hot air," she said quietly. "I wish I could say that he was, but some of the stuff Audrey saw would give you nightmares for years." Should she say more, tell him about some of the terrible things the demons had done to her friend? Maybe that was Audrey's story to tell, and yet, Rosemary thought Caleb should know what kind of monsters they were dealing with. "This stuff is dangerous, though," she added. "The demons burned down Audrey's house."

He sat up straight in his chair, eyes widening with shock. "They *what?*"

"Well, first they trashed it. Then I guess they decided that wasn't enough, so they burned it to the ground. All to mess with her head, to put her off balance so she wouldn't be an effective force against them."

"Holy shit." Caleb scrubbed his hands through his hair, clearly trying to come to grips with this latest revelation. "Are you—are we in danger?"

"I don't know," she said frankly. "I mean, other than that visitation from Madeline the other night, I haven't seen any signs of supernatural interference with what we're doing. And really, I don't think Madeline was interfering…not really. As far as I can tell, she was only trying to help."

"By sending us to find a box of DVDs of a cable special that came out three years ago?"

How Caleb had known that particular bit of information about the DVDs they'd found, Rosemary wasn't quite sure, although she supposed if he'd been a fan of Colin's work, then he might have kept track of his various projects. Anyway, that wasn't the point. At the moment, she couldn't think of a single reason why they'd gone to the Los Feliz house. Analise had said there were no personal belongings left in the house itself, and the only thing they'd found in the garage had been less than useless, frankly. Short of digging up the backyard to see if Colin had buried the missing footage out there, she wasn't sure what else they could have done.

She kind of doubted that Analise and Henry would have been too happy about her and Caleb taking a shovel to their immaculate yard. No, that sort of behavior probably would have prompted a quick call to L.A.'s finest.

"No," Rosemary said, "I have to admit that I have no idea what Madeline was thinking. Which I know isn't exactly helpful, but at least we can scratch that house off our list."

Caleb's lip curled. "That house was basically the only thing on our list."

True. She began to shrug, and was interrupted by the sound of a distant doorbell.

"Food's here," he said, rising from his chair.

Rosemary began to get up as well, but he shook his head.

"No, I'll get it. You stay here and enjoy the sunshine."

Which was probably his way of making sure she didn't try to pay for their lunch. Although she wanted to argue, she knew the best thing to do was just sit here quietly and let him handle things. After all, she had no idea how big his last paycheck had been. Maybe he'd only been late with his electric bill because he'd been waiting on a large payout.

And the air felt great. She closed her eyes and breathed it in, telling herself to be grateful for where she was now, for this beautiful view and this beautiful day. Yes, they were both feeling frustrated, as if they'd hit a brick wall, but even brick walls couldn't stand forever. Sooner or later, they'd figure out the next step they needed to take, the one thing they'd overlooked that would lead them down the trail to Colin's missing footage.

A few minutes later, she heard Caleb come back out onto the patio, and she opened her eyes. Not only did he have their lunch on a tray, but he'd brought along a bottle of white wine and some glasses.

"I noticed the other evening that you liked wine," he said. "I don't know much about it, but I hope this is okay."

A glass of wine sounded like the perfect way to ease some of the sting of their strike-out at Colin's former rental. "Better than okay," she responded with a smile, and his mouth lifted in response.

"Great." He set down the tray, which was full almost to capacity, thanks to the plates and cutlery and glasses he'd loaded it with, in addition to the two covered foil dishes from the restaurant. Working quickly, he set a plate, knife, and fork in front of her, then arranged his own place setting at the spot where he'd been sitting. Nothing matched, and, just as she'd done back at Michael's house, Caleb was using paper towels instead of actual paper napkins, but Rosemary didn't care about any of that.

She recognized the label on the bottle of wine —it was a pinot grigio she'd bought at Trader Joe's on more than one occasion. It made sense that he'd shop there, since one of the original TJ's locations was just up the street on Eagle Rock Boulevard.

Once everything was laid out and he'd poured a decent measure of wine into each of their glasses, Caleb lifted his wine glass toward her. "Better luck next time."

There was a sentiment she could get behind. "To better luck."

They clinked glasses—well, plastic, actually, because she realized the stemless drinkware they held was acrylic, probably a souvenir from some sort of wine festival or something like that—and she took a decent swallow of wine. Yes, that was much better. Already she could feel the tight little knot of tension at the back of her neck begin to loosen.

He dished some antipasto on her plate, being careful to avoid giving her too many slices of meat. It was a small gesture, but one she appreciated. Once again, she thought of how considerate he seemed to be. Possibly his gentlemanly behavior was just an act, although she didn't think so. She'd been around men who pretended to be nice guys, but those façades had always managed to slip at some point. With Caleb, there didn't seem to be anything to slip because he actually was that nice.

After they'd both taken a few bites of salad, he asked, "Are you really going to try to summon Madeline Nash's ghost?"

When she'd first made that comment, Rosemary had known it was born out of frustration with their current situation and not because she actually thought she would do such a thing. Now, though, she wondered if she should give it a try. Really, the worst that might happen was that Madeline simply wouldn't appear. This wasn't like summoning a demon; whoever she had been in life, her spirit had seemed benign enough, nothing that would constitute a threat.

"I'm thinking about it," Rosemary said. "I don't have a lot of experience with this sort of thing, but maybe if I get my sisters to help…."

"Are they mediums?"

She picked up her glass of wine and sipped from it, enjoying the way it glinted pale gold in the sunlight, even as she savored the tart, crisp, cool flavor against her tongue. "No. Their psychic talents are pretty similar to mine. I guess I mostly thought that this sort of thing might be more successful if the three of us combined our powers."

Caleb seemed to ponder her reply for a moment. His fingers tapped against the edge of the table; for the first time, she noticed a paler band of skin at the base of the fourth finger of his right hand, as if he used to regularly wear a ring there but had stopped for some reason. Well, she could see why he might have avoided wearing a ring or a watch while he was working, and maybe he'd decided it was easier to go without.

"Do they know about Madeline?"

There hadn't been any condemnation in his tone, only simple curiosity. Rosemary supposed he'd already figured out that the three sisters were fairly close. They sort of had to be, since they ran a business together. "Isabel does," she replied. "Which means Celeste probably does, too, even though I haven't heard much from her this week. But her little boy is two, and he takes up a lot of her time and energy."

Caleb absorbed this reply without comment, taking a sip of his own wine. Then he said, "But they'd be willing to help."

"I think so." Or rather, she hoped so. Isabel would probably utter words of warning, and Celeste would be on guard against getting dragged into something that might take up too much of her time, but in the end, Rosemary knew her sisters would come through for her. "I'll ask them tonight."

"'Tonight'?" he repeated, his tone sharpening a bit.

Was he surprised she had plans for her day after this? Part of the reason she'd suggested going over to Los Feliz in the morning rather than later in the afternoon was that she had a standing dinner date with her sisters at their mother's house. Some people might have argued that the McGuires already had plenty of family togetherness, but they'd begun the ritual years earlier, right after Rosemary and Celeste and their mother moved into Grandma's house in Sierra Madre. After their grandmother died and their mother inherited the house, they kept up the practice—easy enough, since Isabel had gone to college at Cal State L.A. and could easily make it back for their Sunday dinners.

"We always have dinner at my mother's house on Sunday evening," she said, hoping he wouldn't think it too strange. But then, he'd grown up in Indiana, in a place she guessed was a lot more conservative and family-oriented than Southern California tended to be. Surely, he'd understand this kind of familial ritual. "It's kind of old-fashioned, but—"

"No, I think it's great," he cut in. "Especially since you must see each other a lot during the week."

"It depends on the season, actually. When it's slow, a lot of the time it's just one of us working at the store, except on Saturdays. During the holidays, all three of us usually end up there six days a week."

"So it was a slow day when I came in?"

Rosemary lifted her glass and felt her mouth curve slightly in a smile. "Well, it was slow *until* you came in."

His eyes met hers, warm, brown…inviting. Before she'd met Caleb, she would have said she preferred men with lighter eyes, just because of their infinite variations in color—even when she'd thought he was an ass, she'd been forced to admit that Michael Covenant had amazing eyes—but now she realized she might have been too narrow in her thinking. Caleb's eyes were gorgeous as well, the bright sunlight picking out shimmering shades of amber and chocolate and deep, deep gold.

"I'm glad to hear it," he remarked. "I mean, not that it was slow, but that things got better after that."

She almost said that they'd gotten much better, but she didn't want to sound desperate, or over-eager. They might have kissed, but a few kisses weren't all that much of a commitment when you got right down to it. "They've been looking up," she said lightly.

He chuckled and reached for the container that held their pesto chicken pasta. "Ready for the main course?"

She nodded, and he dished some chicken pesto for both of them. As they ate, he talked a little about the new show for Netflix he was hoping to get hired for—some kind of detective thing, which wasn't really her deal at all, but of course she still wanted him to get the job—and she spoke some more about the store, about how the people in Glendora were first a little skeptical about a woo-woo kind of venture like a metaphysical bookstore, but then came to embrace the shop as a vital part of their downtown scene, a place that attracted shoppers from all over the San Gabriel Valley because of its carefully curated collection of books. Yes, you could get the same books for possibly a little cheaper online, but you wouldn't have someone who could hand-sell you the exact book you wanted...even if you hadn't known beforehand that it was the one you'd been looking for all along.

As they talked, they ate as much of the excellent food as they wanted...and managed to make their way through the whole bottle of pinot grigio as well. Rosemary wasn't exactly sure how that had happened, but she found she didn't care all that much. The time had somehow managed to slip past three o'clock and wind its way on toward four, but she didn't have to be in Sierra Madre until six, and that gave her plenty of time to sober up before she got on the road.

Eventually, the sun had slanted far enough to the west that the patio umbrella wasn't giving them the protection they needed, so she and Caleb gathered up their empty plates and the few leftovers that remained, and brought everything inside to the kitchen. The interior of the house felt cool and dark after spending so much time out in the bright daylight, and she blinked.

"Let me get you some water," he offered, and she sent him a grateful smile.

"That would be great."

He poured a couple of glasses for both of them, then handed one to her. She drank, and looked up from her glass to find him gazing at her.

"What?" she asked, wondering if she'd gotten fried while sitting out in the sun, patio umbrella or no.

"Nothing," Caleb said before adding, "or maybe everything."

A little tipsy, she shook her head at him. "What are you talking about?"

"This," he replied, and stepped closer to her. He took the glass of water from her hand, then knotted his fingers in hers and pulled her to him, his mouth touching hers.

Oh, yes, that was what she'd been wanting. Or at least, she *thought* she wanted it. Maybe it was just the wine doing its dirty work, but the whole time they'd been out on the patio, she'd had to force herself not to stare at Caleb's face, to not think about how good it had been when he'd kissed her, and how much she wanted him to do it again, if only to prove to herself that she was crazy for thinking she might not be as interested in him as she thought she was.

Well, he was kissing her now. She opened her mouth to his, tasted the sweet-sharp tang of the pinot grigio on his tongue, overlaid with the coolness of the water he'd just swallowed a moment earlier. Since they were completely alone, there was nothing to keep her from pressing her body against his, to let him wrap his arms around her and hold her close…so very close.

And now his kisses were moving down her throat, pausing at that delicious spot just below her ear. Rosemary let out a small gasp, and he paused.

"Should I stop?" he asked, his tone husky and yet still so gentle.

"No," she whispered. Her body was telling her the last thing she wanted was for him to stop. Head spinning slightly, she realized she wanted…

…she wanted all of him. So what if they'd met less than a week ago? She'd spent enough time with him to know how much she liked him, how much she enjoyed being around him.

"Don't stop," she added, her tone fierce.

His mouth came down on hers again, hungrier this time, even as one hand slid from where it had been touching her arm to cup her breast. Now the gasp that escaped her lips was much louder, almost a moan. Yes, there was a bra and a blouse between his fingers and her skin, and yet she could practically feel the heat smoldering through his fingertips.

"Yes?" he said, and she nodded, still feeling swimmy and disconnected and not quite herself.

"Yes."

In the next moment, his arms were sliding under her, and before she could begin to react, he'd lifted her from the floor as if she weighed nothing, was carrying her out of the kitchen, through the dining room, and down a short hallway. They went into a bedroom that must have been his, with posters of old classic monster movies on the walls.

He set her down on the bed and kissed her again, pushing her down against the covers…and for some reason, all the eagerness she'd felt a few moments before abruptly disappeared, replaced by an odd reluctance, as though something deep within was telling her she shouldn't be doing this, that this was wrong. Why she'd be thinking something so crazy, she had no idea. She wanted Caleb, and she certainly wasn't worried about her "virtue"—that ship had sailed years before.

But as his hand began to slide up under her

blouse, she found herself pulling away, a voice that didn't sound much like hers saying, "No."

He stared down at her in confusion. "What's the matter?"

Oh, there was a very good question. She honestly had no idea what had gotten into her, but when that inner voice spoke to her this loudly, Rosemary knew she needed to pay attention. "Sorry, I'm—I don't know. It just feels…like we're rushing things."

His mouth tightened, and he pushed himself off her and stood. She supposed she should be relieved by that, should have been glad he hadn't tried to force the issue. If he had, there wasn't much she could have done about it.

But no, Caleb wasn't like that. He was a good guy. He'd just misinterpreted the signals she was sending him—not terribly surprising, since she hadn't correctly read them herself, either.

"Okay," he said, his voice sounding as tight as his mouth had looked a moment earlier. "I'm— well, okay. I didn't think you were like this, Rosemary."

"Like what?"

He paused, then pulled in a breath. "Never mind. I guess I made a mistake."

Oh, shit…there it was. He thought she was a mistake. Maybe fine to spend time with if it looked like he was going to be able to get her in the sack sooner rather than later, but....

Face burning, she got up from the bed as well. As much as she would have liked to stalk out of the house, make some kind of grand gesture, she realized they still had that damn missing footage tying them together. She wouldn't cut him off completely, not when it was so important to him.

"If I hear anything else from Madeline, I'll let you know," she said.

His expression softened somewhat. "Sure. That would be great."

"I'll just get going."

Out of the bedroom then, grabbing her purse from where she'd left it on the kitchen counter before she fled the house and headed toward her Fiat, still parked at the curb where she'd left it. At least this was no walk of shame in broad daylight, since nothing had happened, really. She'd have to stop home first and get herself cleaned up a little before she went over to her mother's house, but not as much as she would have had to do if...if.

She really didn't want to think about that.

Hand shaking a little, she opened the car door and got in. Some part of her wondered if Caleb was going to come outside, maybe wave goodbye, but the front door remained resolutely shut. Probably, it was better that way. She had no idea if this was even fixable.

Did she *want* it to be fixable? She liked Caleb…thought she could do much more than simply like him…and yet she couldn't ignore what her inner voice had been trying to tell her.

Something was wrong. She just had no idea what that problem might be.

Chapter 11

THE WARM SMELL OF CHICKEN PAPRIKASH filled the dining room as the McGuire family gathered around the big oak table that was as much a fixture in Rosemary's life as the house itself. Her mother Glynis sat at the head of the table, while Isabel and Rosemary were on her right and Celeste and her husband Kevin sat to Glynis's left, two-year-old Tyler sandwiched safely between them. That evening, he seemed better behaved than usual—probably because Kevin had taken him to the park that afternoon and kept him running around so he'd crash sometime during the meal and could be laid down on the comfy couch in the family room while the rest of them talked.

No one seemed to notice anything of Rosemary's currently unsettled mental state, and she let out a little inward sigh of relief that none of the McGuires' psychic powers seemed to be directed at her for the moment. Maybe her mother had worn the slightest of frowns as she hugged her daughter, but then she'd only said that Rosemary was looking well and left it at that.

Luckily, the reflection gazing back at her from the mirror when she went home to get tidied up had looked completely normal, betraying nothing of what had just happened back at Caleb's house. She'd used some rice paper blotters to get the shine off her nose and forehead, reapplied lip gloss, and then finger-combed her hair and dampened it slightly with a spray bottle to get the curls to bounce back into shape. Once she was done, she looked fit for company…and she had to hope that no one attending that night's dinner would have any reason to ask her about the "new man" in her life.

But after everyone had dished up their helpings of chicken paprikash and buttered egg noodles and steamed zucchini, Glynis fixed her daughter with a pair of too-sharp blue eyes and commented, "Isabel was saying you'd met someone. Why don't you tell us about him?"

Because Rosemary had been expecting as much—secrets were hard to keep in her family, no matter what she might have secretly hoped for— she'd already prepared an answer, something neutral but providing enough facts that, with any luck, no one would ask too many follow-up questions. "His name is Caleb, and he works in the film industry. We went out on Friday night, and I saw him again earlier today for lunch."

Her sister Celeste looked impressed. "A follow-up date only two days after your first one? It must be serious."

Up until earlier that afternoon, Rosemary had thought things between her and Caleb were serious, or at least, well on the way there. Usually, a guy who wasn't interested wouldn't have pushed for that date Friday night, or asked her to stay at the house for lunch after they were done with their fact-finding expedition in Los Feliz. Unfortunately, her last-minute reluctance had definitely derailed that particular train. She still didn't quite know why she'd reacted in such a way, but there wasn't much she could do about it now, except allow some time to pass and see what happened. Maybe by then she'd figure out what had been going on in her head...and maybe after a day or so, he'd cool off and be ready to give things another try.

If that was even what she wanted. Right then, she honestly didn't know what to think.

"Well, I don't know about 'serious,'" she said, figuring she might as well start setting expectations now in case things were truly over between her and Caleb. "I mean, he seems like a great guy, and we get along together pretty well. But I'm not going to start throwing the S-word around quite yet."

"That's probably wise," Isabel observed. It looked as if she'd planned to say something else, but instead, she reached for the glass of wine by her plate and took a sip. "You might as well take it slowly and see what happens."

Rosemary speared a piece of chicken with her fork and chewed, giving herself time to think. Obviously, she didn't want to come out and say that she and Caleb had had a fight before she came over here—if that weird little scene could even be classified as a "fight"—but she also wanted to set it up so it wouldn't seem that strange if she ended up not spending any more time with him.

"We are taking it slowly," she said. "I actually don't even know when we're going to see each other again—he's up for a job on a new show with Netflix, so he's waiting to see if it comes through before we make any concrete plans for the coming week."

There. That sounded downright responsible. As Rosemary spoke, however, she wondered if Caleb would even let her know whether he got the job or not. They'd left things open-ended in terms of their "investigation," but maybe he'd already decided to forge ahead without her. He hadn't said anything about a location shoot, and so she supposed his employment status might not have as much of an effect on their hunt for the missing footage as she thought it might, but she didn't know for sure. About all she could do was wait and see how everything panned out.

"So, what does Caleb do, exactly?" her mother asked.

Since it was Glynis, Rosemary knew the question wasn't the standard "what does he do for a living?" inquiry that most mothers might make about someone their daughter was dating. No, her mother was merely curious as to what role Caleb played in television production, not how much money he made. Even though it was easy to be unconcerned about material things when you'd gotten a comfortable inheritance and didn't have to worry about housing costs or day-to-day finances, Glynis McGuire had always been like that. She took people on their own merits, not how much they earned or who they were related to.

"Honestly?" Rosemary lifted her shoulders and reached for her glass of pinot noir. "I'm not totally sure. I got the impression that he's mostly just a P.A., or general assistant. He's not a cameraman or anything like that."

Glynis didn't seem too put out by that reply.

"It must be fascinating to work on a television show, though."

Across the table, Kevin chuckled, then quickly reached out to grab his son Tyler's hand before it could close on the paprikash-covered fork he'd left a little too close to the rim of his plate. "It's not that fascinating. I worked as an extra a couple of times when I was in college. Mostly, it's a lot of standing around."

"So is working in a bookstore," Celeste pointed out with a grin.

He smiled back at her. "True. But with fewer paparazzi."

Everyone chuckled then, and the conversation moved on to different topics, for which Rosemary was grateful. While what she'd been doing probably couldn't be classified as lying, she still didn't like having to misrepresent the situation to her family. And as time went on and she didn't mention Caleb again, they'd probably figure out that the relationship had gone nowhere after all and wouldn't ask. That was what she hoped for, anyway.

Eventually, things began to wind down, and Celeste and Kevin started to look as though they were ready to get up from the table and head home. Tyler had conked out about a half hour earlier and was already asleep on the couch in the family room—luckily, his parents could keep an eye on him from where they sat—but it was almost nine o'clock, the time when these get-togethers usually started to break up.

And though Rosemary had come to the family dinner with the intention of enlisting her sisters'—and possibly her mother's—help in contacting Madeline Nash's spirit, for some reason, she'd never been able to come up with a good way to insert that topic into the dinnertime discussion. Now, as she glanced over at the clock that hung on the far wall, she realized she was running out of time.

Apparently, that was when Izzie's psychic powers decided to kick in, because she said, "You should tell Mom and Celeste about what happened to you on Thursday night."

Both of them swiveled their heads to stare at Rosemary. Since mother and daughter were so similar in appearance—both with the same curly brown hair and clear blue eyes, just like Rosemary herself—the effect was a little disconcerting, although she told herself she should be used to such incongruities by now. "What happened?" Glynis asked, even as Kevin, on the other side of Celeste, crossed his arms and frowned.

"I had a…visitation," she said. "A harmless spirit. She was trying to tell me something, but I'm not sure the message came through the way she intended."

Celeste leaned forward slightly, her expression more curious than worried. "Who was it?"

"A woman named Madeline Nash." Rosemary hesitated there, wondering how much she should tell everyone. But then, she needed their help. It wouldn't be fair to withhold information from the very people she was going to ask for assistance. "Actually, it turns out she was once involved with Colin Turner, the man who was producing *Project Demon Hunters.*"

"The man who was murdered," Isabel said. It wasn't a question.

"Yes, him." Rosemary toyed with the base of her wine glass and wished they hadn't drunk all of the pinot noir during dinner. She could have used a few fortifying sips right then. "But Madeline died of natural causes years ago, so she had nothing to do with the show."

Their mother was silent for a few seconds, gaze troubled. She ran a finger over the smooth turquoise stone in the heavy silver bracelet she wore, as if focusing on the polished surface might help her decide what to say next. When she spoke, however, her voice sounded serene as ever. "On the surface, possibly not, but the world of the spirits doesn't work quite the same way as ours. They're not as anchored in time as we are."

Celeste raised an eyebrow. "You're not saying

demons had something to do with her death, are you?"

"No. But they could be the reason why she appeared to Rosemary."

"That's what I was wondering," Rosemary put in, thinking she needed to add her own thoughts to the conversation before it veered off in a direction that would eventually prove fruitless. "But even though I did as she asked, nothing came of it. Now I'm wondering if I just didn't understand what she wanted."

"What did she ask you to do?" Kevin inquired.

"I thought she was telling me to go to the house Colin was renting when he died. But there was nothing to find. Audrey and Michael had the place completely cleaned out, and whoever they hired did a good job."

Isabel and Celeste exchanged a glance across the table. What they were both thinking, Rosemary had no idea. The two of them had always seemed closer to each other than they did to their youngest sister, probably because of the age gap, and she knew they were better at reading each other's cues than she herself was.

"What were you hoping to find?" Isabel asked then.

Although Rosemary had known the question would come up, she still hadn't thought of the best way to reply. But since she'd vowed to tell the truth, she figured that was the only answer she could give. "I was hoping she was telling me where to find Colin's copies of the *Project Demon Hunters* footage. I'm almost positive he made copies for himself, copies he was planning to release but didn't have the chance."

"Because the demons got to him first," her oldest sister said, and she nodded.

Celeste shook her head. "They killed him to stop him from releasing the tapes?"

"No one knows for sure."

"But it's possible," Kevin said. Although he usually seemed like one of the sunniest, least troubled people Rosemary had ever met, right then he looked downright worried.

"I suppose," she allowed.

"Then it's probably a good thing you didn't find what you were looking for, even if a spirit told you to go and find it," Isabel remarked. She was also fiddling with the base of her wine glass, as if she wished there had been more to go around as well. "Frankly, you should probably take a step back from all of this."

Rosemary sent a beseeching glance in her mother's direction, but Glynis also didn't appear to be very enthusiastic about her youngest daughter's latest quest. "I have to agree with Isabel," she said quietly. "While I can understand wanting to solve a mystery, it's not worth putting your life at risk."

"It's not at risk," she protested, but even as she spoke, Rosemary honestly didn't know whether her assertion was true or not. All right, no one had attacked her —yet—or had done anything to make her feel less than safe, and yet she couldn't argue that Colin had lost his life over that footage and his plans to spread it all over the internet. Or at least, Michael and Audrey thought that was why he had died, and they had a better idea as to what the demons were capable of than anyone else she knew.

As Rosemary looked at the worried expressions her mother and both her sisters wore, she realized that asking them to help her summon Madeline's spirit wouldn't do any good. Most of the time, they were extremely supportive, but in this case, they would only think she was doing something dangerous and would do what they could to stop her.

That didn't mean she was going to abandon the quest she and Caleb had been pursuing. It only meant that she knew she couldn't expect her family to provide any assistance.

"Well," she went on before any of them could speak, "I've pretty much hit a dead end anyway, so it isn't like there's much more I can do."

"Good," Isabel said, her expression one of

grim satisfaction. "That project seemed doomed from the start."

Rosemary protested, "That's a hell of a thing to say—"

Glynis said quietly, "Girls."

Only the one word, but it was enough. Rosemary knew that arguing with Isabel about *Project Demon Hunters* wasn't going to change her sister's mind. Of course, she'd helped Audrey back when she'd first come into the store, looking for someone to tell her she wasn't crazy, that she really did need to find a way to protect herself from the demons that had come into her life, but all of the disasters that had befallen the show's cast and crew afterward despite those precautions only proved to Isabel that the entire project should have been abandoned.

Which it was…only not before Audrey lost her house and Colin lost his life.

"Fine," Rosemary said. "It's getting late—I need to get home, since I'm opening tomorrow."

No one pointed out that the store didn't open until ten and it was only a little after nine now. They all realized she wanted an excuse to get herself away before she said something she might regret later.

As she rose from the table, Celeste and Kevin murmured something about fetching Tyler, and Isabel said she'd finish clearing the table. Once they were alone, Glynis looked over at her daughter and touched her arm.

"I know you're trying to do the right thing, Rosemary," she said, her tone quiet. "I think I can even understand why it's so important to you to find Colin's missing tapes. But none of us want any harm to come to you."

Although she was still annoyed, Rosemary knew that her mother and sisters loved her and were just trying to make sure she stayed safe. The knot of tension at the base of her neck eased itself slightly, and she let out a very small sigh. "I know. Isabel warned me…she said she felt as if she could sense something dark on the horizon, although she didn't know what it was."

To Rosemary's surprise, her mother nodded. "I've been feeling something similar these past few days, but I couldn't think of what it might be, since everything seemed to be going well with you girls and I've been doing just fine, too. It's out there, though, like storm clouds building up behind the mountains. You really need to take care, Rosemary."

"I am," she said, although she didn't know whether that was the actual truth. If she'd actually been as careful as she claimed, she probably wouldn't have even allowed Caleb Dixon into her house that first time, let alone spent so much time with him. "Michael's house is safe, Mom. I know I told you that."

"Yes," her mother replied, still with that faint frown line etched into the fair skin between her brows. "But you can't be home all the time."

ALTHOUGH IT WAS NEARLY NINE-THIRTY BY the time she got back to Pasadena, Rosemary fought a losing battle with her pride and checked her phone once she was safely inside the house and had the alarm turned back on. It was probably stupid to look; even if Caleb had decided to relent and get back in touch with her, he probably wouldn't have contacted her so soon.

Only…she had missed a text from him. It was very brief, time-stamped a little after eight o'clock.

Call me when you have a chance.

Now she sat on the couch in the family room, staring down at the phone and wondering if she had the guts to call or not. Maybe it would be better to leave it until the next day. Or maybe never.

Or maybe…maybe she'd overreacted. He hadn't tried to force her, had backed off as soon as she told him no. Had she created a crisis because she liked him too much and was trying to keep herself from getting hurt the way she invariably did? For all she knew, Will Gordon's intrusion into her thoughts was only the other side of the same coin. Letting another man draw focus from Caleb could be yet another defense mechanism.

That explanation seemed distinctly possible. She also guessed she was still trying to shake off the negativity she'd experienced at dinner. Honestly, she hadn't expected that kind of reaction from her family, had thought her sisters or at least her mother would understand what she was trying to do. But it was pretty clear they all thought she'd gotten in over her head.

If her family wasn't going to support her, then it seemed obvious that she needed to reach out to the only person who might. She touched the screen and made the call.

Caleb picked up on the third ring. "Hi," he said. "I was beginning to wonder if I was going to hear from you."

He sounded completely normal, as if they hadn't had their little spat at all. Quite possibly, he was the kind of guy who preferred to ignore that sort of thing and move on. While Rosemary was all for avoiding confrontations whenever she could, she wondered if that kind of behavior was precisely healthy. But then, this was definitely not the time to bring it up. Also, it seemed clear enough that he'd been worried whether she was going to blow him off. It was always nice to know she wasn't the only one battling a host of inse-curities.

"Dinner went later than I thought," she replied, which was true enough.

A pause, and then he said, "I'm sorry. I guess I didn't do as good a job of picking up on your signals as I thought I had."

She hadn't been expecting an apology this early in the game, and realized his response was a surprise. Also, a stab of guilt went through her. It wasn't that he'd misinterpreted the signals she was sending him, only that she'd had a sudden change of heart. Her prerogative, of course, and yet she hated for him to think this was all his fault. Not quite sure what to say, she hesitated, then told him, "It's okay." Should she leave it there? Maybe. But…. "I guess I realized that things were going too fast for me. I'm sorry about the mixed signals."

"It's all right. I'm just glad you called me back." Then, his tone changing, he asked, "How'd dinner go?"

There wasn't anything beyond simple curiosity in his voice—as well as an obvious desire to change the subject. They'd hadn't completely patched things up, but she figured it was better to leave matters as they stood and move on to some-thing a little less fraught. "Not as well as I'd hoped. My sisters and mother made it pretty clear that they thought doing anything to find the missing footage was a really bad idea."

"Ouch," Caleb said, sympathy obvious in his voice. "I know you were hoping they'd be able to help you out."

Rosemary shrugged, then realized it was a wasted gesture since he couldn't see her. "I was, but it's not the end of the world. I'll just have to try to reach out to Madeline on my own."

"You're okay with that?"

Was she? Since she'd never done anything like this before, she honestly couldn't say for sure. But she'd have to try.

Because she hadn't answered right away, Caleb went on, "I mean, I don't want to ask you to do something you're not comfortable with. We can figure something else out."

"You didn't ask me, I offered," she said. "I probably won't try until I get off work tomorrow, though—it's been a long day."

"I totally understand. Whenever you have a chance." He paused for a second or two, then said, tone noticeably brighter, "I got a call about the Netflix gig."

"On a Sunday?"

"Normal business hours go out the window in the entertainment industry. Anyway, they want me to come in tomorrow for an interview. If it goes well, then I'll start on Tuesday."

That fast? she thought. For some reason, she found the thought vaguely disappointing, although she knew she should be happy for him… and probably glad that they'd have a chance to allow some time to pass before they saw one another again. If he got the job, that meant there wouldn't be a repeat of last Wednesday's digging around in the garage. Not that they really had anything to dig at the moment, unless Madeline decided to show up and be a little more helpful in providing actionable information than she had on the first go-'round.

"Oh, that's great news," Rosemary said, hoping she sounded appropriately enthusiastic.

"Well, I have to get past the interview, but a lot of the time, it's just a formality when you've already worked for a particular production company. But since I might be back to work soon, I was hoping we could get together tomorrow night. I want to make this up to you."

He sounded hopeful…but also cautious, as if he fully expected to get shot down. And maybe she should say no. That would be the adult thing to do, wouldn't it? But he so obviously wanted to start over, and at the moment, she wasn't having any feelings of foreboding, nothing warning her that this was a bad idea.

"Sure," she told him.

"Great," he said, sounding relieved. "Do you want me to come over there, or…?"

It would make more sense to meet here at the house, and yet something about that arrangement didn't feel quite right. Madeline Nash was proving elusive enough that Rosemary thought it a good idea not to upset the vibrations here at Michael and Audrey's house. With the unresolved tension between her and Caleb right now, meeting in Pasadena probably wasn't a very good idea.

However, there wasn't any reason why he couldn't meet her at her own house in Glendora. If they met there, she wouldn't have to drive all the way back to Pasadena, and it wouldn't matter as much if she got stuck late at the store for some reason. Also, by the time Caleb came by, the construction workers at the house next door would have called it quits for the day and it should be fairly quiet in her neighborhood.

She wouldn't quite admit to herself that having him come there would be an extra olive branch, a way to show that she'd forgiven him and trusted him enough to let him know where she lived when she wasn't housesitting for Audrey and Michael.

"Actually, why don't you meet me at my place in Glendora?" she asked. "There's nothing wrong with the house except that there's a construction zone next door. But that won't matter by the time you get there…is around seven okay?"

"Sounds great," he said. "I'd like to see your place."

Perfect. She gave him the address, and then wished him good luck on his interview before ending the call. As she set her phone down on the nightstand, she realized she really hadn't given herself any time to contact Madeline the next day. Seeing Caleb was probably more important, but….

Suddenly resolute, she left the bedroom and went back downstairs, flicking on lights as she went. This house might be perfectly safe, but that didn't mean she was going to try summoning a spirit in utter darkness…or at least, as dark as this house ever got. Michael had nightlights everywhere. Just being careful, or were they part of his defense system against the demonic hordes?

She banished that thought as soon as it popped into her head. The last thing she needed to do was imagine an army of demons lurking out in the darkness somewhere, just waiting for an opportunity to pounce.

There was a white pillar candle sitting on a marble dish on top of one of the bookcases in the library. She got out the long-tipped lighter that was kept in one of the desk drawers and used it to light the candle, somewhat reassured by the warm, gentle illumination it provided in the space. Moving carefully so she wouldn't snuff it out, she brought it with her into the family room, then set it down on the coffee table. Why she'd chosen that particular space for this summoning, she wasn't sure, except it was in here that Madeline had first appeared to her, so she figured she might as well stick with someplace which possibly felt familiar to her spirit.

Although she'd never sat down to summon a ghost before, Rosemary realized she should also burn some incense, a practice that accompanied most rituals. Luckily, she had brought an incense burner and some of her favorite white sage incense with her when she came to stay in Michael's house. The incense and its burner sat on a side table, so she went and got some of that going and let it fill the space with its clean and yet somehow warm scent.

She sat on the couch and closed her eyes for a moment, still seeing the glow of the candle's flame from behind her eyelids. Breathe in, breathe out. Leave the day behind, all its highs and lows and the moments in between. Peace and calm, an openness to the universe, a willingness to reach out to someone who no longer walked on this earth in a corporeal form.

"Madeline," she breathed, the syllables falling in a hush on the absolute stillness of the house.

No response, but Rosemary hadn't been expecting to get one right away. She allowed herself to sit calmly and breathe in and out, letting the gentle perfume of the incense surround her, just as she felt surrounded by the light of the white candle on its base of dark green marble.

"Madeline," she said again, more clearly this time, remembering the words of an invocation spell she'd read years before…never thinking she might actually have to use it. "I, Rosemary, call to you. Come again to this place…leave behind death's embrace."

The candle's flame wavered, but she couldn't see any change in the room, couldn't sense that any presence but hers was here. Probably a draft had caused the flame to flicker, and nothing more.

"You sent us to the house, Madeline," Rosemary went on. "There was nothing to find. I need your help…*we* need your help. Tell me what we need to do."

There, at the very edge of her vision. Cold creeping down her spine, she made herself shift slightly on the couch and look over at the doorway that opened on the foyer.

The woman was barely more than a faint pale outline against the darkness, her long, near-black hair blending with the gloom of the entry, since that was the one place where Rosemary hadn't bothered to turn on any lights. Her clothing was dark as well, a plain, long-sleeved sheath that Rosemary realized was probably the dress she'd been buried in.

It was so hard to remain sitting there calmly, to not get up from the couch and flee upstairs and shut the door behind her. Somehow, though, she made herself stay where she was, even as the ghostly figure moved from where it stood in the doorway to come farther into the room.

Now closer, Madeline seemed to be a little more solid. Maybe that was an optical illusion, or maybe the glow from the candle had given her the energy she needed to become more corporeal. No one would have ever mistaken her for a living, breathing woman, but now Rosemary could see more clearly the gracefully sculpted bones of her face, the wide dark eyes, the full mouth that once probably hadn't been nearly so pale.

That mouth moved, and the faintest of whispers emerged from her lips. "Go to the house."

Fingers clenching in frustration on the knees of her skirt, Rosemary said, "We went to the house. There wasn't anything there."

Her words didn't seem to have the desired effect. Rather than respond directly, Madeline said, "It's in the house. You have to go to the house."

"Madeline—"

And then she was gone, dissolving into the air

as if she'd never been there at all. Rosemary got to her feet and looked around wildly, as though she somehow thought the ghost had merely slipped off into another room. But no—she truly had disappeared.

For a long moment, Rosemary stood there next to the couch, not moving, hoping that if she just remained where she was, then maybe the spirit would return. But as the clock in the next room ticked away, sounding off the seconds while they passed, she realized she could stand here for the rest of the night and not get any satisfaction. Madeline wasn't coming back…at least, not any time soon.

"Damn it," Rosemary said, and bent to blow out the candle.

Chapter 12

ALTHOUGH SHE'D HAD NO REASON TO BELIEVE Caleb wouldn't come to see her at the appointed time, Rosemary hadn't realized how anxious she was about their upcoming meeting until she turned the corner on her street and saw his dingy black truck parked outside the small cottage-style house that was her real home.

Then again, maybe she'd been anxious because she was worried he actually *would* be there.

Stop it, she told herself. *Just...relax. Go with the flow and see what happens.*

Easier said than done.

Resisting the impulse to glance in the rearview mirror and make sure her hair and her lip gloss were still intact from the last time she'd checked—which had been right before she locked up the store and headed out to her car—she turned into the driveway and parked. No point in pulling into the garage if she wasn't going to be staying here tonight, after all.

As she got out of the Fiat and came toward Caleb's truck, the driver's-side door opened and he emerged. The smile he sent her was so hesitant, she figured it was probably better if she spoke first.

"Have any trouble finding the place?" she asked, figuring that was a neutral enough opener.

"No," he replied, looking relieved that she'd been so casual with her greeting. "I just let my phone nav me in." He went on, "I have an interview tomorrow."

"For the Netflix job?"

"Yes."

"That's great news!" she exclaimed, experiencing a surge of relief, which she knew should tell her something. At least now his days would be just as busy as hers, and he'd be distracted by other things. "We should celebrate," she added quickly. Was that a bad idea? No, celebrations could be neutral enough. They didn't have to be romantically charged, after all. "There's a nice wine bar here in downtown, or I know a fun Mediterranean place down on Route 66 that's basically one big patio."

"The Mediterranean restaurant sounds good," Caleb said. "We might as well enjoy this weather while we can."

Secretly, she'd been hoping he would want to go to Eden Garden, too, so that made things easier. It was a fun spot, but definitely not intimate or particularly romantic. However, she figured she should give him one minor warning. "It's Monday, so there won't be any belly dancers."

"'Belly dancers'?" he repeated, looking startled.

"The restaurant has belly dancing on Friday and Saturday nights. But you can get a hookah any night of the week."

Now Caleb appeared more amused than anything else, his former hesitancy gone. "You've smoked a hookah?"

"A few times. It tastes good, actually."

"I'll take your word for it."

Rosemary grinned but didn't press the issue. And actually, the couple of times she'd shared a hookah at the restaurant, she'd only done so after downing a few too many glasses of wine. Thank God for Uber.

Not that she planned to drink to excess tonight. One glass would be safe. Anything else… not so much.

"Do you want to come inside first?" she asked then, realizing that they were still standing somewhat awkwardly on the sidewalk in front of the house.

"Sure. You can give me the nickel tour."

"That's about all it'll be—the house isn't very big."

In response, he only shook his head, as if he wasn't quite buying her deprecating tone. Well, he'd see for himself soon enough. She loved the place, but she knew it could never compete with Michael and Audrey's three-thousand-square-foot Craftsman showplace.

At least she'd come by earlier to check on the house, and had done a little dusting and wiping down of counters when she was there. Everything looked presentable enough, although she thought the place seemed awfully bare with all her house-plants residing in Pasadena for the duration. Still, Caleb had never seen the house before, so he didn't have any basis for comparison.

"I like the purple couch," he remarked as they came inside.

"Thanks," she said. Should she take that as a good sign, that they meshed better than she wanted to admit right now? Even her mother, who tended to be pretty relaxed about that sort of thing, had worried that Rosemary might get tired of the sofa after a while, but she'd had it for almost two years now and still smiled every time she saw it. "Obviously, this is the living room. Dining room over there"—she pointed toward the cramped space off to one side, which was barely large enough for a small round table and four chairs—"and there's the kitchen. Down here is the guest bath, in case you need it, and my office. And the room at the end of the hall is the master bedroom."

He nodded. "It's nice. Homey."

"Thanks," she said. She'd always thought so, thought the house walked the line between being cozy and a little too boho, but it was nice to hear he felt the same way. "And here," she went on, then stepped over to the French doors that opened on the backyard, "is the back patio and the yard. I don't quite have your view, unfortunately."

No, she didn't. But she'd had the yard professionally landscaped, and since the house was oriented north and south, she had the San Gabriel Mountains framed nicely between the slender silver-dollar eucalyptus trees that had been planted along the back wall.

"I like it," he said. "Do you entertain much?"

"Sometimes I'll have my sisters over—they live close enough that they can walk. The place really isn't big enough for too many more people than that."

What she really didn't feel like telling him was that she actually didn't have any close friends outside her family. Lots of acquaintances, people she'd met while working at the store, or fellow psychics who worked the various shows and fairs and expos. But someone she could confide in, someone she'd allow to see the worst of her, knowing that they'd still be her friend? Not really. She'd thought she and Audrey might get to that point one day, although their friendship had been interrupted by Audrey's necessary relocation to Tucson for the duration of her doctoral program.

Anyway, confessing any of that to Caleb didn't feel right. If their relationship managed to progress from where it currently resided, then she'd let him find out how narrow her circle of friends really was, how she tended to feel like an outsider when she wasn't around her immediate family. The last thing she wanted was for him to feel sorry for her, or, even worse, worry about possibly being with someone who might come to depend on him too much because she didn't have anyone else in her life.

Luckily, he seemed to accept her explanation —no one could argue that her house and its accompanying yard weren't very large—and after that, they went back outside and got into his truck, with her giving him directions to the restaurant. Since it was still relatively early, the place wasn't all that crowded, and they were given a prime table at the far end of the patio, near a water feature that splashed gently in the background.

"It's different," Caleb said as he glanced around, apparently taking in the expansive trellis overhead, woven with faux greenery, the concrete walls that had been formed to look like rough-hewn rock. Lively Middle Eastern dance music played in the background, although not so loudly that it threatened to overpower their conversation. "It's not the kind of place I'd expect to find in Glendora." His gaze warmed as he went on, "But then, you're not the kind of girl I'd expect to find in Glendora, either."

"Oh?" she said, figuring she should take the remark as a compliment, even as she wondered whether they should really be back at the compliment stage after what had happened between them the day before. Still, she thought she'd play along for the time being. "What kind of girl *would* you expect to find here?"

His shoulders lifted, and he picked up his menu. "I don't know...someone a little more prosaic."

"I'm not prosaic?"

He chuckled. "Hardly."

"Good."

A waiter came by and asked if they wanted drinks, and Caleb ordered a bottle of Shiraz. Rosemary felt her eyebrows lift slightly, then decided if she protested, she'd only prove to him that she was still uncomfortable with the situation. As long as she only had the one glass of wine that she'd promised herself, she'd be fine.

"I thought you had an interview tomorrow," she said as the waiter departed, promising he would be back in a few minutes with their wine.

"I do," Caleb replied, looking unperturbed. "But it's not until the afternoon. That'll give me plenty of time to recover. Anyway, half a bottle of wine isn't quite enough to put me over the edge."

She supposed she should be reassured by that. Anyway, she wasn't his mother; he could do what he liked. Also, they could have the waiter cork the unused portion of the bottle, and Caleb could take it home for later.

They were silent then, both of them perusing their menus. Once he'd set his aside, though, he looked across the table at Rosemary and said, "I went through the box of DVDs."

"What?" she said, taken off guard. She put down her menu as well, figuring she'd go with chicken shawarma since she hadn't had it for a while.

"The box of DVDs we got from the garage at Colin's rental house." Caleb looked as if he wanted to say more, but the waiter returned right then with the bottle, and they both had to wait until he'd opened it, poured some wine for both of them, and then took their orders. Eventually, though, they were left alone again.

Because the conversation had already been

derailed somewhat, Rosemary lifted her glass. "To the new job."

"Job interview," Caleb corrected her with a slight curl at the corner of his mouth, but he went ahead and clinked his wine glass against hers anyway.

"So, the DVDs…."

"Right," he said. "The box was still sitting in the back of my truck, so I pulled it out and brought it inside. Then I started thinking, what if Colin hid the footage in plain sight? He could have burned a couple of DVDs that contained everything he'd shot, then put them in the cases from an entirely different show."

That made some sense, but…. "I thought they were all shrink-wrapped," Rosemary pointed out.

"They were, but someone like Colin would have known where to get them rewrapped."

"And?"

Caleb expelled a disgusted-sounding breath and drank some of his wine. "Nothing. I opened up all twenty-four of those DVDs and put them in my Blu-ray player one by one, and they were all the same old haunted cemetery special. So much for my Hardy Boys impersonation."

"It was a good idea, though," Rosemary said. Yes, it was disappointing to learn those DVDs weren't anything more than what they'd appeared to be, but at least he'd tried. Was that what he'd been doing while she was having dinner at her mother's house? It was probably a better use of his time than sitting there alone and trying to figure out what he'd done to turn her off so quickly. Pushing that somewhat gloomy thought aside, she added, "I suppose I should have thought of something like that, too. Sounds like we've both been striking out, though—I tried to summon Madeline last night, but that turned out to be a bust as well."

Caleb frowned. "She didn't show up?"

"No, she appeared, but she only told me the same thing. I have no idea why she wants me to go to the house when we've already figured out it was a dead end."

"Maybe Colin really did bury the footage in the backyard."

"I don't think so." Rosemary recalled how pristine the yard of the Los Feliz house had been, with barely a fallen leaf out of place. There hadn't been any obvious signs of digging—and honestly, not that much space to dig in the first place, since so much of the property's real estate was taken up by the large swimming pool directly behind the house. "No, I think there's something else going on here."

Caleb held up his wine glass and swirled the liquid inside in a contemplative way. The setting sun slanted through the Shiraz, awakening sparks of garnet and ruby. "Maybe there is, but it sure isn't very obvious."

"I can try summoning Madeline again," Rosemary began, but he only shook his head.

"What's the point? It's kind of obvious that she isn't going to tell you anything valuable."

Or maybe the information the dead woman was trying to impart seemed to make sense to her and something was getting lost in translation. Even though Rosemary wasn't a medium and didn't pretend to be, she knew that messages from the dead often seemed incomprehensible because their frame of reference was so different.

And Caleb was right. If she kept summoning Madeline, she might end up irritating the spirit rather than accomplishing anything worthwhile, so it was probably better to leave things alone for now.

That was sort of a depressing thought, though, and Rosemary was glad the waiter reappeared a moment later with their food. She and Caleb seemed to tacitly agree to leave the topic of Madeline Nash's cryptic communications aside for the moment, and instead talked about safe topics—the food and the restaurant, his upcoming interview, the massive community trick-or-treat that took place the day before Halloween on Glendora's main street. Even though it was chaos, Rosemary always loved the event because she got a kick out of seeing all the kids in their costumes. This year, her nephew Tyler would be going out on his very first trick-or-treat, and she couldn't wait to see how Celeste and Kevin were going to dress him up. The exact costume was a closely guarded secret, but because her sister was a pretty talented seamstress, Rosemary could only imagine they'd come up with something extremely clever and fun.

Once they were done with dinner, Caleb drove her home. After he'd walked her to the front door, she hesitated, wondering what she should do next. If she invited him inside, would that be an open invitation to more intimacies? The one glass of wine she'd had with dinner had helped to relax her, but she knew she wasn't *that* relaxed. For whatever reason, she still wasn't ready to range into that territory yet. He seemed to understand, because his next words were innocent enough.

"I'll call you as soon as I know about the job," he said.

"You'll get it," she told him, her voice firm, even as she let out an inner thank-you to the universe that he'd apparently picked up on her vibe.

"A psychic flash?" he asked, although he didn't sound as if he was teasing her.

"A feeling."

"Well, I trust your feelings." He reached over

and gave her fingers a very gentle squeeze but then let go quickly. "Have a good night, Rosemary."

She stood on the doorstep and watched him stride down the front walk to his truck. It wasn't until he'd pulled away from the curb that she allowed herself to finally let out the sigh she'd been holding in. Should she have given him a signal, let him know that it was okay for him to kiss her good night, if only on the cheek?

Problem was, she didn't know if it would have been okay. She still felt jangly and strange, despite the glass of wine she'd had with dinner. Maybe that strangeness stemmed from standing here on the front porch and wondering whether she should even go inside or not. Yes, she'd thought she'd come back to the house and test the lights, make sure everything was still working okay, since she hadn't been here after dark since she moved into Michael and Audrey's place. Now, though, she couldn't decide what to do.

Well, standing on the doorstep like an idiot isn't helping, she scolded herself. *Either go inside, or get in your car and go back to Pasadena.*

All right, she'd go inside. It would be stupid to waste the opportunity, especially since she had no plans to hang around this late in Glendora any time in the near future.

A quick fumble for her keys, and then she was standing in the entry. By instinct, her hand went to the switch next to the door, and she turned it on, illuminating the torchiere lamp that stood in the corner past the couch.

After that, she went into the kitchen and checked the overhead fixture there, then headed down the hall toward the backyard and looked outside. The outdoor lights were all solar-powered, and seemed to be functioning just fine. Just as she'd thought, everything seemed okay here, and she realized she'd been worried for no reason.

Since she figured she could use a little extra time to let the wine from dinner wear off before she got on the road, she went to her purse and got out her phone. It wouldn't hurt to check and make sure she hadn't missed any messages while she was out with Caleb, since she'd put the phone on vibrate to keep it from interrupting their dinner.

There was one missed call—from Audrey's number—and a new voicemail. Wondering what that was about, Rosemary went and sat down on her couch, feeling obscurely comforted by the warm, nappy sensation of the purple velvet against her bare legs. Maybe it was just her being silly, but she'd missed that couch, no matter how comfortable the furniture at the Pasadena house might be.

To her surprise, when she retrieved the new voicemail, she heard Michael's voice rather than Audrey's. Maybe he'd called on Audrey's phone in the hope that she'd pick up when she saw a number she recognized. Well, the call had only come in a couple of hours ago, so at least it wasn't as if she'd ignored it all night.

"Hi, Rosemary," he said. "I'm still working on Madeline Nash's background—or at least, my source is. She was an actress, which I'm guessing is probably how she met Colin. She was originally from San Jose—went to college up there, then moved down to L.A. after she graduated. However, I'm still having a hard time pinning down where she lived during the two and a half years before she died. I'm assuming it was with Colin, but he also has a blank spot in his rental history around then. Anyway, we'll keep plugging away at it. Something's bound to turn up. Mostly, I just wanted to let you know where things stand right now—and also to be careful, and make sure to call Will if anything strange comes up."

Well, she'd already done that. Actually, Michael's admonition made her feel a bit better about the situation, if only because his words seemed to indicate that Will hadn't told him anything about their meeting. Obviously, he considered their conversation confidential, and she felt her respect for him increase.

Oh, it's respect now? she jeered at herself.

It was something. She just hadn't figured out what. If only things hadn't gone sideways between her and Caleb. Yes, they'd started to patch up their relationship, but she still didn't have a very good idea of where they stood.

But she could figure out all that later. Now she needed to get out of here and head back to Pasadena. She got up from the couch and slipped her phone into her purse, then realized she had to go back to her bedroom and shut off the light there before she could leave. She turned toward the hallway, figuring she'd pause just outside her room and reach inside to hit the light switch. However, she'd only taken a step before she halted abruptly, her purse slipping from her suddenly icy fingers and falling to the floor with a heavy *thunk*.

Someone was standing in the hallway, blocking the door to her bedroom.

Not just anyone, though. The hall wasn't directly lit, but there was enough illumination emanating from the open door of her room to outline the intruder's face, to highlight his features even as a jolt of terror shocked its way through her body.

The man in the hall was Colin Turner.

A ghostly pale Colin, though, with two cavernous black pits where his eyes used to be. Was that what the demons had done to him? Gouged out his eyes? Audrey would never say exactly how he'd died.

Rosemary's veins might as well have been

filled with ice. Somehow, though, she managed to hold her ground and say, "Colin? It's Rosemary. Do you need me to help you?"

No reply, only his sightless figure staring at her as if he could still somehow see where she stood despite the grotesque black wells that were all that was left of his eyes. His mouth opened, and she tensed. Was he going to tell her where his footage was hidden? Had he come here because he was frustrated with Madeline's inability to explain why Rosemary and Caleb needed to go to his house?

No words escaped those pale, parted lips, however. Instead, a strange pale green mist began to drift from his mouth, moving toward her, coalescing into the form of some hideous creature, with glaring red eyes and bony hands that began to form into claws....

She left out a terrified little shriek, then bent and grabbed her purse where it rested near her feet before backing toward the front door. The thing emanating from Colin's mouth snarled, clawed fingers reaching toward her, but somehow she managed to wrench open the door and slam it behind her, not bothering to lock it, thinking only of her car a few yards away in the driveway.

Once she was outside, she bolted for the little green Fiat, scrabbling inside her purse for the key fob, pressing down on it. While she was still a few feet away, she heard the reassuring *clunk* of the door unlocking and threw herself forward with a sob. Her fingers closed on the handle and she yanked it open, then fell into the seat and pressed the lock with her left hand while her right touched the starter button.

A pale greenish mist was beginning to ooze its way around the front door, as if that was the only way the creature or entity or whatever it was could get past a physical barrier. She sure as hell wasn't going to wait to see what it might do next, though. No, she mashed her foot on the accelerator and felt the car jump backward, and she reversed out of the driveway at a speed the Fiat's engineers had probably never intended. Once out on the street, she quickly shifted into drive and peeled out of there, leaving a few whiffs of smoke and the acrid scent of burned tires behind her. She risked a glance in her rearview mirror as she left, but the green mist didn't appear to be following her.

Still, she wasn't going to slow down until she got back to Pasadena and was safely barricaded behind the doors of Michael's demon-proof house. And then…and then she'd try to figure out what the hell she should do next.

First, though, she needed to call Will.

Chapter 13

ALL SAINTS WAS A LARGE GOTHIC-STYLE church on the outskirts of Pasadena's downtown. Even though Rosemary had never been there before, she knew exactly where it was located—mostly because its grounds backed up to an open plaza it shared with a California Pizza Kitchen, of all places. By some miracle, she was able to find a parking space right out in front, thus saving her from having to park in the price-gouging public garage under the restaurant.

The night before, she'd had to convince Will that she was all right, that he didn't need to come charging over to the house to check on her. Okay, he hadn't exactly used the word "charging," but she could tell he was very worried about her. However, as soon as she stepped into the Pasadena house, she'd known she was safe. Whatever that...

thing…was back in Glendora, it couldn't follow her there. And she'd been feeling rattled enough that having Will over hadn't felt like a very good idea. She managed to talk him down, but only by promising to come see him the next morning.

She fed a dollars' worth of quarters into the meter, then paused on the sidewalk for a moment, trying to get her bearings. Although she'd managed to get some sleep, she still felt exhausted and yet on edge, starting at every stray sound, every odd movement caught in her peripheral vision, despite her reassurances to herself that nothing could pass Michael's wards.

And as much as she hated to bail on the store, she knew she was feeling way too rattled to go into work that day. Luckily, Isabel said she would cover for her, and didn't even ask what important business had come up to prevent her younger sister from being at work the way she was supposed to. Maybe she felt a bit guilty about not being more supportive at dinner on Sunday night, but whatever the reason, Rosemary was just glad she didn't have to come up with any explanations for her unexpected absence.

Right then, she honestly wasn't sure what she could have said.

She hadn't called Caleb, either. The last thing she'd wanted to do was upset him right before his job interview. They'd talk after he was done with the interview and knew he'd gotten the job. Since she'd taken what precautions she could—she'd turned on the alarm system, smudged every damn room in the house, and left white candles burning everywhere as well—she didn't see the point in upsetting Caleb when there really wasn't anything he could do. No specters had appeared, and no monsters had crawled out from under the bed or from inside the closet. As Michael had said, his house was safe.

Obviously, her own place was an entirely different matter.

A pause as Rosemary stared up at the façade of the church, at the square tower and the intricate stained-glass window that faced out on Euclid Avenue where she stood. She hadn't been raised to find any particular comfort in a church, and yet something about the elegance and strength of the building reassured her, as if something was telling her that she'd done the right thing by coming here.

She hoped so. Deep down, she couldn't help wondering if this was a huge mistake, considering the way Will Gordon had been haunting her thoughts ever since she first met him. Problem was, she didn't know what else to do. Her psychic abilities couldn't exactly protect her from specters or demons or whatever the hell that thing had been inside her house. With Michael and Audrey nearly five hundred miles away, the only recourse Rosemary had was to reach out to the one person in the area who possessed the expertise she needed.

A deep breath, and she smoothed the folds of her flowing embroidered skirt, a half-nervous, nearly unconscious gesture. Today was a little cooler than the weather had been for days, so she'd put on a short-sleeved wrap top rather than the tanks she'd been wearing lately. Hopefully, that would be appropriate enough attire for a church.

Or at least, church grounds. There was no need for her to go into the chapel; Will had told her to come around the side, to the wing of the building where the actual offices were located. Feeling more hesitant with every step, she made her way to the back of the large structure, following the signs that directed her to the rectory. When she entered the building, she was a little surprised to see how institutional it looked, with very little of the Gothic style shown in the chapel itself.

She walked slowly down the hall, reading the signs placed next to each door. When she got to the end of the hall, she heard her name.

"Rosemary?"

Will stood in the last doorway on the left. Just like the last time she'd seen him, he was wearing a dark shirt and pants, no priestly collar in evidence.

Her heart made an odd little skip at the sight of him. "Hi, Will," she replied, glad that she sounded relatively normal. Too bad there really wasn't anything normal about the situation…or, apparently, the way she reacted to his presence.

He didn't appear to notice anything wrong, thank God. "Please, come in."

She entered his office, which was a pleasant jumble of bookcases and tropical plants. Bright light streamed in through the open windows, offering a sunny view of the public courtyard area outside. The setting helped put her a little more at ease; it was hard to imagine getting attacked by anything supernatural in such a warm, friendly place.

"Let me get those out of the way for you," he went on, his tone a little apologetic, as he bent down to pick up a stack of books from where they'd been resting on the room's only visitor's chair.

"Thanks." She sat down and watched him put the books on top of one of the bookcases—there clearly wasn't any room on the shelves themselves.

Instead of taking a seat behind his desk, which was also littered with books and an alarming number of file folders, he perched on one corner, hands resting on the dark oak surface as he regarded her. "I'm glad you're all right. I was worried about you."

"Oh, I'm fine," she replied, even as her voice gave the lie to her words. Damn it, she really hadn't planned to sound quite that shaky. The whole morning, she'd held herself together as well as she could, but there was something about the sympathetic light in William Gordon's clear gray eyes that made her fragile self-control feel as if it was about to fall apart like a house of cards.

"You're sure?"

She nodded. "Yes, the house was quiet. Nothing happened—just as I knew it wouldn't." That was also a lie. She'd *hoped* everything would be okay, but she hadn't known. Not completely.

His expression was very serious. "I still wish you'd let me come over to check on things."

About all she could do was manage a lift of her shoulders. "Once I was back at Michael's house, I figured I was as safe as I would be anywhere."

Will didn't respond right away, although his brows were drawn together, as if he was quietly considering what she'd just told him. In silence, he went over to the shelf behind him and lifted the basket that sat on top. "Tea?" he asked.

Now Rosemary saw that the basket held a variety of small packets, presumably of different flavors of tea. "Sure," she said, figuring maybe it would help to steady her nerves. "Do you have any green tea?"

"Absolutely."

He busied himself for a moment, fetching a couple of mugs from the shelf below the one where he'd gotten the tea, then pausing to lift an electric kettle from where it sat on top of an old gray metal file cabinet. Obviously, he'd been expecting to offer her some refreshment, and so had gotten the kettle going some time before the hour when she was supposed to arrive.

Once he'd handed her a heavy brown-glazed mug with her green tea steeping inside—and had gotten his own drink as well—he settled back against the desk. "Tell me again what happened."

It was too soon to drink her tea. Too bad, because her throat felt suddenly dry. She really didn't want to relive those terrifying moments all over again. But she could understand why he wanted to hear her story once more, if only to get it from her when she wasn't on the phone and stammering as she tried to relate what she'd seen at the Glendora house.

His eyes were fixed on her, filled with sympathy. "It's okay," he said, his tone gentle. "This is a safe place. Nothing can harm you here."

Rosemary had already gotten that feeling from the rectory, but it was nice to have her impressions corroborated, especially since she'd had the awful thought as she drove over here that maybe the entity in her house couldn't follow her to Michael's, but it just might be able to get her if she was someplace that wasn't warded. She wrapped her hands around her mug and inhaled the fragrant steam, hoping that doing so would give her some courage even though the tea itself was still far too hot to drink. Another breath, another reminder that she'd survived last night's encounter, terrifying as it had been, and so she didn't need to fear talking about it now.

As calmly as she could, she explained how she'd gone out for dinner, and that after her date had said good night and gone home, she listened to her messages, and decided to check the house one last time before she headed back to Pasadena. Then she went on to explain to Will how she'd seen what at first she thought was Colin Turner's ghost, but had realized soon enough it was no benign entity like Madeline Nash's spirit had been. Maybe the terrifying apparition was the dark energy her sister Isabel had sensed. That seemed to make sense, because whatever the thing truly was, she knew it had to be evil.

"And that's when I ran," Rosemary said simply. "Just bolted and got the hell out of there. Um…heck, I mean. Sorry."

One corner of Will's mouth lifted in what

looked like a hastily smothered smile. "It's okay if you swear, Rosemary. We're not in church."

No, but close enough to one that she figured she'd better be on her best behavior.

He went on, "Did you get any sense of evil from the entity you saw, or was it only that you were so startled, you figured it was better to get out of there and try to figure out what was going on once you were safely away?"

She frowned at that question. What *had* she felt from the entity? Well, besides being scared shitless at the very sight of the thing.

"I felt cold," she said at last. "Maybe that was just my own fear talking to me, but I remember feeling as if all the blood in my veins had turned to ice."

That response made Will nod, as though in comprehension. However, he didn't speak right away, but instead lifted his mug of tea to his lips and took a slow, deliberate sip.

Which meant her own tea was probably safe to drink as well. Rosemary brought the heavy mug to her mouth and allowed herself a small swallow. It was still fairly hot, but not at a tongue-burning level of heat. Besides, its warmth felt good going down, reassuring her that at least everything here in this cluttered office seemed relatively normal.

"That's often how people react to the presence

of demons," he said after a moment. "A sensation of overwhelming cold."

"I thought Hell was supposed to be hot," she quipped, and he tilted his head at her as though he'd taken her comment seriously rather than viewing it as the half-joke she'd intended it to be.

"Do you believe in Hell?" he asked.

"Well...." She let the word trail off, then glanced down at the mug she held, not quite sure she wanted to meet his eyes. "A few months ago, I would have said no. I'm not exactly what you'd call a Christian."

Will didn't seem particularly perturbed by this revelation. "What changed your mind?"

Another sip of tea, and then she leaned over and set her mug down on a stone coaster that apparently had been put on the bookshelf near her chair for that very purpose. "Seeing what Audrey and Michael went through. I mean, if demons exist, then I guess the place they're supposed to come from has to exist, too, right?"

"Right." Unlike her, Will didn't seem inclined to abandon his tea, but took another swallow. "Demons are very real, unfortunately. Most people can allow themselves to doubt their existence because their paths will never cross, but once you've had an encounter with demons—even one by proxy like you have, thanks to being friends with Michael Covenant and Audrey

Barrett—then it's a lot more difficult to fly below the radar, so to speak."

Great, so her very friendship with Michael and Audrey had made her more vulnerable to demonic intervention. Rosemary didn't like that idea, no, not one bit. However, rather than allow herself to start freaking out about an existence where demons would interfere with her life at every turn, she thought it better to focus on the problem at hand. "So...that was a demon in my house last night?"

"Very likely. A regular ghost or spirit wouldn't have behaved in such a way. You never saw Madeline Nash's ghost do something like that, did you?"

A shiver went through Rosemary at the very thought. "No, she always seemed pretty benign, although it's still unnerving to have a ghost popping in and out of your immediate vicinity, benign or not." Rosemary paused for a moment and looked up at Will. His expression was thoughtful, but patient as well, as if he was content to stand there leaning against his desk for as long as it took to tease out the important threads of her story. She hadn't mentioned the missing video during their first conversation, but she figured there was no point in trying to avoid the topic any longer. "Did Michael tell you about the footage?"

A nod, and then Will drained the rest of the tea in his mug and set it down in one of the few clear spaces on his desktop. "He did. I can see why you'd be trying to track it down. It's immensely valuable."

Which was pretty much what Caleb had said, even if he hadn't used those exact words. She refrained from mentioning that, though, mostly because she preferred to keep him out of this if at all possible. All right, he was the one who'd roped her into looking for the lost footage in the first place, but despite that, she didn't want him getting tangled up with demons and ghosts and God knows what else. No, he was going to get that new job and, with any luck, be safely away from anything that might put him in danger.

Because if what Will had just said was correct, then she'd been in trouble long before Caleb came on the scene. She'd already been pinging the demons' radar…and it didn't seem as if there was much she could do about that unfortunate fact.

"I suppose it is worth a lot," she conceded, not wanting to commit to anything more than that. "But I haven't been able to come up with any leads, so it looks like the footage is going to stay missing."

Will spread his hands, as if to indicate he wasn't going to say one way or another what his own opinion on the matter might be. "We can leave that aside for now, I suppose. Right now, I want to go take a look at your house."

Although she'd been fearing he would make such a request, she couldn't quite keep herself from shooting him an alarmed look. "Do we have to?"

To her surprise, he smiled. "If you ever want to live there again, then yes. I assume that Michael and Audrey will want their own house back at some point."

"True." Rosemary played with the amethyst ring she wore on her right hand, twisting it around nervously. Not looking up, she added in a low voice, "I'm scared to go back there."

"Which is completely understandable." Will straightened then and gazed down at her, again with a slight smile touching his lips. "But it's broad daylight right now, and I'll be there with you. The circumstances are very different."

She supposed she could protest that some pretty scary shit had gone down at the Whitcomb mansion in the middle of the day—and at Audrey's house, for that matter. But Will was right; she'd have to go home sooner or later, and better to check it out now while she had some expert assistance.

"Okay," she said, then got up from her chair and brushed at her skirt. "Do you want to follow me? I'm parked out front on the street—the light green Fiat."

"That should be easy enough to follow," he responded. "But give me your address, too, just in case."

He went around the back of his desk and got a Post-it note and a pen out of the middle drawer. Rosemary told him her address, along with the nearest cross street.

"I'll pull in the driveway, and you can pull in behind me," she added. "It's about fifteen minutes from here."

"Got it," he said, and tucked the little yellow slip of paper in his breast pocket. "I'll come around on Euclid and meet you there. I'll be driving a black Dodge Challenger."

She nodded. So that's what that impressive-looking muscle car was. Again, she wondered what he was doing driving a vehicle like that, but she supposed it probably didn't matter one way or another.

There wasn't much to do after that except go back outside and wait while he locked the door to his office, then wave as she headed out to Euclid Avenue and he went in the opposite direction, presumably to wherever the staff at All Saints had their designated parking spaces. When she got back out to the street, she saw that the time on her meter had already run out, but, luckily, no over-zealous meter maid had yet descended to give her a ticket.

After she started the engine, Rosemary sat there and idled while she waited for Will Gordon to appear so he could follow her back to Glendora. His sleek black muscle car came around the corner, and she could feel her eyes widen as it approached. Up close like this, it was even more impressive, the restrained thunder of its engine audible even through the rolled-up windows of her own car.

With a slight shake of the head, she turned on her signal and pulled out from her spot at the curb, heading north so she could pick up the frontage road that ran parallel to the 210 Freeway and eventually get on at the Lake Avenue on-ramp, since there wasn't any freeway access closer than that. The whole time, Will Gordon's car stayed right behind her, not too close, but close enough that even an aggressive driver would have had a hard time inserting himself between the two of them.

Then they were safely on the freeway, heading east. As the miles passed and they got closer and closer to the Grand Avenue off-ramp in Glendora, Rosemary could feel her fingers tensing on the Fiat's steering wheel, could feel a lump of dread begin to form in her stomach. She didn't want to go back to her house, didn't want to risk another encounter like the one she'd experienced the night before. Sure, she could sit here and tell herself that she would have Will with her and that everything would be just fine, but she didn't know that for sure, did she?'

Despite her roiling thoughts, despite the tension that knotted the muscles at the back of her neck, she dutifully exited the freeway at Grand, then headed north to the neighborhood that had been her home for the past five years. Everything looked serene and peaceful as she turned onto her street. Well, except for the usual hubbub at the construction site next door. You'd think the racket would be enough to drive off any marauding entities, but she wasn't sure she could count on the noise of hammers and power saws being sufficiently disruptive to work as an anti-demon deterrent.

She pulled into the driveway and Will turned in a minute later, then stopped a few feet behind her car. They both got out at the same time, with him giving a quick, surveying glance around as he transferred the black satchel he held to his other hand so he could lock the car door.

For a few seconds, she stared at the satchel, slightly puzzled. Then she guessed what it must contain.

Holy water.

Well, Michael apparently never left the house

without it, and she supposed Will must take the same precautions. He came over to stand next to her, and even though he wasn't wearing his clerical collar, Rosemary thought that anyone looking at him must know he was a member of the clergy, in his plain black shirt and black trousers, not exactly typical attire for a warm October day in Southern California.

If he had any idea how conspicuous he was, he didn't give much sign of it. Instead, he looked down at her, his expression encouraging and not at all afraid. "Let's go in, shall we?"

"Are you going to do anything first?"

One dark eyebrow lifted slightly. "What were you expecting me to do?"

"I don't know," she replied, flustered. "Sprinkle holy water all over the place or something."

Her comment made his mouth quirk, and there was no mistaking the amused light in his clear gray eyes. "I'll have it ready," he promised. "But things seem to be quiet for the moment, so I'd rather not attract any undue attention."

He had a point, so she only gave him a resigned nod and got her house keys out of her purse, then realized there was no need to unlock the front door—she'd slammed it as she fled but hadn't paused to lock it, so it was still open.

"Let me go first," Will said.

While her first instinct was to say of course he didn't need to do that, she realized this was exactly what he'd come here for. He was the expert, not her. "All right."

Hanging back a bit, she watched as he entered the dim interior—all the drapes had been closed when she fled the place—then touched the light switch next to the hall closet. The fixture in the microscopic entryway came on at once, illuminating the living room and some of the dining room.

Rosemary wasn't sure what she'd been expecting. Possibly to find the house trashed the way the demons had destroyed the interior of Audrey's home before they decided to get really serious and just burn the whole place down. But, as far as she could tell, her own house looked untouched.

Will advanced farther inside. She'd been so busy looking around that she hadn't been paying much attention to what he was doing, but she realized he must have retrieved one of the bottles of holy water from the satchel he carried, since he now held a vial of clear liquid in his right hand. "It seems okay so far," he said quietly. "Come inside."

Trying not to bite her lip, she stepped into the entryway, then closed the door behind her but didn't lock it in case she needed to make another precipitous departure. Moving with care, she walked over and stood next to him. Maybe she was being regressive and completely unliberated, but right then, it felt better to be close by Will, to allow his height and calming presence to reassure her. If she'd known him better—and if she was just a little less affected by his presence—she might have reached over and taken his hand. She had a feeling he probably wouldn't have stopped her, but she decided that would be utterly too weird.

"Do you sense anything?" he asked, still in the same undertone as when he'd spoken a moment earlier. "Anything at all?"

Although she really didn't want to reach out and use her extra senses to probe the atmosphere inside the house, she knew she had to. Will wasn't psychic, and so he didn't have any special abilities that would allow him to tell if something dark and malignant still lay in wait here. Yes, he'd said that he could sometimes feel when demons had lurked in a particular location, but she had no idea how infallible such a sense might be.

She breathed in and willed her mind to be as still as possible. Now was the time to let that strange inner sense which told her sometimes of things that were yet to come, or possibly might be happening at the very same moment, or occasionally spoke to her in dreams, do its thing. It wasn't perfect, of course— she hadn't noticed a damn thing until she'd actually seen the demon or whatever it was standing in her hallway—but on many occasions, she'd been able to tell if something terrible had happened in a place, or simply whether the tensions between the people who lived in a house had built up their own dark residue, laden with the anger and resentment that had grown over time to take on a life of their own.

Here, right now…she couldn't sense a damn thing.

Feeling her mouth twist, she looked up at Will and gave a small shake of her head. "I'm not getting anything."

"Nothing at all?"

"Nope."

He didn't appear too troubled by her reply. Instead, he went farther into the living room, then glanced over at the dining area and the kitchen. Good thing she'd tidied up the last time she was here, just in case Caleb might come inside. That hadn't happened, which was just as well. She had no idea how he would've reacted to the entity that had manifested in the hallway.

"The bedrooms are down that hall?" Will asked.

"Yes," she replied. "Well, I use the second bedroom as an office, but it's in the hallway that the entity appeared."

"Good," he said, although Rosemary didn't see

anything particularly good about the situation. However, she followed him as he moved down the hall, vial of holy water still held at the ready in his right hand.

A brief pause as he stopped and looked into her office, although a glance past his shoulder told her that everything seemed to be in order there, the desk looking somewhat blank and empty, since her laptop was still safely over at the Pasadena house.

But then he turned and continued to her bedroom and stepped inside, while she had no choice but to follow him. At least the bed was made and everything was tidy enough, but she still found it almost excruciatingly uncomfortable to have him standing in her bedroom.

His face was completely impassive, so she had no idea what might be going through his head right then. Probably a good thing. "Did you come in here that night?"

"Not really," she said, glad that at least her voice sounded steady, even if she couldn't do anything about the telltale rosiness of her cheeks. "I checked my phone messages, then realized I needed to come back in here and turn off the light. It was as I started to come toward to the bedroom that I saw him—it, I mean—standing in the hallway."

"Here?" he said, and took a step or two back so he stood a foot or so outside the door.

At least that got him out of the bedroom. "Maybe. I'll have to go back into the living room and look down here to tell for sure."

"Go ahead and do that, then."

She moved past Will, doing her best not to brush against him, although she felt a fold of her skirt touch his pant leg as she went. Maybe he'd felt it…maybe he hadn't…but he didn't react either way, for which she was grateful. She still wasn't quite sure how to act around him. All right, there wasn't any harm in thinking someone was attractive, but it felt wrong in some way, as though she was betraying Caleb.

And you've got way more important things to worry about right now, she scolded herself as she walked back to the living room so she could position herself in the same spot she'd occupied the night before when she saw the entity. *Figure all the rest of this stuff out when you're not getting attacked by demons breathing green mist, okay?*

Duly chastised, she stopped in more or less the same place where she'd been standing when she first saw that dark shape in the hallway. "I think I was standing somewhere around here. And I think you're just about where it was, too."

Will nodded and looked up at the ceiling above him, and down at the polished oak floor before glancing from side to side. What he thought he would see, she didn't know; the hallway looked the same as it ever had, with the soothing sage green paint on the walls and the neatly framed family photos that had always hung there.

But then he frowned and reached with his free hand to dig something out of his pocket. As she watched, she realized it was a keychain…a keychain with one of those mini Mag lights attached to it. Flicking the flashlight on, he shone it up toward the ceiling and directed the beam toward the flush-mount light fixture there.

"Do you see something?" she asked. A little chill shivered its way along her spine, but she made herself walk back toward him.

"I think so. Come here."

Hoping she didn't look too reluctant, she moved closer and paused less than a foot away from him. This close, he seemed taller than ever, and she felt herself swallow.

"Look up there," he said, then pointed up at the light. "See those markings around the lamp?"

As she squinted up at it, she realized there was a ring of strange symbols etched into the off-white paint that covered the ceiling. They looked as if they'd been scratched there with the point of a knife, and because they were white against white and she hardly ever turned on the hall light, she realized they could have been there for some time without her even noticing their presence.

"What are they?" she asked.

"Sigils of summoning," Will replied, looking grim. "Probably not so different from what Michael and Audrey found in the basement of the Whitcomb mansion, although, since I didn't have a chance to see those marks before they were destroyed, I can't say for sure."

Now that icy sensation was moving along her limbs, although the house was actually stuffy and too warm, thanks to the closed windows and the sun beating down on its roof. "Who put them there?"

"I have no idea." He shut off the flashlight and returned the keychain to his pocket. "I know one thing, though."

"What's that?" Rosemary asked, even though she wasn't really sure she wanted to know the answer.

"Whoever scratched those sigils on your ceiling definitely wanted to hurt you."

Chapter 14

Rosemary watched, arms crossed, as Will climbed up on the ladder he'd fetched from the garage and carefully scratched out all the sigils that had been carved into the ceiling plaster. Once he was done, he got out his vial of holy water, dabbed some on his fingertips, and smeared it into the surface while he murmured something under his breath. The water left grayish blotches on the paint, although she hoped it would dry without staining too badly.

Then again, what did she care? Someone had been attracting demons to this house on purpose. In that moment, she was fairly certain she never wanted to spend another minute there. Housing prices in SoCal were going through the roof, and she was pretty sure she could more than recoup her investment in the place. Better to take the money and run, get a nice, safe, unhaunted condo somewhere....

"I think that should do it," Will said. He stared up at the ceiling, eyes narrowed, as if to make sure he hadn't missed a single mark.

"Thanks," she told him, but she really wasn't feeling very thankful. No, the emotions bubbling inside her were a toxic mixture of anger and fear. Part of her was simply offended that someone had come in her house and defiled it in such a way... but she was also nearly scared out of her mind that anyone would wish that kind of misfortune on her. As far as she knew, she hadn't done a single thing that would have attracted the wrath of a person who dabbled in such dark practices.

Will came down the ladder and folded it, then leaned it up against the wall. With that task completed, he sent her a piercing glance. "Are you all right?"

"No. I don't know." She tucked a stray curl behind her ear and added, "I want to get out of here."

"I understand. Well, I'm done, so there's no reason to stay."

Thank God.

In silence, they exited the hallway and went back out through the front door. This time, she did lock it, although she realized that the house had been open all night and no one had come in.

Well, part of the home's selling point had been the safe neighborhood where it was located, and she supposed her haste the night before had only proved that fact.

Will appeared concerned as she pointed the fob for her Fiat at the car and unlocked the door. "Are you sure you're okay to drive?"

"Of course I am," Rosemary snapped, even as she realized her reaction had been completely uncalled for. None of this was his fault.

"You seem a little shaken—"

"Maybe I am, but it's not going to stop me from driving back to Pasadena. I want to get the hell out of here."

"Fair enough." He hesitated, hands shoved in the pockets of his black trousers. Tone gentle, he went on, "I think this house is safe now."

"Maybe it is," she returned. "But I don't have any reason to be here, so there's no point in my hanging around." Something was nagging at her, although she guessed that having this discussion while standing in her driveway maybe wasn't the best idea. But they were here now, and she had to ask. "Why, though? I mean, anyone who's this invested in sending the demon hordes after me has to know that I'm not even living here right now. It seems like kind of a crap shoot."

His keen gray gaze rested on her for a moment. She didn't know him well enough to guess what might have been going through his mind. Was he considering responses and then discarding them when he feared she might react negatively? Or did he simply not know what to say?

When he spoke, however, his voice sounded sure enough. "I think whoever it is probably knows you're staying at Michael and Audrey's house, and are therefore protected. This was, as you said, a crap shoot. They also probably know you come back here somewhat regularly to check on the property. You're always alone when you do that, aren't you?"

"Yes," she said, still feeling cold all over in spite of the warm sun that shone down on them both. Vaguely, she realized it wasn't even noon yet. If she wanted to, she could head over to the shop and still put in a full afternoon's work. Not that she would; she'd told Isabel she needed the whole day off, and she figured that finding out someone had just put a demonic hex on her property was a good enough excuse for taking a mental health day.

"And the demon didn't appear last night until after your date left for the evening."

Well, to be perfectly accurate, he'd never even come inside the house, but she had a feeling that if she'd invited Caleb in—if they'd talked or kissed or gotten even more intimate—the demon still would have stayed away while he was there.

"You're right," she said. "So, the demon wanted to make sure I was alone?"

"It's just a guess, but it seems plausible."

"But I'll be fine at Michael's house." It was a statement, not a question. After all, she'd survived the night before without any further demon encounters. Still....

Will nodded. "Yes…but I want to follow you back there, just to be safe."

Rosemary opened her mouth, a protest bubbling to her lips…but then she realized it was probably better that way. For all she knew, the unknown person or persons who'd scratched those sigils into the ceiling in her hallway had also put the whammy on her car, although probably if the Fiat really had been hexed in some way, it would have acted up before now. Still, having Will follow her to the Orange Heights house seemed the safest thing to do. Besides, the route wasn't horribly out of his way, since he had to go back to Pasadena to return to All Saints anyway.

"Okay," she said. "I'm not sure it's necessary… but thanks."

He offered her a reassuring smile and then headed over to his own car so he could get behind the wheel. Once again, she had to wonder at a clergyman driving such an impressive piece of muscle. Probably a story there.

Would they ever know each other well enough that she would find it safe to ask?

She climbed into the Fiat and waited for Will to back out of the driveway so she could exit as well, then drove with exaggerated care through the quiet residential area that surrounded her house and on to the larger street leading to the freeway. Just as on the drive over here, he stuck fairly close behind and didn't let anyone cut in between the two of them. Was he also worried that her car might have been tampered with in some way?

To her relief, though, it performed flawlessly as ever on the short drive back to Pasadena. Will pulled up to the curb in front of the big brown Craftsman house, watching as she made her way up the driveway and parked in the garage. Normally, she would have gone through the side door and headed into the house through the entrance in the kitchen, but this time she let herself out through the gate and came around to the front door so he could see that she'd gotten safely inside. Once there, she entered the code for the alarm…and just as quickly reengaged it. When she looked back out through the window, she saw that the shiny black Challenger was gone.

For some reason, a little stab of disappointment went through her. That was ridiculous, though. Will had done his duty, had figured out why the demon had entered her house, had come back here with her to make sure she got home safely.

Only…this wasn't really home, was it? Just a borrowed refuge, one she was all too glad to have, but she couldn't say it was actually hers.

"You can figure all that out later," she told herself, speaking aloud because she needed to hear the sound of her own voice right then, needed to have it reassure her that she really was all right and that she'd survive this, just as she'd survived everything else life had thrown at her so far. "Michael and Audrey won't be back here for almost two years."

A lot could happen in two years. For now, though, she guessed she might as well get some lunch…not because she was particularly hungry, but because it would give her something to do until she heard from Caleb. His interview was at one, so she doubted she would get a call from him until after two at the earliest.

As she'd thought, putting together a salad kept her somewhat occupied. By the time she was done, she realized she was hungrier than she'd thought, and she sat down in the family room with her salad and some ice water, and turned on the local noontime news. She really didn't care what the newscasters had to say, but their brisk, businesslike voices reminded her that the world was still rolling along out there, far away from her own scary universe of demons and spells of summoning.

Of someone who wanted to hurt her.

Which drove her back to the central question.

Why?

She'd lived her life as blamelessly as she could, had never wittingly—or willingly—hurt anyone. Sure, like almost any other female in her twenties, she had a couple of messy breakups in her past, but they weren't the sort of thing that would have made any of her exes thirsty for revenge. Not that any of them were exactly the demon-summoning type, either. Maybe nasty notes on a car windshield or a barrage of texts pleading for her to rethink things, but demons?

Not really.

Rosemary wondered if Will had stopped for lunch on his way back to the church, or if he'd had to hurry over to his office because he had an appointment with a parishioner. She realized then that she didn't know much about what a minister really did from day to day. True, Michael Covenant was a minister as well, but he didn't practice or have a congregation. It was more like he'd gotten ordained because he thought it would help him in his demon-hunting vocation, and not the other way around. Whereas Will must have felt a true calling, or why would he have gone into what she couldn't help seeing as a pretty thankless profession?

She wasn't sure what to think about that. Overly religious people had always made her uncomfortable, mostly because she feared that they'd start trying to convert her as soon as they found out she was a self-proclaimed pagan who didn't believe in God. Not that Will had tried anything like that, and actually seemed fairly laid-back for an Episcopal minister, but there was still a chance he could bust out with the proselytizing at any moment.

He won't, she told herself as she picked up the remote for the television and began idly flipping through the channels. *Michael probably told him you wouldn't buy what he was selling if he tried anything like that anyway.*

The thought reassured her a little. At the same time, she realized she was slightly annoyed with herself for continuing to think about Will Gordon when she really should have been focusing on Caleb, if only to send some good vibes out into the universe so he'd get the job and wouldn't have to worry about his finances for the next few months.

And if he didn't get the gig…well, something else would come along. Of course, he hadn't confessed all that much to her about his money situation, and so she honestly didn't know how much of a cushion he had to fall back on if his unemployed period stretched out for too long. It sounded as if his current housing situation was pretty solid, though. She guessed that he might be able to skate along for a bit before things got too bad.

Her thoughts darted this way and that. Rosemary knew she was distracting herself with Caleb's imaginary troubles because it was easier than dwelling on her own, but she didn't know what else she should do.

Just as she was wondering whether she should go out and do some shopping, more because the thought of being surrounded by people was obscurely comforting than because she needed anything in particular, her phone rang. Since she'd put it down on the coffee table as she was eating her lunch, all she had to do was reach over and pick it up.

Caleb's number.

"Hey," she said. Good, she sounded upbeat and cheerful, and not at all like someone who had discovered a bunch of demon-summoning sigils carved into her ceiling a few hours earlier. "How'd it go?"

"Great," Caleb replied. His voice was a little tinny, so he must have been driving someplace that didn't have good cell reception. "I got it. Like I thought, I start tomorrow."

So soon. Yes, he'd warned her that such a thing was distinctly possible, but she still had to hold back a stab of disappointment. If nothing else, she wanted to see him so she wouldn't have to sit here by herself and obsess over who might be calling up demons to kill her. "Congratulations!" she said, doing her best to drive that unpleasant thought out of her head. "You'll have to let me take you out to dinner to celebrate."

He chuckled. "I thought we were celebrating last night."

"That was just for the interview. This would be for the job itself. And it's my treat."

"You don't have to do that."

"Maybe not, but I want to. Anyway, I'm in Pasadena, so we can pick someplace around here, or I can meet you at your place."

"'Pasadena'?" Caleb repeated, his tone slightly confused. "I thought you had to work today."

Damn it. She'd been so eager to get things set up for dinner this evening, she'd let that particular tidbit slip right out. Even though she really hadn't wanted to get into this over the phone, she knew if she tried to hem and haw, he'd guess right away that something was wrong. "Well, there was an… incident…last night after you dropped me off."

Immediately, his voice sharpened. "An incident? What happened? Are you okay?"

"I'm fine," she reassured him. "Nothing happened to me. I had a sort of visitation, I guess."

"Madeline Nash's ghost?"

I wish. "No," she said carefully. "Something else. Something that looked like Colin but wasn't. I got out and came back to Pasadena since I knew I'd be safer here."

"Jesus." He sounded shaken. "But you're sure you're okay?"

Once again, she decided it was better not to mention Will Gordon...or his visit to the Glendora house and what he'd found there. Maybe at some point, she'd have to explain to Caleb why she had no plans to go back to her home in the near future, but that could wait. "I'm okay," she said. "Honestly, I'd rather forget about it. But now you know why I'm not at work."

"I wish I could have been there for you. Why didn't you call me?"

A very good question. However, she doubted Caleb would be too happy to have her tell him that she'd called an Episcopalian minister to come to her assistance instead because she'd had a feeling that an indie filmmaker from Indiana wasn't exactly the best person to help out with marauding demons. "I was sort of on autopilot," she confessed. "I just bolted and came back here. But nothing else happened…or has happened. Everything's okay."

A pause. "I'm not sure if it sounds okay," he said, his tone clearly dubious. "But as long as you're safe—"

"I am."

He let out a breath, then said, "I wish I could come over there this afternoon, but I've got to sign some paperwork, and then there's a production meeting I'm supposed to attend. That's where I'm driving right now."

Rosemary realized she'd been hoping he was on his way home, because then they could have gotten together much earlier than she'd thought. It didn't sound as though anything before dinner was in the cards, though. "It's okay," she lied. "I need to go run some errands anyway."

"Is it safe?"

She had to hope so. "Of course, it is. I was just going to run over to Trader Joe's and maybe swing through Old Town. There'll be lots of people everywhere I go. What could be safer than that?"

Her answer seemed to convince him, because he said, "Well, that sounds pretty harmless. I'm not sure when I'll be done this afternoon, but I'll call you as soon as I get home. Sound like a plan?"

"Sure. And don't worry about me—everything's been quiet over here, and I don't see any reason why it won't stay that way. Have fun at your meeting."

"I will. And you—you be careful, Rosemary."

She made an affirmative sound and then touched her phone's screen to end the call. A small sigh escaped her lips as she bent to put the phone back down on the coffee table.

It looked as though she was going shopping after all.

ACTUALLY, THOUGH, BEING SURROUNDED BY the moms shopping at Trader Joe's before they headed out to pick up their kids—by far the largest percentage of shoppers at the store at two-fifteen on a weekday afternoon—made Rosemary feel a bit better about life. It was all so relentlessly normal, something she thought she could use in her world right about then. The same with wandering around Old Town Pasadena after she'd picked up the few odds and ends she needed at TJ's, although the crowd in Old Town looked more like college kids than suburban mothers. She spent way too much money on a pair of dark teal-blue flats but allowed her better judgment to steer her away from a shocking orange sweater in another store, then hiked back to the parking garage where she'd left the Fiat and got her car out of hock.

For some reason, though, instead of heading straight up Fair Oaks so she could jump on the freeway for a few miles and save herself a little time, she turned right on Colorado, then zigged left on Euclid...a route that would send her right past All Saints. Why, she wasn't sure; if Will had been all that concerned about her, then he would have stuck around rather than jetting off the second she was safely inside the house...which meant he probably wouldn't appreciate a drop-in visit.

I'm not going in, she told herself as she drove slowly down the narrow street, just a block over from Pasadena's municipal center. *I'm just...checking.*

Yep, that sounded exactly like the sort of thing a psycho ex-girlfriend might say. Not that she was anything close to a girlfriend of Will Gordon's, not even really a friend, just someone whose safety he'd been charged with. Or at least, she had a feeling Michael had made it very clear that she needed looking out for, even though if he'd said such a thing to his face, she would have told him she could take care of herself, thank you very much.

Except she hadn't been doing such a great job of that lately, had she? When was the last time the tough, resourceful heroine in an action movie had run screaming out of her house? Ellen Ripley or Sarah Connor probably would have flame-throwered that demon right out of existence. Hell, even Audrey Barrett had stood shoulder to shoulder with Michael and beaten a goddamn demon lord and sent him back to Hell. But Rosemary McGuire?

Wimp.

She grimaced and allowed herself a quick glance over at the church as she drove by. Everything appeared calm and serene, which was about what you'd expect of a church on a weekday afternoon. Maybe they had evening services or some kind of community programs later in the day, but at the moment, she couldn't detect a single sign of activity. Was Will back in his office, dealing with paperwork? On the phone with a parishioner? She wouldn't allow herself to stop and find out, even though she spotted a convenient parking space just a few car lengths ahead.

You need to stop thinking about him, she told herself sternly. *There are roughly a million reasons why acting like this is completely stupid. You have a date with Caleb tonight, remember?*

Well, sort of a nebulous date, since she didn't know when he was going to get home or what they were going to do once he got there. Still, Rosemary knew she needed to come up with some kind of plan, just so they wouldn't waste any of the precious time they had this evening. She'd been trying to take things slowly, but now she wondered if they shouldn't just go to bed, get it over with so there wouldn't be this weird tension between them.

And what a wonderful way to think about something that should be magical. Still, she'd always disliked this stage of a relationship, when it was pretty obvious where things were going to end up but neither of the parties involved had taken the next step to get there. Wouldn't it be better to go ahead and sleep with him, and put all this awkwardness behind them? She enjoyed his company and was obviously physically attracted to him, or she wouldn't have had to slam on the brakes the way she did on Sunday afternoon. Actually, now she was annoyed with herself for pulling back, for not allowing matters to progress to their logical conclusion. Maybe then she'd have her head screwed on a little straighter when it came to William Gordon.

Father William Gordon.

Oy.

She decided to skip getting on the freeway at all and crossed over the 210 on Los Robles, heading north toward home. As she went, she tried to come up with some kind of idea that would make this date with Caleb special, but her brain didn't feel as if it was firing on all cylinders. It didn't help that she knew next to nothing about Eagle Rock or the restaurants there. All right, there was the Italian place where they'd gotten take-out for lunch that one time, but she didn't think that was special enough.

Her mood hadn't improved one bit by the time she got back to the house. She told herself that getting all riled up over something so inconsequential wasn't a very good use of her mental energies, but if anything, such inner cajoling only made her that much more irritated. Scowling, she got her shopping bags out of the trunk and stalked into the house, then put away the groceries she'd purchased with a bit more slamming of cupboards than was strictly necessary.

As she shut the refrigerator door, she saw Madeline Nash standing there in the kitchen, dark, sad eyes fixed on her.

"Holy shit," Rosemary blurted, then added quickly, "I mean…hello, Madeline."

The ghost only continued to stare at her. "It wasn't him," she said. Her voice sounded different today, clearer, stronger. And she was barely transparent. Just a little bit more solid, and she would have looked like a regular person.

Rosemary wasn't sure what these changes meant…nor why the ghost had appeared in the middle of the day, in broad daylight, when before she'd only manifested during the evening hours. Frowning slightly, she asked, "Who wasn't him?"

"The thing in your other house. It wasn't Colin."

A glance down at her bare forearms told Rosemary that goosebumps had formed on the lightly tanned skin there, even though the house was almost a little too warm, since she hadn't turned on the A/C today. "It was a demon, wasn't it?"

"Yes."

Madeline seemed much more communicative today, which had to be a good sign. "What was it doing there?"

"Sent...to stop you."

"To stop me from doing what?"

The ghost paused and looked over her shoulder, although at what, Rosemary had no idea. Still, just the way Madeline had stared at the empty space behind her made an uneasy chill trace its way along Rosemary's back. "Finding it," the ghost said simply.

"The footage?"

A nod.

"Then you have to tell me where it is," Rosemary pleaded, knowing how desperate she sounded. Still, she didn't know what else to do. Maybe Madeline thought she was being clear in her instructions, but she might as well have been speaking in a foreign language for all the help her advice had been.

"I told you," she said. As she spoke, she seemed to be growing fainter, dissolving even as her voice began to fade away. "In the house...."

And then she was gone.

Rosemary stared at the empty space where the ghost had been standing—or maybe floating... she'd never really looked to see whether Madeline's feet were actually touching the ground—just a minute earlier. Once again, frustration boiled up in her, but she knew there wasn't a damn thing she could do to change the situation. Obviously, the dead woman had one piece of advice she was going to provide, and that was it.

Trying not to swear under her breath, Rosemary went back to the family room, grabbed the remote for the television, and sat down on the couch. If the universe intended to throw up roadblocks for her, then fine. She'd sit here on her ass until she heard from Caleb, and then she could try to salvage this wreck of a day.

What other choice did she have?

Chapter 15

"I'M REALLY SORRY," CALEB SAID, SOUNDING breathless, as if he'd run out to his car to make the call—which, Rosemary reflected, was probably exactly what had happened. "But the meeting sort of turned into a dinner thing with the crew, and I can't really beg off—"

"It's fine," Rosemary told him, even though she knew it wasn't really fine. But what else was she supposed to do? It wasn't as if she was going to tell him to inform his director that he already had plans for dinner and needed to leave. At the same time, though, she wished she had something else she could be doing tonight, anything but sitting alone in this big empty house. A sudden thought occurred to her, and she added, "I might go over to my mom's place. She was just complaining the other night that the two of us never get much of a chance to talk anymore."

"Oh, good," Caleb replied. He sounded relieved, although she wasn't sure whether that was because she wouldn't be by herself if she went to her mother's house, or simply that if she also had plans, he wouldn't need to feel guilty about bailing on her.

No, that wasn't very fair. Pretty much everything she'd seen of him so far seemed to indicate that he was a considerate person. Most likely, he was thinking of her frightening encounter the night before and was glad she had someplace to go so she wouldn't have to spend the whole evening alone.

"You just let me know when you'll be getting a break, and we can go out then," Rosemary said. "A delayed celebration is still a celebration."

"You're the best," he replied. "We may be working on Saturday, but it doesn't sound as if we'll have to come in on Sunday, so maybe then."

Great. A whole six days from now. But she told herself she'd gotten along just fine for the past year without much of a social life—unless she counted the various family dinners and other McGuire get-togethers she'd attended—so it wasn't as if she couldn't survive another week without male companionship.

And you might see Will Gordon somewhere

in there anyway, her brain told her, although she tried to push that traitorous thought out of her mind. Yes, it was possible she might need Will's assistance over the next few days if any more weirdness cropped up, but asking him to protect her from the next demonic visitation wasn't exactly the same thing as going out on a date.

"No problem," she said blithely. "I work pretty much every Saturday anyway. So, just give me a call when you can."

"I will. Gotta go—talk to you later."

The call ended there, but she remained where she was, staring down at the phone for a moment, long after the screen had gone dark. Once again, she had to push back the urge to curse out loud. Unfortunately, swearing wouldn't change anything and would only put more negative energy out into the universe. She had enough of that to deal with already.

Instead, she texted her mother and asked if it was okay if she came over this evening. The reply came back right away.

Of course, sweetheart. Any time. I have a pot of minestrone going right now.

That sounded like her mother. She loved to make big batches of soup, then keep some for herself and send the rest home to her daughters, or give it away to neighbors if Rosemary and Isabel and Celeste weren't available to come over and pick up their care packages. But at least going to Sierra Madre tonight wouldn't be an imposition, wouldn't make her mother feel as if she needed to whip up an elaborate meal when she'd just fixed one for the whole family two nights before.

Feeling somewhat more at ease, Rosemary went upstairs to the bathroom to get herself tidied up, then cast a suspicious glance around the hallway. Madeline Nash had never materialized anywhere except the ground floor of the house, but there was a first time for everything.

However, no ghostly presences announced themselves, so Rosemary got her purse, set the house's alarm, and headed out to the garage. Instead of taking the freeway, though, she headed east on Orange Grove, then cut up to Sierra Madre Boulevard at the east end of town. Despite the traffic and all the stoplights, she preferred to take this route, since she found it more relaxing to drive through residential neighborhoods rather than being stuck in bumper-to-bumper traffic on the 210.

About twenty minutes later, she pulled up into the driveway of her mother's house, parked the Fiat, and got out. Even as she was climbing the porch steps, the front door opened and Glynis peered out.

"I thought I heard a car," she said. "How was the drive?"

"Fine," Rosemary replied. Or at least, as fine as an eastbound weekday drive in the early evening could be. Despite that, though, she felt relieved to get out of the house. Michael's place was safe from demon incursions, true, but having a ghost popping up all the time wasn't exactly the most reassuring thing in the world, either.

Her mother's gaze lingered on her face for a moment, as if Glynis was seeing something Rosemary would much rather have remained hidden. However, all she said was, "Come on inside," and opened the door a little wider so her daughter could enter the house.

Since the weather had been cooler that day, all the windows were open to catch the breeze. A collection of antique vases held roses from the backyard garden, their colors ranging from pink-tipped white to a velvety red verging on black. *Grandma's roses,* as Rosemary always thought of them, even though her mother had been tending the bushes for the past six years, ever since this house had come to her.

Something about being here, about being surrounded by the familiar jumble of antiques and pictures and knickknacks, made the tense little knot she'd been carrying inside her for the past few days gradually begin to loosen. She couldn't say why the house was having this effect on her now, when she certainly hadn't felt this way when she'd been here on Sunday night, but maybe it was simply that she was alone with her mother now, rather than having the entire family here.

"Let's go to the kitchen," her mother said, and Rosemary followed her toward the back of the house, to the large, cozy room that had been such a central component of her later childhood years. Yes, Glynis had finally updated all the appliances a couple of years ago, and they were now gleaming stainless steel instead of the brown 1970s relics that used to occupy the space, but the creamy tile with its red and green accents was the same, as was the enormous wrought-iron pot rack that hung over the island in the center of the space.

An enticing aroma filled the room, its source the large stock pot that sat on a back burner of the big Viking stove, the gas flame turned down to its lowest setting. Without saying anything else, Rosemary's mother went over to a cupboard and extracted a pair of wine glasses, then lifted an already opened bottle of Chianti that had been waiting on the counter.

"Planning ahead, I see," Rosemary remarked, and her mother smiled.

"I knew you'd be over soon enough…and I knew you probably would need this."

Sometimes, having a psychic parent could be a

good thing. Rosemary took the glass of wine her mother handed her and said, "To surviving Tuesdays."

"And all the rest of the week, I hope," Glynis responded as they clinked glasses.

"I guess I'll just have to see how it goes."

That remark made her mother lift an eyebrow. "That bad?"

"I don't know." Another sip, and then the words seemed to pour out of her in a rush—that terrifying encounter with the not-Colin demon in the Glendora house, the sigils she and Will had found in the hallway ceiling…the completely unhelpful ghost of Madeline Nash.

Rosemary's mother listened to all this, her finely arched brows—the same brows all her daughters had inherited—pulled together in a slight frown. When she spoke, however, her comment seemed to come from out of left field. "I noticed you didn't say anything about Caleb. The other night at dinner, you seemed very impressed with him."

"Well, I didn't mention him now because he didn't have anything to do with any of this," Rosemary replied. A stab of annoyance went through her, although whether that irritation had been caused by her mother's seemingly random question, or by the simple fact of Caleb's defection this evening, she wasn't sure. "He was off at a job interview today. We were supposed to have dinner tonight, but that fell through."

"I'm sorry." A long pause as her mother sipped some wine. It seemed as if she'd intended to say something else, but instead, she set down her glass and went to the cupboard to fetch a couple of bowls. "Let's get dinner on the table."

The subtext seemed to be that she would prefer to get some food in her daughter's stomach before the discussion went any further. Since Rosemary was hungry, she didn't protest, only got a bowl of salad out of the fridge as her mother instructed, then took it in to the dining room table. Two place settings had already been laid out at one end, so she set down the salad bowl there and went back to retrieve the wine while her mother brought out the soup.

Once they were both seated, however, Glynis fixed her daughter with a very direct look. "Why don't you tell me some more about this William Gordon?"

Nonplussed, Rosemary stared back at her mother. "What's there to tell? He's someone that Michael Covenant knows. He's sort of working as Michael's relief pitcher while he and Audrey are out of town. So to speak."

"Your voice changes when you talk about him."

Oh, great. Now her mother was going to go

all psychic on her and attempt to see hidden nuances that didn't really exist. "Well, I'm grateful to him," Rosemary said, spearing a cherry tomato with her salad fork. "If it weren't for him, I don't know whether I would have ever discovered the sigils on the hallway ceiling."

"He knew what he was looking for?"

"I'm not sure it was exactly that." She paused, replaying the scene in her mind. Will had stood where the demon appeared and then inspected his immediate surroundings with care. Obviously, he'd guessed there had to be some reason why the entity had chosen that particular spot to manifest, and that was why he knew to look for the summoning symbols. "Or rather, he's probably encountered things like this before and so had a checklist of things to try. Honestly, I really didn't ask him. I was just glad he was able to figure it out. And then he scratched out all the sigils so they couldn't be used for another summoning. I'll need to get the hallway ceiling repainted at some point, but since I'm not planning on moving back there any time soon—"

"Rosemary."

Three small syllables, but they were enough to make her pause and gaze over at her mother. Glynis's expression was serious enough, and yet Rosemary detected a very faint lift at one corner of her mouth, the sort of small tell that seemed to indicate she was secretly amused even if she was doing her best not to let it show.

Another flicker of annoyance flared then, and Rosemary wondered if she was PMSing or something. Usually, she didn't allow every little thing to set her off. "What?"

"You're telling me what he did, but you're not telling me *about* him. Not really."

"Because I don't know much about him," Rosemary protested, which was only the truth. "He's a minister over at All Saints. You know, the big Gothic-style church on Euclid."

Glynis picked up her glass of Chianti and sipped from it, still with that small quirk touching the right side of her mouth, although Rosemary guessed her mother's amusement now probably stemmed from this revelation of Will's occupation. But because she didn't reply, just nodded slightly, it seemed as though she wanted her daughter to continue.

"Anyway, it's not as though we've had a chance to have any heart-to-heart talks or anything. He's from the East Coast, I think, and I think he's in his mid-thirties, but I really don't know anything more than that. Not how he and Michael met, not how long he's worked at All Saints, not his favorite color or football team or whatever else people are supposed to know about each other."

After delivering this not-quite diatribe, Rosemary took a sip of her own wine before turning her attention to the bowl of minestrone in front of her. Seriously, she didn't know what the point of this inquisition actually was. Well, okay, one or two direct questions didn't exactly an inquisition make, but still.

Her mother seemed to absorb the minimal information Rosemary had provided and tapped her fingers against the bowl of her wine glass, still without speaking.

And although Rosemary had resolved not to say anything else on the subject, somehow the words slipped out anyway. "I suppose you think it's funny that I might be attracted to an Episcopalian priest."

Now her mother smiled outright. "Well, that's better than a Catholic priest, isn't it?"

True. As awkward as the situation might seem to her, Rosemary reflected that it could be a lot worse. "Probably. But I think maybe I'm just trying to sabotage myself by thinking I'm attracted to him, instead of focusing on whatever might be happening with Caleb."

"Which is?"

Good question. Everything had seemed to be going well—maybe too well—until she got cold feet after their dinner at the Eden Garden Café and decided to slow things down. But just because she'd been going through an awfully long dry spell, it still didn't mean she should have jumped right into bed with Caleb Dixon. Or at least, that was what she'd tried to tell herself, although once again she thought it might be easier if they just did they deed and moved on from there.

"We get along well together," she said. "He seems like a nice guy." A nice, normal, good-looking guy, one who didn't seem to have any particular hang-ups or neuroses, except maybe his dedication to tracking down Colin Turner's missing *Project Demon Hunters* footage. Even that small obsession, though, seemed pretty harmless. In a town crowded with wannabes, Caleb was just looking for something that would make him stand out.

Even as the thought crossed through her mind, though, she realized his obsession might not be quite so harmless after all. Before they'd started on this quest, she hadn't had to deal with wandering ghosts or mist-spewing demons. Her life had been a lot quieter before he crossed her path.

"I'm sure he's very nice," her mother said.

However, her tone was neutral enough that Rosemary set down her spoon and gave her a sharp look. "Is there something you'd like to tell me?"

"I'm not having a psychic flash about Caleb, if that's what you mean."

In a way, Rosemary wished she had. If her mother was getting some bad vibes about him, then at least she'd know what to do. But life was rarely that cut-and-dried. She liked him a lot, enjoyed spending time with him, and yet she hadn't experienced anything close to the strange little zing that had gone through her when she'd looked into Will Gordon's clear gray eyes for the first time.

"But…?"

"But…nothing, really." Glynis glanced away, gaze moving toward the window, although Rosemary wasn't sure what she could see out there, except for the red-leaved Japanese maple planted in the side yard, and possibly a span of redwood fence. "You're my daughter, Rosemary, and I want whatever is best for you. If you think that's Caleb, then I'll be happy for you. It's just that I've seen you settle in the past, and I don't want you to do that again."

She wished she could say her mother was wrong, but she'd pointed out a truth that Rosemary had tried to ignore. Meeting decent men seemed to be getting more and more difficult, no matter what all the dating apps liked to say on the subject. Being a self-proclaimed psychic only made matters that much worse. She seemed to attract either kooks or guys who wanted to prove to her that her supposed "powers" weren't anything more than the power of suggestion. When someone halfway decent crossed her path, she tended to give them far more benefit of the doubt than they probably deserved, simply because they appeared so much better in comparison with the other men who'd tried to pursue her. After her last relationship collapsed more than a year earlier, she'd basically washed her hands of the whole thing. Celeste could be the one sister with the perfect marriage and the happy family and the adorable rescue dog, because it sure didn't look like either she or Isabel were going to be able to achieve that particular triple-word score.

"I'm not 'settling,'" Rosemary said then, and poured herself some more Chianti. "I've only been out with the guy twice. And since it looks as though my third date with him is on hold indefinitely, I doubt we have much of a future."

Her tone was casual as she spoke, but a pang went through her at the thought of not seeing Caleb again. She loved her sisters and her mother, loved the closeness of their family, and yet sometimes it was really nice to have some male companionship. Then she told herself to stop borrowing trouble. He'd pretty much told her that he wanted to see her on Sunday, so there was no reason for her put on a mask of tragedy and act as though she'd been outright abandoned.

But was that because he really did want to see

her, or only because he hoped she might have gotten some leads on the missing footage in the intervening time?

And Will…probably better not to think about him too much. There wasn't any reason for her to be in contact with him unless she had another strange encounter. And as much as she wanted to see him again, she wasn't sure she was willing to deal with another invading demon just to have an excuse to call him.

Her mother sat quietly, no doubt watching the shifting expressions on her face and trying to figure out whether it would be better to say something reassuring, or whether she should allow her daughter to sift through this problem on her own. When she spoke, it was clear she'd decided to change the subject.

"What are you going to do about the house? Will it need to be cleansed in some way?"

"Probably," Rosemary replied. While she didn't like to think of how her pretty little house had been defiled, she realized the problem would have to be addressed sooner rather than later. Will might have erased the summoning sigils, but he hadn't done anything to remove the psychic taint the demon had left behind. "Maybe you and I and Isabel and Celeste can go there one night this week and smudge the hell out of the place."

"Literally," her mother said with a smile. "I

have my book club on Wednesday, but otherwise, I'm free any time you girls are. Just let me know when you work it out with Celeste and Isabel."

"Sounds like a plan."

From there, the conversation moved to more harmless subjects, like the book her mother was reading for her club, and how Halloween was rapidly approaching, only a little more than two weeks away. Every Samhain, the family met here at the Sierra Madre house to have their own observation of that ancient holiday so they might honor their dead and show proper respect to the world beyond the veil. The past week had been so tumultuous, Rosemary had almost forgotten how they were inching ever closer to the day when the barrier between this world and the next would be at its thinnest.

Not that it had seemed all that thick lately to begin with, thanks to the way Madeline had been popping in and out of existence in Michael's house.

Eventually, however, the two of them had eaten their fill of soup and salad, and Rosemary helped her mother take the dirty dishes back into the kitchen, then insisted on rinsing everything and putting it away in the dishwasher. Knowing better than to protest, Glynis had waited off to one side until her daughter was done, then thanked her.

"I'm sorry your date was canceled, but I'm glad you were able to come over and visit," she said as Rosemary closed the dishwasher door. "It's been too long since we were able to chat like this. And even though things may seem muddled now, I have faith that you'll be able to find your way through in the end."

She wished she had her mother's confidence. At the moment, it seemed as though she didn't know what she should do next. Well, sometimes the best thing to do was to do nothing, to relax and allow the universe to tell you where you should go.

Still….

She tucked a curl behind her ear and then leaned against the counter, arms crossed. "What's the point in being psychic if I can't even tell what I need to do next?"

"Oh, sweetheart." Glynis came over and wrapped her arms around her daughter, the hug brief but infinitely reassuring. Somehow, the faint scent of the lemony perfume she always wore seemed to ground Rosemary, to remind her that her family would always be here for her. Too often lately, living alone as she did, she'd allowed herself to forget that very important fact. "Just because we've been gifted with heightened perception doesn't mean we can see everything…and I'm glad

317

we can't. Would you really want that kind of power?"

Even though she knew the correct answer to that question, Rosemary gave a helpless little lift of her shoulders. "I don't know. I mean, would you have married Dad if you'd known he was going to leave you the way he did?"

For a long moment, her mother was silent. Then, to Rosemary's surprise, she smiled a little. "Of course, I would have. Because even though that relationship wasn't meant to last, my marriage to your father gave me you girls, and you know I wouldn't give you up for anything in the world. We're all on the path we're meant to be on. Always remember that."

Rosemary gave a reluctant nod. Well, she would try to do her best…no matter where that path might lead her.

Chapter 16

THE DAYS THAT FOLLOWED ROSEMARY'S Tuesday night dinner with her mother seemed interminable, but possibly that was only because nothing of any note occurred to break up the monotony. Yes, the McGuire family converged on her house on Thursday night to look for more sigils—they found none, though—followed by a thorough cleansing, but even then, nothing tried to stop them from ritually smudging every room, or walking through the place afterward holding white candles as they murmured ancient invocations of protection. She wondered if she should have an alarm system installed—an expensive security measure that she'd been doing her best to avoid—but then decided to leave it alone for now. Although she hated the noise of the construction zone next door, she had to admit that having her neighbors' property swarming with construction workers at least ten hours every day was probably a good deterrent for any would-be intruders. Yes, someone could still attempt to break in late at night after the work crews on the adjacent property were gone, but she had to hope that the precautions she and her family had taken would keep away anyone trying to summon another demon.

Even if they did, joke was on them. She had no intention of sleeping in the place any time soon…especially since she didn't have to worry about Caleb meeting her here in Glendora for another date.

Oh, he kept in touch. He hadn't, as she'd worried he might, ghosted her, using the excuse of his new job to pull a disappearing act. Maybe he didn't call every night, but he called on Wednesday and again on Thursday, although she missed him that time because she was in the middle of cleansing the Glendora house with her mother and sisters. And he reached out to her on Friday to let her know he definitely had to work Saturday, but that so far Sunday looked open.

"It's the best I can do," he said, sounding genuinely apologetic. "But I'll make it up to you, I promise. What would you like to do?"

"Rummage through more storage units?" she suggested, and he chuckled.

"Did you find another key?"

"No," she replied. "No sign of Madeline lately, either. That dead end is staying dead, as far as I can tell."

"And...everything else is okay?"

By the hesitant way he'd phrased the question, Rosemary guessed he was asking whether she'd had any more demonic visitors. "Everything is fine," she told him, wondering if she sounded a little too emphatic. Well, that couldn't be helped. Plowing ahead, she added, "My mother and sisters went to the house and helped cleanse it. I don't think my little demon friend is going to make a repeat appearance any time soon."

"I'm glad," he said. "I couldn't stop thinking about that...worrying about you."

But you weren't worried enough to come check on me in person, she thought, even though she realized she was being grossly unfair. Not many people had the kind of freedom in their jobs that she enjoyed, couldn't take off at a moment's whim if something strange or unexpected occurred. All she had to do was ask one of her sisters to fill in for her if she needed to get away for a few hours or even a whole day, but Caleb didn't have that luxury. He had to make sure he stuck with this production until it wrapped—and do well enough at it that he'd be recommended for another one if at all possible.

Besides, it wasn't as if Will Gordon had exactly been beating down her door to keep tabs on her, either. He'd sent her a text on Wednesday morning, asking if she was okay, to which she'd answered that everything was hunky dory. All quiet on the Western front. Which was only the truth, but even as she'd sent Will her reply, she found herself wishing that things *weren't* hunky dory, just so she could ask him to come over and offer some assistance.

"You don't need to worry," she assured Caleb, doing her best to jerk her thoughts back to the here and now, and not a mythical visit from Will Gordon that was never going to materialize. "Honestly, this has been a pretty boring week. I hope you're having more fun than I am."

He chuckled then, and she could almost imagine him shaking his sandy blond head at her, his brown eyes twinkling with amusement. "Actually, I am. The crew on this show is a lot of fun. They make the long hours seem, well, not so long."

"Are you going to tell me what it is?" She'd asked the question before, but each time, she hoped he might change his mind and let her know a little more about the show that was currently consuming pretty much all his waking hours. Yes, he'd told her it was a detective show of some kind, but that was it—nothing about who was in it or when it would be released, not even the smallest detail about the premise.

"No, I have a little NDA that sort of prevents me from telling you anything more than I've already said."

"Just a hint?" she said, knowing how wheedling her tone sounded as she asked the question.

Another chuckle. "Nope. Sorry. You don't want to get me fired, do you?"

Of course, she didn't. And mostly, she'd been teasing.

"Anyway," he went on, "like I said, I want to do something fun on Sunday. Whatever you like."

"Even going to the beach?" Rosemary wasn't sure why that idea had popped into her head, but it had been ages since she'd seen the ocean, and the thought of getting far, far away from Pasadena and Glendora and all the other land-locked places she'd been hanging out lately was sounding better and better.

"Isn't it kind of cold? The water, I mean."

Now it was her turn to chuckle. "Not to go swimming. Just to…go. Have you ever been to the Santa Monica pier?"

"No," he said. "I've lived in L.A. for three years, but I still haven't made it much farther west than Century City."

"Then the beach it is. Sounds like a moral imperative to me."

"Well, I definitely don't want to ignore a moral imperative." He paused then before saying, "I've missed you. Maybe that makes me sound like a dork when we've just started seeing each other, but...."

"No, I get it," she said, wishing she could be just be happy that he missed her and wanted to see her. Absolutely nothing had happened between her and Will Gordon, and yet she couldn't quite rid herself of a feeling of guilt. She forced herself to add, "I feel kind of the same way."

The relief in his voice was obvious. "Good. Then I'll give you a call tomorrow night to firm everything up, but for now, let's plan to meet at my place and then I'll drive from there. Is around eleven okay?"

"Works for me," Rosemary replied, inwardly relieved he'd been so concrete about a day and time for their date. If he'd really been planning to let things sort of die with a whimper, she doubted he would have done that much. "I'll talk to you on Saturday, then."

They said their goodbyes, and the end result of the conversation was that she was in a much better mood when she went in to work on Saturday than she'd been expecting. No, she hadn't heard anything from Will, but she hadn't really been expecting to, either. And while she knew she could always reach out to him instead of sitting around and waiting for a phone call like some ingenue from an old black and white sitcom, what in the world was she supposed to say? There was no need for her to see him, none at all.

Well, except that she wanted to hear the sound of his voice, wanted to have that cool gray gaze meet hers once more.

Not going to happen, she told herself as she headed out for a delayed lunch, Celeste manning the cash register so Rosemary could get something to eat. *You have a firm date with Caleb tomorrow, and you're pining away for Will Gordon like he's the star quarterback on the high school football team. Get a grip, woman.*

These bracing inner admonitions didn't do much to improve her frame of mind. It probably also didn't help that the long run of warm, sunny days they'd been enjoying had come to an abrupt halt; the weather was cool and cloudy, feeling more like January than mid-October. She hoped it would clear up before the next morning, because she'd been envisioning a day in the sun with Caleb, not shivering in a jacket or sweater while rough ocean winds made the air feel even colder than it already was.

Usually, she liked to walk over to the park and eat out of doors if the weather was at all amenable, but since it was so dreary that Saturday afternoon, she went into Ed's Place, a tiny hole in the wall a block down from her store that only served breakfast and lunch, and ordered a garden omelet since she wasn't in the mood for a sandwich. Luckily, she was able to grab a small table for two up against one wall rather than sit at the counter—most of the time she didn't mind eating there and chatting with Ed or one of the other cooks, but that particular day, she wanted to sit at a table and be left alone.

After she placed her order, she got her phone out of her purse and checked for any missed calls. She hadn't been expecting any, so she was surprised to see that she had a new voicemail from Michael.

Unfortunately, he didn't leave any details, only said, "I have some new information about Madeline. Give me a call when you have a chance."

Rosemary glanced around, relieved to see that no one appeared to be paying any attention to her. Figuring it was safe enough to make the call here —and definitely better than making the same call from the store, where she knew there was a good chance she'd be interrupted by a customer—she pressed the button on her phone's screen to have it call him back.

Only to have his phone ring and ring, then go to voicemail. She supposed she shouldn't have been too surprised, since it was Saturday and there was a good chance Michael and Audrey were out running errands, but still, Rosemary hated the idea of playing phone tag, especially if the reason for Michael's call turned out to be important. Since there wasn't much else she could do, she left a brief message, telling Michael she'd gotten his voicemail and that he might as well wait to call her until after five-thirty, when she'd be safely home again. She would have preferred not to wait so long, but she knew what Saturday afternoons at the store tended to be like. There was no way she'd have any privacy at all until she was done with work for the day.

Even though she knew she shouldn't expect another call, she still couldn't help but be disappointed when she checked her phone at the end of the day and saw she hadn't missed a single thing. No calls, no texts, just junk email that could be safely ignored for days.

"Everything okay?" her sister Celeste asked as she slipped the receipts and cash from the register into the pouch they used to transport their money to the bank. They would have to wait until Monday morning to make their deposits, but Celeste was the one who took the precious bundle home with her at close of business on Saturdays, since she had a safe at her house. Her expression was concerned, but at the same time, Rosemary could tell that CeeCee just wanted to get home to her husband and little boy, and probably had no desire to get delayed by any lengthy explanations as to what was going wrong in her younger sister's life.

"Sure," Rosemary said easily. "I was just thinking about my date with Caleb tomorrow. We were planning to go to Santa Monica, but if the weather stays like this...."

"I'm sure it will clear up," Celeste replied, although Rosemary guessed her sister's statement was based more on a blithe belief that everything would work out just fine than because she'd spent any time actually checking the weather forecasts. "But even if it doesn't, I'm sure you'll have fun."

The best response was a nod and a smile, even though she wasn't feeling all that cheerful at the moment. "Of course we will," she said. "Have a good weekend!"

"You, too," her sister responded, and Rosemary headed out the rear entrance to the store, the one that opened onto the parking lot out back. She took her time going to her car, a ritual she followed to make sure Celeste got everything locked up safely and was able to get in her own vehicle without incident—which she always did, of course.

But then her sister started backing her Ford Flex out of its parking space, a signal that it was safe to get on the road. As she headed away from the store, Rosemary's spirits began to lift somewhat. It was silly to get bent about the weather, after all; no one had forecast any torrential rainstorms, so her day with Caleb should work out just fine, cloudy or not.

She really hoped it would be better than fine. What she wanted was a spectacularly fun day, one so obviously diverting that she'd realize the chemistry with Caleb had been there all along, and she'd just been too blind to see it. Then she'd be able to give up this weird little crush she'd developed on Will Gordon and get on with her life.

Well, that was the plan, anyway.

When she got home, she took a suspicious glance around, halfway expecting to see Madeline Nash lurking somewhere, ready to deliver more cryptic information. However, there was no sign of the ghost, and the house remained serene and still, albeit a little darker than usual because of the heavy overcast. Rosemary flicked on the overhead lights in the kitchen and went to the refrigerator, figuring she'd pour herself a glass from the open bottle of Sauvignon blanc she had in there. Maybe the wine wouldn't relax her all the way, but she needed to start somewhere.

For good measure, she lit the white pillar

candle that still sat on the coffee table in the family room. Its soft, soothing glow filled the space, and she settled herself on the sofa and regarded the candle for a moment, allowing the gentle illumination to wash over her even as the wine she was sipping began to do its work in mending her frayed nerves.

Just as she leaned back against the cushions and let out a sigh, her cell phone rang—from the kitchen, where her purse still sat and where the phone was hidden in one of its interior pockets.

So much for relaxing and getting all Zen. Hastily, she put her wine glass down on a coaster and hurried into the kitchen, where she scrabbled inside her purse for the phone and allowed herself a glance down at the screen to see who was calling.

Michael—on his own phone, not Audrey's.

"Hey, Michael," Rosemary said. Irrationally, her heartbeat had speeded up a bit, even though she tried to tell herself that just because he might have discovered more information about Madeline Nash, it didn't mean he'd found anything that could be of any real use to them. "What's up?"

"Some good news," he replied.

"I'm ready for some of that."

A chuckle, and then he said, "Well, I think we've finally figured out why both Colin and Madeline seemed to go off the radar housing-wise for a few years. She'd gotten a chunk of money from a pilot that was filmed but never aired, and the two of them pooled their resources and bought a house together for cash. That was why we couldn't find a rental history for them."

Made sense. But…. "If they owned a house, shouldn't you have found the title when you packed up Colin's stuff?"

"That's the tricky part. They transferred the title to a trust they set up not long after they bought the place. Protecting their assets, I guess, but that would be why neither of their names came up in any of the usual searches you can perform when you're trying to find out if someone owns property."

"What happened to it?" Rosemary asked. While she didn't understand how it all worked from a legal standpoint—at least, not exactly—she knew that trusts were a thing simply because her mother had set one up so it would be easier to transfer her home and other assets to her daughters upon her death. "Did Colin sell the house after Madeline died?"

"No, he still owned it up until—well, until he was killed. Apparently, he was using it as an income property and had a real estate attorney handling the whole thing." Another pause, and then Michael went on, sounding somehow grim and partially amused at the same time, "The guy he'd been working with didn't even know Colin was dead. It sounded as if they didn't communicate very much unless some kind of emergency came up with the house. Because he was sending money orders to Colin's mail drop, the attorney had no idea they weren't being deposited. It wasn't until the current tenants moved out a few weeks ago and he couldn't get hold of Colin to approve a new application that he realized something was wrong."

Damn. Rosemary supposed she could see how such a thing might happen—since the house was paid for, and presumably Colin paid the property taxes once a year, no one would necessarily know that its owner was dead until those became delinquent. "What happens with the house now?"

"I suppose that's something Colin's sister has to decide, since she's the executor of the estate. The house is still vacant, obviously, because Colin's attorney can't rent it out with things in limbo as they are. In a way, that's probably a good thing—I have a feeling that Emma will want to sell it, unless she'd rather keep Colin's arrangement with the real estate attorney in place. But I only just notified her about the house earlier today, so she hasn't really made a decision yet…I think she's just trying to absorb this latest revelation."

Rosemary nodded, even though she realized Michael couldn't see her and such a gesture was basically useless. At the same time, a sudden thought struck her, one that seemed so obvious, she wondered why it hadn't occurred to her the minute he'd mentioned the house Colin and Madeline had bought together.

"Michael, where is this house?" she asked.

"In Glendale, not too far from the community college."

"Can I have the address?"

"Why?"

"Because," Rosemary said, her voice shaking with excitement, "I think I know where Colin hid the missing footage."

MICHAEL HAD BEEN RELUCTANT TO GIVE HER the information. She could tell he was worried about her going off on some hare-brained chase with no backup, but once she assured him she'd call Will first and have him accompany her before she went to look at the house, he'd told her what she needed to know.

1830 Las Flores Drive.

After they ended the call—and after Michael said he'd get in touch with the attorney who'd been care-taking the place so he could put a key in the mailbox for her—Rosemary set down the phone, then went and retrieved her glass of wine. Not to drink the rest of it, tempting as that felt, but to put it back in the fridge. There were a few pieces of veggie pizza left in there from the take-out she'd gotten the night before, and she quickly ate one of them, knowing she needed some fortification before she headed off to the house Colin had once owned with Madeline Nash.

Afterward, she paused in the middle of the kitchen and called out softly, "I understand now, Madeline. You were trying to get me to go to the house where you lived with Colin. Isn't that right?"

No reply, no ghostly figure materializing to tell her that she'd finally figured it out. Somehow, though, Rosemary knew Madeline was watching and giving her silent approval.

Enough of that, though. Time to get to work.

Dutifully, she called Will's cell phone…and got his voicemail. For just the barest second, she hesitated, wondering if she should even bother leaving a message. But she'd promised Michael that she'd get in touch with Will, so she briefly told him what Michael had discovered and where she was going, and if he got the message in the next half hour or so, to go ahead and meet her at the Las Flores Drive address.

With that taken care of, she went upstairs and changed out of her flowy skirt and ballet flats, trading them for some jeans, low boots, and a long-sleeved T-shirt. She had no idea where Colin might have hidden the footage, but better to be prepared in case the task required her to root around in the garage or the yard.

At least the house was unoccupied, so she wouldn't have to explain herself to the current tenants. And since she'd have a key, it wasn't as if she was breaking and entering. Michael had said he'd tell the real estate attorney who'd been managing the place that she was an agent for Colin's sister and was going over to snap some photos so Emma could make a decision as to whether she should sell the house or keep renting it out. If he thought it seemed strange to have someone go out there on a Saturday evening rather than wait for Monday morning, well, so be it. Luckily, the guy was apparently a local, so he wouldn't have to drive far to drop off the key and then go about his business.

Rosemary paused to blow out the candle she'd lit earlier, turned on the alarm, and then went out to the garage. As she was backing out of the driveway, she wondered if she should give Caleb a call as well. After all, if it hadn't been for him, she would probably never have gone chasing down the footage in the first place.

Oh, that's exactly what you need, she thought. *Will Gordon and Caleb Dixon in the same place at the same time. Because that wouldn't be awkward or anything.*

Better to wait and see if this theory panned out at all. Michael wanted Will Gordon with Rosemary because of all the weirdness that had been dogging her lately. Once Will had assured himself that no demons were popping out of the basement—if the house even had a basement, which she kind of doubted—then presumably he would leave, and she'd be free to call Caleb and let him know she'd finally found what they were looking for. In fact, if he was done with work, she could stop by and they could look at the footage together. His house was on her way home.

Easy.

Not that any of this had been particularly easy. The silence from Will bothered her a little. Shouldn't he be calling her back? True, it was nearly seven on a Saturday night, but Episcopalian priests weren't known for their active social lives, were they?

Well, he could call her back, or not. She was going ahead with this, no matter what. A sureness drove her, spurred her on, because she somehow knew that she was on the right path here. Maybe it was her psychic powers or pure gut instinct, but either way, she had a very strong feeling that Colin had hidden the footage at his former residence simply because it was a place no one could have connected with him unless they were willing to do some very serious digging. Yes, Michael's "source" had eventually tracked down that information, but not many people had those sorts of resources. And even he had taken days to locate the house.

She drove west on the 210 Freeway, speeding even though she knew Saturday evenings were generally not the best times to be thumbing her nose at the law. And thank God the traffic actually was moving that night—too often, a concert at the Rose Bowl or some other event in Pasadena really jammed up the works, but she was able to get past the interchange with the 134 Freeway without incident.

From there, it was only a few more miles to her exit, Glendale Boulevard. She turned right as she got off the freeway, heading toward the foothills, although her destination lay closer than that, in a modest neighborhood a few blocks from Glendale Community College. Or rather, while the houses here might have looked simple enough, one-story homes built in the 1950s or '60s, she knew that they had to be worth a ton simply because of their location.

Colin's house was in the middle of a block and looked much the same as the homes that surrounded it—single story, with a two-car garage and a neatly landscaped yard with low palm trees and decorative planters out front. It was far less showy than the Mediterranean-style house he'd rented in Los Feliz...and probably the last place anyone would go looking for illicit footage that contained images of real-life encounters with demons.

Rosemary parked in the driveway and got out of the car. By then, it was nearly dark, and she was glad of the solar lights marking the path that led to the entrance. She followed the stamped-concrete pathway and went to the mailbox by the front door. Even as she lifted the lid, she wondered if the real estate attorney had really done as Michael asked and left her a key. Yes, she could still snoop around the backyard, but....

Her fingers touched something cool and hard and metallic, and she let out a sigh of relief. One less thing to worry about.

Key clutched in her fingers, she turned toward the front door and inserted the key in the lock. It turned easily, and in the next moment, she was inside.

She couldn't see much, and she fumbled on the wall next to the door, hoping a light switch might be located somewhere in the vicinity. And yes, there it was. A flick, and the recessed lights in the entry came on, revealing an empty, open space that was probably supposed to be the living room. The floors were pale gleaming oak, the walls nearly white. At one end of the living room was a small fireplace, its brick painted to match the walls. It all seemed very minimal and plain, although she supposed the house would look a lot livelier with some rugs and furniture and plants.

That's not why you're here, she told herself. *Start looking.*

Despite that internal admonishment, she remained where she was for a moment, trying to think of the best place to begin her search. Would Colin have even left anything in the house itself? It seemed a strange place to hide something so valuable if the place had been rented out. But she knew the footage had to be here someplace…most likely in a spot where the tenants wouldn't have been able to find it.

She turned toward her right, where she'd spied the kitchen. Instead of peeking into the cupboards, however, she went to a door that she guessed led into the garage. Sure enough, there it was, empty except for some cans of paint off to one side and a few boxes of unused floor planks, presumably left over from the last time the house had been remodeled.

On the other side of the garage, though, were a series of built-in cupboards. While those seemed like too obvious a hiding place, Rosemary carefully opened each one and looked inside. They were all empty, just as she'd feared. And there weren't any overhead storage areas, so it looked as though the garage was a bust.

Frowning a little, she went back inside and began poking through the kitchen cabinets. The same story here, although she found a wine bottle opener someone had left behind and a couple of rubber bands and paper clips in what had probably been the "catch-all" drawer for the former tenants.

"All right, Colin," she said aloud. "Where'd you put it? Is it hidden in the backyard? Stuck in a waterproof container in one of the toilet tanks?"

She sincerely hoped not. While hiding the footage in a toilet seemed like just the sort of thing Colin might do as a joke, such a hiding place had to be far too risky. One toilet that wouldn't stop running, and the game would be up.

As she stood there, wondering where to go next, her phone rang from inside her purse. Thinking it must be Will, she quickly unslung the bag from her shoulder so she could dig out her cell.

However, the number on the screen wasn't Will's, but Michael's.

Getting her excuses ready—*no, Michael, I really did call Will, but he wasn't answering*—she put the phone to her ear. "Hi, Michael, I—"

"Are you at the house? Is Will with you?"

"Yes, I am, and no, he isn't. I left a message, but—"

He cut in, his voice urgent. "You need to get out of there."

"What?"

"It's not safe for you to be alone. Get in your car and drive over to All Saints, and call Will again. But even if he's not there, you should be safe at the church."

Even though she had no idea what the hell he was talking about, a cold trickle of fear ran its way down her spine. "Michael, what's going on?"

"My source just contacted me again. I had him look into Caleb Dixon—"

"You *what?*"

"I told you I would. That doesn't matter."

Dimly, Rosemary recalled how more than a week ago, Michael had told her he planned to do more digging into Caleb's past...and how she'd been annoyed at the presumption that there would be anything to find. However, before she could say anything else, he continued.

"His name isn't really Caleb Dixon."

"So?" she responded, even though she knew the bravado in her voice rang far too hollow. "Lots of people change their names when they come to Hollywood."

Michael ignored her comment and went on, "His name is Caleb Lockwood. His father is

Charles Lockwood. Charles Lockwood is one of the current trustees of the Underhill trust."

Somewhere in her brain, an alarm went off, even though consciously, she still wasn't making the connection.

"The trustees are all cambions, Rosemary… half-demon offspring of the original demons Belial brought to this world to do his bidding.

"Your Caleb is the grandson of one of those demons."

Chapter 17

THE WORDS CAME OUT AUTOMATICALLY. "HE isn't 'my' Caleb."

"Whatever. You didn't tell him about the Glendale house, did you?"

"No." She almost had, though. She'd almost picked up the phone and let him know where she would be. Another shiver went through her despite the stuffiness of the house, the stale air of a place that had been closed up for days on end.

"Well, thank God for that," Michael said, and he did sound relieved. "But now you need to get out of there."

"I just started looking—"

"I don't care, Rosemary."

She could practically feel his frustrated worry shimmering across the hundreds of miles that separated them. Was Audrey somewhere in the background, listening in anxiously and praying that everything was still okay over there in California?

"Okay," she said. "I'll go. But I'm coming back here with Will just as soon as I figure out where he is."

"If you must. Never alone, though."

Through her worry, irritation raised its head. Did Michael think she needed a babysitter?

Apparently, he did…mostly because her supposed new boyfriend had turned out to be part demon. And she'd kissed him, let him touch her, had almost….

Her brain shied away from that thought. Shaking now, she went to the front door and let herself out, then locked it behind her and hurried down the front walk to the spot where she'd left her car in the driveway. A quick glance around told her the street was deserted except for a few parked vehicles. She got in the Fiat, turned on the engine, and backed out, looking over her shoulder the whole time.

No one there, not even someone taking their dog for a late walk.

"Are you still there?" Michael asked, and Rosemary realized that, in her shock, she'd forgotten to end the call.

"I'm here," she said as she pulled onto Glendale Boulevard. "I'm fine. I'm just getting on the freeway now. I should be at All Saints in about ten minutes."

"Good," he replied. "Call me when you get there—whether or not Will is around."

"Okay—gotta go," she said, then actually remembered to touch the little red button on the screen to hang up. Without looking, she dropped the phone into her purse and maneuvered her way over to the left lane so she could get on the eastbound 134 Freeway.

The icy chill that had wound its way down her back a few moments earlier now felt like a blanket of ice surrounding her entire body. Her hands wouldn't stop shaking, even when she clenched them around the hard leather of the steering wheel.

Caleb was part demon. How was that even possible? All right, she knew Michael had mentioned a few things about the trust Belial had set up while he was wearing Jeffrey Whitcomb's human form, but to be honest, she hadn't paid a huge amount of attention. Belial had been defeated and sent back to Hell, and whatever he'd done while here on Earth, it seemed as though he'd been rendered impotent. What she'd somehow managed to forget was the demon lieutenants who'd lived here on Earth as well, who had—according to Michael—married human women and had children with them. Those original demons might have "died," or relinquished their human forms so they could return to Hell, but their offspring had remained here, and obviously, those offspring had had children of their own.

One of whom just happened to be Caleb Dixon. Lockwood. Whatever.

Was that why she'd stopped things so suddenly when it had looked as if they were about to fall into bed together at his house? Had something in her recognized his otherness and recoiled, even though at the time, she couldn't have said exactly why she hadn't wanted matters to progress to their natural conclusion?

Possibly. Because even as shaken as she felt at the moment, she realized the situation could have been a whole lot worse. How would she be feeling right now if they actually had slept together?

He seemed so normal. So much like a regular guy. It had to have all been an act, though. He must have approached her because he needed to get his hands on the footage, and he figured she was the best way to go about it, a convenient loose end in need of a tug. Had he simply not believed she was psychic, or did he have a few demon tricks up his sleeve that made her powers useless around him?

She didn't know. There was just so damn much she didn't know.

However, now she knew for sure what Isabel had been talking about. Caleb himself was the dark force that had entered her orbit.

Fingers still clenched on the steering wheel, Rosemary got off the freeway at Fair Oaks before heading south so she could cut left on Walnut Street and then turn onto Euclid. When she reached the small side street where All Saints was located, she saw it was far more crowded than she'd thought it would be on a Saturday night. City Hall was closed, so there shouldn't have been as much overflow parking as there was during the day. Whatever the reason, she had to keep driving past the church and go another block so she could park in the public garage there.

Michael would hate me doing this, Rosemary thought as she left the Fiat in a spot near the stairwell. Parking garages were always mildly spooky in the first place, and now that she knew she'd been consorting with a part-demon intent on using her for his own ends, her nerves jangled all over the place. True, she had the little can of pepper spray in her purse...although she had to wonder whether mere pepper spray would do anything against a demon, or even a part-demon.

She glanced around before she headed down the stairs, but she didn't see anyone. Still, she practically took the steps at a run and nearly careened into a couple around her age as she emerged on the street.

"Dude, watch it," the guy said, although he didn't sound too upset—probably because it was pretty obvious that he and his date had been throwing back more than a few drinks over the course of the evening.

"Sorry," she said breathlessly as she trotted toward the street corner. The light was green, and so she didn't have to wait, could keep going across Union. Another pause while she waited for the light there, her eyes still scanning her surroundings. All clear, which wasn't so surprising; she'd left the shops and the restaurants mostly behind her, since this block had the back side of the City Hall complex on one side and All Saints and a large square apartment building on the other.

Except....

She hadn't noticed the man because he'd been lurking under the colonnade that led to the courtyard behind the municipal buildings. As she waited for the interminable light to turn green, she realized that he'd begun to walk toward her, his gait slow and steady, not wavering at all as he came closer and closer.

To hell with the light. She bolted across the street, running toward the church. The sound of feet slapping on concrete echoed off the tall buildings on either side, and she risked a glance over one shoulder to see that the man had started to run as well. It was still too dark for her to see him distinctly, but she didn't think it was Caleb—he seemed shorter and wider, his hair black instead of sandy blond.

Maybe the stranger was just a lone creeper preying on unaccompanied women…or maybe he was something far, far worse. Continuing to look back at him would only slow her down, so Rosemary forced herself to run faster, to flee for the front doors of the church as if all the demons of hell were pursuing her.

All right, probably not *all* of them, but even one would be bad enough.

And there were All Saints' doors—large and wide, barred with dark metal.

And very, very locked.

She tugged on them once, twice, and realized they weren't about to budge. So much for leaving the sanctuary open at all times for anyone who might need refuge inside. A panicky little sob escaped her throat, and she turned and fled toward the back of the church, thinking she could go to Will's office—even as she realized with mounting panic that of course no one would be there at nearly eight o'clock on a Saturday night.

But if you keep running, there's the California Pizza Kitchen, she told herself. *There'll be people there. You'll be safe.*

All right, maybe a CPK wasn't the best sanctuary in the world, but at that particular moment, she'd take it.

The footsteps behind her were getting closer. In a way, that fact was strangely reassuring. If her pursuer really was some kind of demon, couldn't he sprout wings and take to the air, come after her that way?

But then she spied lights in the building to her right, and realized that beyond Will's office were apparently meeting rooms of some sort. There was even a little sign out front that read "ACA," whatever that meant. It wasn't important, though. What mattered was that the place wasn't quite as deserted as she'd feared.

She ran for the door, flung it open, and hurried inside—only to find about twelve pairs of eyes fixed on her, pairs of eyes that belonged to a group of people who sat on folding chairs in a loose circle. Will sat there as well, although he rose to his feet as he looked at her in some astonishment.

"Rosemary?"

"Someone—after me," she panted, and immediately he came to the door, sharp gray eyes fixed on her face.

"Who?"

"I don't know," she said, voice still breathless. "Michael told me to come here, so I did, but as I was walking from the parking garage, a man started following me."

"Stay here."

He slipped outside and shut the door behind him, while Rosemary waited and sent an awkward smile at the people in the folding chairs. Some kind of support group, she guessed.

"Sorry about the interruption," she said.

A kind-faced older woman got up from her seat and came over to her. "You look all shaken up, dear," she said. "Do you want some water, or maybe some tea?"

What Rosemary really wanted was to look outside and see what was going on with Will, but she managed to nod and reply, "Water would be great."

The woman led her over to a refreshment table and poured her some water from a large clear glass container with a metal spigot. As she sipped at it, Rosemary saw the door open and Will come in. He gave her a very faint shake of his head, then turned toward the group.

"I'm sorry," he said. "It looks like a false alarm. Rosemary, we're just about done here. Would you mind waiting in my office? Take my keys—you can go through that door there and down the hall."

He reached in his pocket and got out a set of keys, holding them up by a single brass one—

presumably the key to his office—and pointed toward a door in the wall opposite the one where she'd come in. About all she could do was quickly say, "Sure. I'm sorry about this," since she had a feeling they wouldn't go on with their meeting while she was still standing there and listening to everything they said.

Then she hurried out of the room, into a hallway that at least was somewhat familiar…as was Will's office. When she unlocked the door, she saw that he'd left a desk lamp on, as though he'd been working in there before he went out to run that AA meeting or whatever it was. Something where people would be talking about personal subjects, which was probably why he hadn't wanted her to stay there until the meeting wrapped up.

While she didn't much enjoy the thought of being by herself after what had just happened, she was glad of the light, glad of the coziness of the space. As Michael had said, it felt safe here inside the church building, although she wasn't sure whether that was the actual truth or whether she was telling herself that so she wouldn't worry so much about being by herself.

At least she'd brought her plastic cup of water with her, so she sipped from it as she did her best to sit in the office's visitor chair and tried not to think about whoever—or whatever—had been pursuing her. Belatedly, she realized Michael had told her to call him when she got to the church. However, she really didn't feel like talking to him right then, so instead she sent a quick text.

Hi—I'm at All Saints. Will was conducting some kind of meeting, so I'm waiting in his office until he's done. I'm safe. Talk to you soon.

There. At least that way, Michael would know she was still alive and hadn't been attacked by demons on the 134 Freeway somewhere around Eagle Rock.

Not too long after she'd sent the message, Rosemary heard footsteps on the linoleum in the hall outside. She stiffened, wondering what she could use in the office to defend herself if necessary—maybe the desk lamp—then let out a relieved breath as Will entered the room.

"I'm sorry—" she began, but he raised a hand to stop her apologies, even as he reached back with the other one to shut the door behind him.

"It's all right," he told her. "I'm glad you came here. I just didn't feel comfortable ending the meeting early, which was why I asked you to come here and wait in my office." For a second or two, he was quiet, his gaze fixed on her face. "What happened?"

"Was there anyone outside?" Rosemary asked. She wasn't sure why knowing such a thing was so important, but maybe she simply wanted to have him corroborate the fact that someone really had been following her, that she hadn't made up the whole incident because of being so utterly on edge.

A pause, during which his clear gray gaze flickered to the window and then returned to her. She didn't know what he could see out there, since even the landscape lighting in the courtyard mainly existed to make sure you didn't trip while you were walking and didn't provide all that much illumination. "I thought I heard someone running —feet on the concrete, moving fast, moving off toward Los Robles. But I couldn't see anyone."

If Will had heard the stranger, though, then that meant he existed, and wasn't just a figment of her paranoid imagination.

Clearly worried by her lack of a response, he went on, "What happened?"

"I tried to call you," she said, and he blinked, then looked apologetic.

"Sorry about that. I put my phone on vibrate when I'm conducting a meeting, but I'd taken off my jacket and had it on a chair, so I wouldn't have felt it."

Of course. Will had his own demands on his time, his own work to do. She realized he hadn't been wearing the jacket when he was conducting the meeting, had on yet another dark shirt to go with his black dress slacks, but he wore it now.

Even though he'd left off the clerical collar, he still looked sort of priestly in the getup.

Rosemary wasn't sure how she felt about that.

"Anyway," she went on after taking a swallow of water to fortify her, "Michael and his 'source' figured out that Colin still owned a house he bought with Madeline Nash before she died. I realized that had to be where she'd been telling me to find the footage, so I headed over there to take a look. But I also tried to call you so you could meet me there, because Michael wasn't very keen on the idea of me going there by myself."

"But you went anyway."

Will's tone was so neutral, she couldn't tell for sure whether he was judging her for her impetuous actions or not. She decided to take his comment as purely observational and forged ahead.

"Yes. I left you a message, though, since I'd hoped you could meet me at the house if you got my voicemail in time." She stopped there for a few seconds, wondering if he was going to apologize again. Since he remained silent, she continued. "I checked a few places in the house and didn't find anything. But then Michael called me again and told me...." When she reached this part of her narrative, Rosemary faltered. She really, really didn't want to tell Will that Caleb had turned out to be part demon. Never mind that no one in the world could have known by looking at him that he was anything except the transplant from Indiana he'd claimed to be. However, she was psychic; she wasn't supposed to make those kinds of mistakes.

Voice very gentle now, Will said, "Michael told you what, Rosemary?"

The words came out in a rush, as if she somehow hoped that by saying it all at once, she could make everything seem less awful. "He told me that his source—whoever that is—had discovered that Caleb Dixon's grandfather was one of the Underhill trustees, that he was a demon in human form. And he told me to get out of the house, that I wasn't safe on my own and that I should come here because it was safe. So I got the hell out of there and drove to Pasadena, but then someone started following me as I left the parking garage, and…I ran. I ran, and I found where you were having your meeting and got away."

"You did the right thing."

The whole time, she'd been staring down at the plastic cup she held, turning it around and around in her hands so she wouldn't have to see the expression on Will's face as he listened to what a screw-up she'd been. Now she lifted startled eyes to his and was surprised to see an odd mixture of emotions in his face—worry for her, yes, but also guilt, as though he was angry at himself for not being there when she needed him.

Not sure how she should react, she said, "I should never have gone to that house alone—"

"Maybe. Maybe not. No one approached you or attacked you there, did they?"

"No."

He stepped closer to where she was sitting, although not so close that she would feel as if her space was being intruded on. Problem was, she wanted him to get in her space. He did seem very tall, though, standing by her chair like that, so she stood up, using the pretense of throwing her empty cup in the trash to cover up the nervousness that had spurred her to abandon her seat in the first place.

Turning back toward him, she asked, "Do you think someone is following me?"

"I don't know," he replied. "It would seem that way, but if that were the case, you'd think you would have noticed someone tailing you back here to Pasadena."

And she hadn't noticed anyone like that, or at least, she couldn't recall any vehicles whose movements seemed suspicious in any way. Then again, she'd been so focused on getting out of Glendale as quickly as possible that she supposed she might have overlooked any pursuers.

But if someone really had been following her,

that meant they knew she'd gone to the house on Las Flores Drive. Maybe they didn't know exactly *why* she'd gone there, but she had a feeling they'd check the place out anyway since it had to have been something important that sent her running out to Glendale on a Saturday evening.

Panic overtaking her, she reached out and grabbed Will by the sleeve. In that moment, she'd completely forgotten that she was supposed to act cool and neutral around him, wasn't supposed to initiate contact of any kind. Surprise flared in his eyes, even as she said, "Will, we have to get back to that house. We can't take the chance of someone else getting that footage."

His left hand closed on hers where it rested on his right sleeve, warm and strong. He didn't try to pry loose her fingers, though, but instead let his hand rest there, fingertips brushing against her skin. Despite the urgency that seemed to thrum through her veins with every heartbeat, she couldn't quite prevent herself from staring up at him.

Their eyes met, held. For one achingly endless moment, neither of them said anything. Will's lips parted, and she thought for sure he was going to tell her that there was no way in hell they were going after the footage, that doing such a thing was far too dangerous.

Instead, he bent and pressed his mouth

against hers. Sudden, aching heat flared through her, making her forget the alarm that had consumed her just a moment earlier, making her forget pretty much everything except the stunning reality of Will Gordon kissing her, his arms circling her waist and pulling her close. His body felt very different from Caleb's, sturdier, stronger, infinitely solid and reassuring. She clung to him even as she wondered what it was that had made Will kiss her now. Was it only that he'd been far more worried about her than he'd wanted to admit, and now needed this physical contact to remind himself that she was safe?

Rosemary didn't know. Maybe it didn't matter. What mattered right then was knowing something of what she felt for him must have been reciprocated, although he'd done his best to hide his feelings from her. She kissed him back, lips parting so they could taste one another, so they could lose themselves in an embrace that seemed as if it had taken a lifetime for them to reach this point.

At last, however, he lifted his mouth from hers, although he reached over at the same time to brush a curl away from her face. Caleb had done the same thing, she recalled, but without any of the infinite tenderness of Will's gesture. It was as if he needed to touch her hair now to show that he still wanted some contact, and had only ended the kiss because they couldn't ignore the pressing needs of the outside world for a moment longer.

And when he spoke, it was only to return the conversation to where they'd left it, with him saying what she'd expected him to tell her just a few moments earlier.

"It's not safe, Rosemary."

"It will be if we go together."

He smiled then, his hands going to cup her face, the caress so simple and yet beautiful that she wanted to stand there forever and feel the gentle brush of his fingertips against her cheeks. At the same time, she realized they didn't have the luxury of lingering here in his office, not when Caleb's minions—or Caleb himself—might be descending on the Las Flores Drive house to claim the footage for themselves.

Before she could continue, however, Will said, dropping his hands, "I'm just an ordinary man, Rosemary. I don't have yours or Michael's powers of the mind. I'm not sure what you expect me to do."

She gazed up at him, at the straight nose and finely sculpted mouth and dark bars of brows over his clear gray eyes. So very handsome…and so utterly unlike Caleb.

Thank God.

"Well, I'm not expecting you to be some kind of action hero," she said, her tone sensible. "But there must have been a reason why Michael asked you to look out for me."

"Because I have some experience with the demonic—"

"And that's exactly what we're dealing with here," Rosemary cut in. "So I think there's plenty you can do. Can't you bring a bunch of holy water or something?"

"I suppose I can," Will said, a flicker of amusement showing in his expression. "Do you really think that will be enough?"

"It will have to be."

For a moment, he didn't say anything. Then she saw his chest move, as if he'd released a sigh too small for her to actually hear. "All right. Let's go."

She shot him a grateful smile, although she sensed a certain weakness in her knees and wondered if she really was up for this after all. However, they had to go back to the house and see if the footage was still there; she had no idea whether the man who had been following her worked for Caleb or whether he'd been an ordinary mugger who'd given up once he saw her enter the church offices, but either way, she needed to do her best to prevent Caleb from getting his hands on the *Project Demon Hunters* files...wherever they might be hidden.

Will led her out of his office and back

outside, where they went to a small, secluded parking lot that contained only his shiny vintage Challenger and a beat-up pickup truck. In fact, spotting that truck made her pulse accelerate for a moment…until she realized it was bigger and painted red, wasn't the oxidized black of Caleb's Nissan.

They got in the Challenger and silently fastened their seat belts. As Will was pulling out of the parking lot, Rosemary told him, "You need to take the 134 and then get off at Glendale Boulevard."

He nodded. "Okay. You can guide me in the rest of the way after we get on surface streets."

Once they were on the freeway and cruising along at a little over seventy miles per hour, she said, gaze focused on the road in front of her rather than over where she could see his expression, "I can't believe I didn't notice anything off about Caleb Dixon."

"Don't beat yourself up about that," Will said immediately. "Remember, these demons have been able to pass themselves off as members of the regular population for decades. And Caleb isn't even a full demon, is he?"

"I don't think so," she replied. "That is, Michael made it sound as if the original trustees married human women, so their children were only half demon. And Caleb is from the generation that came after the half-demons, so he must be only a quarter."

"More human than not," Will observed, and she supposed he was right.

For some reason, though, his pointing out that fact didn't make her feel much better about the situation. She hated for him to think that she'd been intimate with Caleb, when nothing had really happened between them. Well, almost nothing, anyway.

"We didn't—" she blurted out. "I mean, he and I—"

"Rosemary," Will interjected in that quiet way of his, and she looked over at him. He had his attention fixed on the freeway in front of them rather than on her, but somehow she could still feel the intensity of her connection to him, the way the memory of the single kiss they'd shared had already created a bond that would be difficult to break. "It doesn't matter. That's between you and Caleb. Whatever happened between the two of you, it doesn't change how I feel. Not a single bit."

Some part of her wanted to ask exactly how he felt, but she knew that would be disingenuous. The intensity of their kiss should have told her everything she needed to know. For now, it was better to accept what he'd told her, and know it was only the truth. He honestly didn't care that she'd been dating a half-demon. Quarter-demon. Whatever the hell Caleb was.

What mattered now was getting back to the house before Caleb did. She consoled herself with the knowledge that he'd been working late that night and so wouldn't be able to leave the set whenever he felt like it.

Assuming the Netflix job was real, of course, as worry began to form a cold, hard knot in her belly. Maybe that had been yet another lie. Obviously, Caleb Dixon was very good at lying.

But they had to try. If it turned out the footage was gone, well, they'd figure out what to do next at that point. Giving up before they even made the attempt was not an option.

She stared at the lights on the freeway as they rushed past, and hoped she and Will wouldn't be too late.

Chapter 18

THE HOME ON LAS FLORES DRIVE DIDN'T look as if anyone had come by during her absence. A single light shone from within, but Rosemary knew she'd left it on when she ran from the house, and she didn't see any other lights besides the one in the entryway. Also, there weren't any vehicles parked on the street that hadn't been there when she left less than an hour earlier. Still, how much did that particular detail even mean? Caleb could have parked one street over and walked to the house, or had one of his minions come over here to do his dirty work. If he even had minions, of course. She was a little hazy on what the perks of being descended from a demon actually were.

Luckily, she'd shoved the house key into an interior pocket of her purse as she fled the scene, so it was a simple enough matter to head up the walkway, Will at her side, and then let the two of them in through the front door. He had his left hand hovering near his jacket pocket, where he'd stashed a couple of small plastic bottles of holy water before they left the church.

However, the house looked empty enough. Rosemary went into the kitchen and glanced around, but nothing seemed to have been disturbed since she was last here.

"How big is the house?" Will asked, his voice barely above a murmur.

"I'm not sure," she replied. "I ran before I had a chance to really inspect the whole place. But it looks as though the bedrooms must be located on the other side of the living area, because over here it's just the kitchen and the garage."

He nodded. "Let's take a look."

Now it was his turn to take the lead, which Rosemary appreciated. Not that she wanted him to face the brunt of any attack they might encounter, but still, he was taller and bigger and obviously stronger than she was. Plus, he had the holy water with him.

The light from the entry was sufficient to reveal something of the hallway on the unexplored side of the house. A few doors opened from it, leading to two bedrooms and a single bathroom. The doors weren't what caught Rosemary's attention, though—it was the opening in the ceiling, one that apparently allowed access to a crawlspace. Even as she reached out to grip Will's arm, a pair of jeans-clad legs appeared in that opening, and Caleb Dixon dropped down into the center of the hallway.

For a single, shocked second, her eyes met his —and he seemed to be almost as surprised as she. But then he grinned, a wide, malicious grin so unlike any smile he'd previously worn in her presence, he looked almost unrecognizable.

"Hey, Rosemary," he said, tone so casual, they might have just met in the produce section at Whole Foods rather than the dark hallway of a house that belonged to a dead man. His gaze flicked over at Will, clearly contemptuous. "What, have you suddenly gotten religion?"

Will only raised an eyebrow. "You're trespassing," he said evenly.

This statement elicited a careless shrug. "I suppose I am," Caleb replied. "But it's in a worthy cause."

For the first time, Rosemary realized he was holding one hand down at his side, a hand that held a small, dark, rectangular object. The light in the hallway wasn't very good, but she thought it looked like a portable hard drive, the sort of multi-terabyte gizmo used to back up a computer.

"You found it."

"What, this?" He held up the hard drive, still

smiling. "I suppose I did. Your own fault, Rosemary—you led me right to it and then bolted before you even figured out where it was hidden. Not very smart."

No, it wasn't. But then, she'd had no idea anyone was following her, although she supposed she should have taken such a possibility into account and been a lot more careful. And if only Michael hadn't spooked her into leaving before she was done looking around the house....

"That's not yours," she said. Pretty feeble argument, but it was the first thing that popped into her head.

"It's not yours, either," Caleb replied. The same smirk still twisted his mouth. How in the world had she ever thought he was good-looking? In a detached way, she was somewhat astonished by how a shift in expression could alter someone's features so radically. This, obviously, was who he truly was. Everything else had been an act, a mask he'd worn to get the one thing he wanted...which sure as hell wasn't Rosemary herself, but the hard drive he mockingly held before her now.

"That hard drive belongs to Colin's sister," Will said. His voice sounded cold and precise, and if he was at all worried about facing down a part-demon adversary, he showed no sign of it. "And since we're here on behalf of her agent in this country, I'll have to ask you to hand it over."

This assertion might have been something of a stretch, but Rosemary wasn't going to quibble right then. She watched Caleb, wondering how he was going to react.

She should have guessed.

He gave a derisive chuckle, then said, "No, I don't think so. You see, my father really wants what's on this disk, wants to make sure no one else sees it."

"Why not?" Rosemary challenged him. "I thought you demons liked feeling important. What's more important than having your existence proved beyond a shadow of a doubt?"

"Oh, but you've forgotten one thing about you stupid humans," Caleb replied. "These files might prove demons exist…but if we exist, then Heaven and Hell exist…and so does God." His nostrils flared as he uttered that one simple word, and he looked as if he'd just tasted something bad. "And we can't have a bunch of people starting to believe in God, not when He's finally starting to lose His stranglehold on large chunks of the population."

Will seemed to absorb this remark, then offered a smile of his own. "I suppose that would make things more difficult for your kind. But I still have to ask you to hand it over."

Caleb's lip lifted in a sneer. "I don't think so."

Quicker than Rosemary would have thought

possible, Will's right leg snaked out and caught Caleb behind the knee. He let out an *oof* of pain and surprise, then stumbled, the hard drive slipping from his shocked fingers. She lunged for it, catching the device before it could hit the hardwood floor.

Unfortunately, Caleb recovered himself quickly, regaining his balance in the next moment even as he turned a baleful gaze on his unexpected assailant. He raised his hands as an odd fiery glow enveloped them, a glow that turned to angry-looking flames.

Those flames leaped out and crashed into Will, knocking him to the floor. His head impacted with the wooden surface with a sharp crack, and Rosemary cried out in dismay as his eyes shut and his mouth went suddenly slack.

"Ooh, that had to hurt," Caleb said, tone mocking. He turned toward her, the flames receding from one hand but still surrounding the other. The hand free of flames reached toward her. "Better give me the drive, Rosemary, so you can check on your priestly loverboy there. I think he might have a concussion."

Angry words sprang to her lips, although she realized this was not the time to be arguing over whether Will was a priest...or her lover. "I can't give you this," she said.

"Then I'll take it."

In the next second, Caleb was next to her, his flaming hand encircling her wrist—although not the one attached to the hand that held the drive, as if he knew those unholy fires could damage the precious information contained in the hard disk. The sensation was excruciating, like being clutched by molten lava, and she gasped in pain.

"I really don't want to hurt you," Caleb told her, his tone almost conversational, as if they were both discussing what to do on their outing to Santa Monica the next day. His eyes narrowed, and the look he gave her made her want to take a bath. "No, there are a lot of things I'd *like* to do to you, but hurting you isn't one of them." Giving the lie to his words, the grip on her wrist increased. "But I'll do what I have to. Better give me the drive, Rosemary, because if I don't let go soon, it's going to leave a scar."

"Asshole," she spat, although tears of pain had begun to leak down her cheeks.

"You're probably right about that," he said. He didn't look offended at all.

And, as if to prove that he'd been toying with her all along, he reached with his other hand to tear the hard drive from her grip…and bent to give her a quick kiss on the mouth at the same time.

She gasped in revulsion and he laughed, then

stepped away from her, his prize clutched firmly in his fingers.

The flames that enveloped his hand cast an unholy light in his dark eyes, making them appear tinged with red. Or maybe that was what they really did look like. "What, you didn't like that?"

"I prefer kisses from men who aren't part demon," she retorted.

At once, Caleb's eyes narrowed, and he looked past her to the place where Will lay unconscious on the floor. "Cheating on me, Rosemary? When we had a date set for tomorrow? Guess I'll have to do something about that."

He slipped the hard drive into the back pocket of his Levi's and then lifted his hands, fingers curling into claws as the flames danced around them. She had no idea exactly what he planned to do, but she knew it wouldn't be anything good. And what she was supposed to do about it, she couldn't begin to guess. She wasn't a fighter, couldn't pull a cool physical maneuver like Will had a few minutes earlier. Then again, that *tae kwon do* move or whatever it was hadn't done him much good.

But she thought of how Michael and Audrey had beaten a far worse adversary than the one she faced now, and they'd been armed only with holy water and their own faith that they'd prevail. Rosemary wasn't sure she possessed that kind of faith, but she still had to call on the powers within her to do what they could.

She hurriedly backed away from Caleb and dropped on her knees next to Will's unmoving form, then reached into his pocket and pulled out one of the vials of holy water he'd hidden there. As her part-demon foe advanced on them, she unscrewed the lid from the small plastic bottle and flung its contents at him.

The flames surrounding Caleb's hands went out, but otherwise, he didn't seem to be affected at all. In fact, he wiped some of the liquid from his face and chuckled. "Oh, you'll have to do better than that, Rosemary. I'm part human—holy water doesn't hurt me the way it would a full-on demon."

Well, shit. She remained crouching next to Will and raised defiant eyes to the man she'd once thought might make a decent boyfriend. Joke was on her.

"You got what you wanted. Now leave us alone."

"Oh, I don't think so," Caleb returned. The smile was gone, but she would rather have seen that mocking smirk than the expression of cruel anticipation he wore now. "This guy is obviously trouble. I think I need to make sure he's safely out of the way."

She didn't even stop to think. On one level,

Rosemary wasn't quite sure what she did, not exactly. It was as if all the years of casting the spells of white light, of protection, had somehow coalesced within her, had allowed her to summon the one thing she hoped might save Will from Caleb's attack. The flames danced around his fingers and shot outward—only to bounce off a shimmering shield of pale illumination that surrounded both her and the man who lay on the floor less than a foot away.

Face twisting with fury, Caleb raised his hands to strike again...and again the baleful fire that shot forth from his fingers skittered off the surface of the light she had conjured, rendering his demon-summoned flames harmless.

"Nice trick," he said. "I didn't know you had it in you."

Neither did I, Rosemary thought, still astonished that her powers or whatever you wanted to call them had managed to manifest in such a useful way.

"But I've still got this," Caleb went on, one hand patting the pocket that concealed the hard drive. "So I guess that means you lose. Oh, and I'm canceling our date for tomorrow. You understand."

Before she could begin to reply, he winked out of existence, disappearing before her astonished eyes in a single blink.

No wonder there hadn't been any sign of forced entry.

She would have to worry about all that later, though. Miraculously, her purse had remained slung over her shoulder throughout the entire confrontation. Her fingers scrabbled through it now, searching for her phone. She pulled it out and dialed 911, told the dispatcher that there was a man who'd suffered a head injury at 1830 Las Flores Drive, and then scooted closer to Will and took his wrist in one hand, feeling for a pulse. It was there, fast and light, but she had to pray he hadn't been hurt so badly that he couldn't hang on until the ambulance got there.

Everything else would have to wait. Caleb… the hard drive…the rest of the world.

It would all have to wait until she knew Will would live.

Project Demon Hunters continues with *Unmarked Graves*, releasing in January 2020.

Also by Christine Pope

PROJECT DEMON HUNTERS

(Paranormal Romance)

Unquiet Souls

Unbound Spirits

Unholy Ground

Unseen Voices

Unmarked Graves

Unbroken Vows

THE DEVIL YOU KNOW

(Paranormal Romance)

Sympathy for the Devil

Charmed, I'm Sure

A Wing and a Prayer

THE WITCHES OF CANYON ROAD*

(Paranormal Romance)

Hidden Gifts

Darker Paths

Mysterious Ways

A Canyon Road Christmas

Demon Born

An Ill Wind

Higher Ground

Haunted Hearts

THE WITCHES OF CLEOPATRA HILL*

(Paranormal Romance)

Darkangel

Darknight

Darkmoon

Sympathetic Magic

Protector

Spellbound

A Cleopatra Hill Christmas

Impractical Magic

Strange Magic

The Arrangement

Defender

Bad Blood

Deep Magic

Darktide

THE DJINN WARS*

(Paranormal Romance)

Chosen

Taken

Fallen

Broken

Forsaken

Forbidden

Awoken

Illuminated

Stolen

Forgotten

Driven

Unspoken

THE WATCHERS TRILOGY*

(Paranormal Romance)

Falling Dark

Dead of Night

Rising Dawn

THE SEDONA FILES*

(Paranormal Romance)

Bad Vibrations

Desert Hearts

Angel Fire

Star Crossed

Falling Angels

Enemy Mine

TALES OF THE LATTER KINGDOMS*

(Fantasy Romance)

All Fall Down

Dragon Rose

Binding Spell

Ashes of Roses

One Thousand Nights

Threads of Gold

The Wolf of Harrow Hall

Moon Dance

The Song of the Thrush

About the Author

USA Today bestselling author Christine Pope has been writing stories ever since she commandeered her family's Smith-Corona typewriter back in grade school. Her work includes paranormal romance, fantasy romance, and science fiction/space opera romance. She makes her home in Arizona.

Don't miss out on any of Christine's new releases —sign up for her newsletter today!

Christine Pope on the Web:
www.christinepope.com